"A multi-layered mystery sizzling with infidelity, abduction, and danger, *Mainely Angst* is a smorgasbord of anxieties caused by the pandemic, political unrest, betrayal, and loss."

—*InD'tale Magazine*

"As readers follow him on journeys that weave through disparate lives and special interests, the mysteries become more than another story of perps, leads, and threats. They consider resolution and motivation, make the perps not just believable, but human, and pair confrontation with understanding in a manner that allows for a touch of romantic inspection along the way. These unexpected twists and thought-provoking considerations keep *Mainely Angst* centered not just on mysteries, but in community interactions, responses, and anxiety. *Mainely Angst*'s special relevance to post-pandemic readers keeps its concerns contemporary and its mystery especially vivid, which will delight genre readers looking for a story firmly rooted in community struggle and current events."

—Diane Donovan, Senior Reviewer, *Midwest Book Review*

D1286578

Novels by Matt Cost
aka **Matthew Langdon Cost**

The Goff Langdon Mainely Mysteries

Mainely Power

Mainely Fear

Mainely Money

The Clay Wolfe / Port Essex Mysteries

Wolfe Trap

Mind Trap

Mouse Trap

Historical Fiction

I Am Cuba: Fidel Castro and the Cuban Revolution

Love in a Time of Hate

MAINELY ANGST

A Goff Langdon Mainely Mystery

MATT COST

Encircle Publications
Farmington, Maine, U.S.A.

Paperback ISBN 13: 978-1-64599-284-4
Hardcover ISBN 13: 978-1-64599-285-1
E-book ISBN 13: 978-1-64599-286-8
Kindle ISBN 13: 978-1-64599-287-5

Editor, Encircle Publications: Cynthia Brackett-Vincent
Cover design and digital illustration by Deirdre Wait
Cover photographs © Getty Images

Published by:

Encircle Publications
PO Box 187
Farmington, ME 04938

info@encirclepub.com
http://encirclepub.com

Acknowledgments

If you are reading this, I thank you, for without readers, writers would be obsolete.

And thank you to the wonderful writing community that has welcomed me with open arms and made me feel at home. This includes so many fantastic people it would take an entire book to note not just writers, but reviewers as well.

I am grateful to my mother, Penelope McAlevey, and father, Charles Cost, who have always been my first readers and critics.

Much appreciation to the various friends and relatives who have also read my work and given helpful advice.

I'd like to offer a big hand to my wife, Deborah Harper Cost, and children, Brittany, Pearson, Miranda, and Ryan, who have always had my back.

I'd like to tip my hat to my editor, Michael Sanders, who has worked with me on several novels now, and always makes my writing the best that it can be.

Thank you to Encircle Publishing, and the amazing duo of Cynthia Bracket-Vincent and Eddie Vincent for giving me this opportunity to be published. Also, kudos to Deirdre Wait for the fantastic cover art.

Dedication

*To the people of the world who have
pulled together to defeat Covid-19.*

Chapter 1

"Somebody stole my wife," the man said.

Goff Langdon thought that was a strange way to complain about a cheating spouse. Perhaps his advertising was misleading, saying that he investigated marital infidelity. Maybe affairs of the heart merely came under the heading of theft. Burglary. *Hello*, Langdon thought, fighting back a grin, *I'm concerned that my wife has been burgled.*

"You mean your wife is having an affair?" Langdon asked, his tone neutral.

This was not unusual. As a matter of fact, the cheating hearts of the greater Brunswick, Maine, area, made up about fifty percent of his business. The rest was mostly insurance fraud, background verifications, and delivering summonses, with the random light-fingered employee thrown in. Of course, there were the occasional cases of a more challenging nature, a recent one coming to mind involving blackmail and murder, a case which had threatened the lives of his family, friends, and self, in that order of importance.

"What? No. Somebody stole her."

"I'm sorry, let's start over. I'm Goff Langdon. Everybody calls me Langdon, and that includes my wife and daughter. What's your name?"

"Rudolph. Rudolph Morin."

Langdon guessed the man was a couple of years younger than his own age of fifty-three. But those years had been kinder to Langdon.

Rudolph had a paunch, wide florid cheeks, a receding hairline, and a bulbous red nose that probably drew a lot of humor at his expense due to his given name.

"What do you do for a living, Rudolph?"

The man curled his lip sullenly. "I'm a lobsterman."

"You live in Brunswick?"

"Out to Bailey Island."

Langdon leaned forward over his worn and beaten mahogany desk and steepled his fingers under his chin. "How long have you been married?"

Rudolph narrowed his gray eyes and counted out on his thick fingers. "Just 'bout seven years."

"What's her name?"

"Ann."

This was the delicate part, Langdon thought, studying the man carefully. "And you say she ran off with another man?"

"Ran off? Goddamn it, no, I told you somebody stole her." Rudolph slammed his meaty hand down on the desk, scars crisscrossing it, proof that he was indeed a lobsterman and had been for some years. Lobstermen got cuts all the time from the wire their traps were made of, the lines they handled, even the hard, spiny shells of the lobsters themselves. "What are you? Stupid?"

Business had been slow for a few months now, otherwise Langdon would've thrown the man out then and there. It seemed that the pandemic was not good for the private investigator business, nor his other occupation as a bookstore owner. But, to be fair, it had not been good for the lobstering industry either.

Rudolph hadn't been happy to put a face mask on, but Langdon had insisted, and he'd grudgingly taken one from the box by the door. It was currently pushed down below his nose. This irked Langdon as well, but he did need the business.

"Are you saying your wife was taken? As in, abducted?" Langdon asked.

"That's what I'm saying, she was stolen."

Langdon thought that it perhaps said a lot about Rudolph that he would refer to the abduction of his wife as her being stolen, as if she were a piece of property, and not a human being. "When did she come up missing?" he asked.

"Four days ago."

"Did you report it to the police?"

"I sure did, but they ain't gonna do shit. The snot-nosed kid who claimed he was a lieutenant said there was nothing to indicate she'd been taken. Asked me if I thought she'd just decided to leave, move on."

Langdon thought it best not to suggest the same thing, even if he was thinking it. Not if he wanted to pay the bills. "You said you've been married seven years. Where'd you meet your wife, Rudolph?"

"You fixin' on finding Ann, or writing a book about my life?"

Langdon drummed his fingers on the desk and said nothing. Patience was often necessary in this business, whether it be sitting in a car with a camera waiting for a curtain to be pulled revealing the carnal embrace of adulterers, or outside the house of a man on disability for a back injury to see whether or not he would miss his weekly golf outing.

"Russia, okay. I met her in Russia."

This, Langdon thought, was indeed a surprise. "What were you doing in Russia?"

"She's a mail-order bride, okay? For immigration purposes, I had to go meet with her at least once, and she came here once, before we done got married."

"Do you have a picture of your wife?"

"What for?"

"I need to know who I'm looking for."

Rudolph grudgingly took a battered cell phone from his pocket. He scrolled through a few items and then offered it to Langdon, who took it. Ann was a stunning blonde, perhaps a bit on the heavy side, full of curves and bearing a wicked smile. She was wearing lingerie that did little to hide her voluptuousness. Langdon felt like he'd just received a crass text message from one of his more unsavory friends and that some joke might be attached to the picture.

"Is this recent?" Langdon asked.

"No. She sent me this right before we got married. Almost eight years ago."

"Got anything more recent?"

"Nope. But she hasn't changed much. Except for gettin' a mouth on her. Learned English so well, you can hardly tell she's Russian no more."

"Do you know her family?"

"She said she had nobody."

"Did she grow up in an orphanage?" Langdon knew that many women were recruited directly out of the orphanages into forced prostitution. Maybe mail-order brides were the same.

"She didn't talk much about her time back there," Rudolph said. "I don't think it was all that good."

Langdon knew he should tell the man to get lost. Chances were the woman had just walked out on this buffoon who lived in a false reality where women could be bought and sold like chattel and where being female meant you knew to only speak when spoken to. But what if the woman, Ann, had really been abducted? If he found her and she didn't want to be found, he could always claim to have come up empty-handed. Langdon believed in what was right and wrong and not necessarily what was written down. And, of course, he did need the money.

"I charge fifty dollars an hour and will need you to put down a retainer for two grand," Langdon said.

Rudolph peeled off twenty hundred-dollar bills from a wad in his pocket. Langdon gathered some more information, had the man sign a few forms, and escorted him from his office, through the mystery bookstore, and out onto Maine Street of Brunswick, the only street in the state with that name.

Chabal, Star, and dog were all waiting for him when he returned to *The Coffee Dog Bookstore*, a mystery bookstore named after dog's predecessor. Chabal had been his first employee back in 1996, had married him in 1999, and now in 2020, she was his partner, confidant, and lover. His other employee, Star—Jonathan Starling—had been around for almost as long, a former lawyer dragged back from the brink of alcoholic decay to become a bookstore clerk, the job somehow turning out to be a boon to his sobriety. The canine, dog, with a lowercase d, was now almost nine, but still full of all the vim and vigor of a puppy.

Langdon had returned to Brunswick from college some thirty years earlier with dreams of being a private detective and opening a mystery bookstore. He hadn't had the funds for the bookstore, and the PI business certainly wasn't cutting it, but then his crazy Aunt Zelda died, leaving him a chunk of cash. Not enough to retire to the islands, but enough to open a fairly well-stocked bookstore right on Maine Street, with no bank payments to be made.

Langdon had always been Zelda's favorite, perhaps because he'd raised his twin younger brothers after their dad left them all in the lurch. Over the years, the bookshop had grown into the finest collection of mysteries in Maine, and most likely all of New England. The shelves housed old school authors such as Dashiell Hammett, Raymond Chandler, and Mickey Spillane. These legends were connected to contemporary authors by giants such as Robert Parker, Marcia Muller, and Sue Grafton. Current best-selling authors James Lee Burke, Michael Connelly, and Harlan Coben were mixed in with as yet unknown rising stars. Langdon was perhaps most fond of his Maine Writers shelf showcasing the likes of Gerry Boyle, Paul Doiron, Bruce Robert Coffin, Richard Cass, and Joseph Souza.

"Hey, earth to Langdon. What'd the fellow want?" Chabal Langdon was just over five-feet tall, had blonde hair that reached her shoulders, cheeks that bulged slightly, and possessed a cracking, caustic wit usually aimed in her husband's direction.

"You mean Rudolph?" Langdon asked.

"That's just wrong, man," Star said.

"I'd guess that dude hits the bottle pretty hard to have a schnozzle that red," Chabal said.

"That's a myth," Star said. "The red nose thing is a condition. Alcohol might be a trigger, but the person is already predisposed."

"Whatever," Chabal said. "What's his real name?"

Langdon chuckled. "No, really, it's Rudolph. Rudolph Morin."

"Son-of-a-bitch," Star said.

"What'd he want with you?" Chabal asked.

"Hired me to find his wife. Said somebody stole her."

"You mean she ran off with somebody else?" Chabal asked.

A customer came to the register with two books, so Langdon sidled down the counter away from the woman, Chabal following suit, as Star rang up the purchases. The counter was twelve feet long, made of maple, and polished to a mirror-like sheen.

Langdon thought it best to wait before discussing private cases in a public space and held back as the woman left and John Dobson, who owned a specialty furniture shop a few doors down, stepped up to the counter.

"Hey, Langdon, do you have a book about poison? Think the author is Dr. Robinson, or something like that?"

"Hi, John." Langdon nodded. "You're looking for The *Queen of All Poisons* by BJ Magnani. The protagonist is Dr. Lily Robinson." He led the man back into the shelves.

Once the man had bought the book and left, Langdon turned back to Star. "I got Tucker coming in at 10:00 to run curbside." He looked at his watch. "Right about now. Will the two of you be okay here without us?"

"Only six allowed in at a time. Should be fine."

"Might take my wife out for a cup of coffee and talk about the latest case."

"We got coffee here. You can go sit in your office, so you don't have to be interrupted by customers and share information with me, if you want." Star looked over at the coffee dispenser behind the counter. Coffee was just one of the perks they offered here at the bookshop—well, coffee was normally on offer until Covid times had required them to stop for reasons of hygiene. The regulars knew they could ask for a cup, though. Local artwork adorned the walls, and once a month, they had an art opening, complete with hors d'oeuvres and free wine. At least they used to, before the pandemic.

Langdon thought it best to not say that it was a gorgeous day outside and that the tables out front of the Lenin Stop Coffee Shop would soon be done for the season. It wasn't normal to pass the mid-point of October in Brunswick and have the temperature at 68°. "Thought we might get a pastry as well."

"Bring me one," Star said. "And take your dog with you."

"Don't suppose you're going to ask me if I want to go?" Chabal asked.

"If we don't hurry, they're going to run out of their brown sugar sticky buns," Langdon replied.

Langdon was the last one out the door. Chabal was almost first before being knocked aside by dog. They emerged onto the wide sidewalks of Brunswick to a dazzling day of blue sky and glittering sunshine. Downtown was a throwback to days of old with shops, restaurants, and banks lining the four lanes that was Maine Street. Crossing the street could be a risky proposition in the summer when the tourists raced up and down, but now, in the fall, it was a rare car that didn't stop as soon as a pedestrian approached a crosswalk.

Maine Street was bordered by Fort Andross, a huge old brick mill repurposed for businesses on the Androscoggin River to the north, and the First Parish Church marking the boundary of Bowdoin College to the south. Portland was just a half-hour away, and the ocean licked the shores a scant four miles from the center of town. Langdon had grown up here, gone to school here, raised a daughter and step kids here, and it was the only home he'd ever known.

It'd taken some time, but dog had finally come to the realization that if he followed a step behind Landon in crossing the street, he would get a treat on the other side. Quid pro quo was the bartering system that controlled the canine's life, food and praise for being a good boy, an arrangement that made everybody happy. More than likely, dog had an inkling of where they were going, and, not above begging, he was bound to capture a lot of booty as he patrolled the outdoor tables.

Once they'd settled into their cast-iron chairs, sharing a pastry between the three of them with two more in the bag for Star and Tucker, Chabal fixed her eyes on Langdon. "Tell me about this *stolen* wife."

"Rudolph sure is a piece of work," Langdon said. "Sounds like his wife, Ann, short for Annika, was a mail-order bride from Russia. This, then, is why he considers her a possession, something he bought and paid for."

"Asshole," Chabal said.

"She's been gone for four days."

"Do you actually think she's been abducted?"

"Of course not. First of all, she's a good twenty years younger than him; second, she's gorgeous; and third, he is indeed an asshole." Langdon broke off a piece of the pastry and split it in two, throwing half to dog, who appeared to swallow his whole, a straight shot down the throat.

"But you took Rudolph's money?" Chabal snickered slightly when she said the name.

Langdon shrugged. "Asshole or not, I guess Rudolph deserves to know where his wife is. Or who she's with."

"What if he drags her back home?"

"She is not, after all, actually property, and we're not in Russia."

"It can be pretty intimidating being a woman in an abusive relationship. She might be too scared to refuse. Fear does funny things to a person."

"True," Langdon said. "How about we find her and then assess the situation? If we determine that she is safer without him knowing her whereabouts, we'll return the money and wash our hands of the whole thing."

"Money would stave off breaking into our retirement funds for a bit," Chabal said.

"Or we could keep the money and call it his penance for being an asshole," he said.

"A morality fine, of sorts," Chabal said.

"And it *is* possible that Ann has actually been taken or attacked in some manner, maybe even murdered. We don't know for sure yet that she ran off on the schmuck."

Langdon's phone buzzed with a text message. It was from Starling.

Got another possible client here looking for you.

Two in one day, Langdon thought, as he pecked out his reply.

Let them know I'll be there in five.

K.

~ ~ ~ ~ ~

Annika Morin sat in the cottage all alone. She didn't much care for the isolation, but it was for a good cause. Being alone certainly was better than being beaten and used by men. The problem was the loneliness. This overwhelming emptiness, the quiet that was suffocating. Soon, it would be all over. Soon, she would have her fairy-tale ending. She'd go off with her knight in shining armor, riding into the westward setting sun to live happily ever after.

The third time was the charm. This is what she told herself. She deserved it. It was her due. Some twelve years ago, she'd been swept off her feet by Taras Kulyk. He'd come into her small village in Russia with those flashing dark eyes and compact body. He was the first man she'd slept with, a far step above the boys she'd climbed into haylofts with for some awkward fumbling that was often over before it even started, for her anyway. Taras took his time, saw that she, too, felt pleasure.

When he asked her to leave with him, there had been no hesitation.

At first it was exciting to be the girlfriend of an enforcer for the Odessa mafia in the Ukraine. To be a member of the *Malina*. Men and women treated her with respect. She had nice things. Ate well. Bought shoes and jewelry and dresses. Annika Andreyevna, as she had been known then, was a *gospozha* who was envied by some and feared by all. To cross the mistress of Taras Kulyk was to invite disaster.

The descent began with Taras ignoring her for increasing stretches of time, disappearing overnight. Then he began to flaunt whores in front of her. This was followed by verbal abuse, the occasional beating, and forcing her to fuck his friends. Annika knew that the only way that was going to end up was with her dead.

One day she stowed away on a steamer headed back to Russia, disembarking in Kuchugury, using her natural gifts—refined by Taras' teachings—to work her way to Moscow. She was too afraid of returning to her village, where she would most likely be shunned by her family as soiled goods, and easily found by Taras. She was forced to perform acts on men just to eat, to buy clothes or a tram pass, to get by. This, she did not mind so much. It empowered her to hold a man in her hand and know that she controlled him, even if only for that little bit of time.

In Moscow, she signed up with a service that matched women with men from America. This was her way out, to somehow get to this place of blue jeans, cinema, and freedom. Annika could envision the fairy-tale ending in her head as the tall American businessman arrived to whisk her back to his seaside mansion where she'd host dinner parties and volunteer her time helping poor children rise above their station. It was a disappointment when it was portly, red-nosed Rudolph who showed up to meet with her, but, she reasoned, some of the best gifts were not always the most finely wrapped, and she did love lobster.

Life with Rudolph might not have been the material of fairy tales, but it was certainly a step up from Russia and the Ukraine.

He only demanded sex once or twice a week, rarely hit her, and wasn't into anything kinky. Things could be far worse. She had food to eat. Little was expected of her except to cook and clean.

One day, Annika realized she was pregnant and became lost in a glow of maternity. A little boy. Even Rudolph seemed to soften. Perhaps this was the fairy tale. To be a mother. She would give birth to a boy and raise him to be a man who was strong, smart, and kind. When she grew old, this boy would take care of her, bringing her to live with him in his mansion.

But that was not the way it had worked out, Annika thought, a tear in the corner of her eye. Not by a long shot.

Chapter 2

Langdon had worked on exactly seven cases since Covid had swooped in back in March and set Maine, or really, the world, into a state of suspended animation, with people retreating into their houses and behind their masks, empty streets and closed stores and restaurants, a barren landscape indeed. Now, across the desk of his windowless office sat potential client number two of the morning. Raven Burke was a light-skinned Black woman with multiple tight braids falling down just past her shoulders. She had dark, flashing eyes, thin eyebrows, and an old scar about two inches long on her right cheekbone.

"What can I do for you, Raven?" He'd already been instructed to call her by her first name.

"I was sexually harass' by my boss and then fire' when I refused his advances." Raven's eyes flared with the promise of anger and vengeance.

Langdon would guess that her dialect was of some sort of Caribbean extract. "Where'd you work?"

"Brunswick Brew Pub."

Langdon was a fan of their beer. He might have to rethink his patronage. "Did you report this incident to the owner?"

"Not that simple a thing, Mr. Langdon."

"Langdon. Just Langdon will do. I'm sorry. Why is it not a simple thing?"

"He *is* the owner," Raven said.

"Rick Strong?" Langdon asked. He knew the man slightly from around town. They both attended Chamber of Commerce meetings and events as well as the in-town group.

"That's the pig-fucker."

Langdon sat back in his chair. *Whoa*, he thought, *this young woman is harnessing some deep anger.* "When did these incidents occur?"

"Last January, soon after I was hire', for about three weeks until I was fire'."

"I believe the statute of limitations for filing a claim is 300 days," Langdon said. "The first thing you'll need to do is file a charge with the Maine Human Rights Commission."

"I di' that," Raven said. "They dismiss' my claim."

"What? What for?"

Raven sighed. "I file' my complaint. Six-weeks later they share' Rick's response, which was that I was lying, been stealing money, and drinking on the job."

"Nonetheless," Langdon said. "I believe they can sometimes take up to two years to investigate a sexual harassment charge. What reason did they give?"

"With the Covi' and all, I went through some tough time'. Got evict' from my apartment. Ha' my phone turn' off. Things were pretty... bad. Then in August I got a job waitressing over at the Wretch' Lobster. Just down the street. You know the place?"

"I sure do," Langdon said. "The owner, Richam Denevieux, is a good friend of mine."

"He a goo' man," Raven said. "He pull' me up by my bootstraps and got me back on my feet. Help' me get a new apartment and get my phone turn' back on. Once things were flowing smoothly again, I check' in with the Commission. The investigator of my case, Carol Smith, was no longer working for them. Took me awhile, but I finally dug out that my case got dismiss' because they couldn't get ahol' of me."

Langdon nodded. He understood that the Commission reserved

the right to dismiss any case in which they were unable to contact the accuser. They were sort of sticklers for that. To Langdon, this seemed to be a real Catch-22. The women who most needed the support were often neglected. "I'm not sure what I can do for you, Raven. Do you want to pursue criminal charges? Or perhaps sue him?"

"No," Raven shook her head. "Seem' like my case was pretty thin to begin with. Carol, the investigator, say that I should've written down the incidents, gotten them corroborated by other employees. I didn't do any of that. It's not like he ran his foul mouth when others were aroun'. Woul' put his hand on my back while he spoke with me and then let it slide down to my ass. But not in front of anybody else, he was too sly for that."

"What sort of things did he say to you?"

"What he want' to do to me. What he want' me to do to him. He'd ask me if I... liked... to do certain things, if I ha' a boyfrien', what my favorite position was." Raven started to cry, silent tears rolling down her cheeks. The scar on her right cheek diverted the flow like a gulley in a flash flood.

Langdon thought it best that Chabal follow up on this line of questioning with Raven at a later time. "How can I help?"

"Men like that aren't one-timers," Raven said. "I wasn't the first, and I won't be the last. Not unless I do something."

"You want me to catch Rick Strong sexually harassing women at the Brunswick Brew Pub and expose him?" Langdon kicked himself internally for the bad choice of words. He considered saying no pun intended, but luckily, thought better of it.

"Ya. He has to be stop'. Either legally or through the court of public opinion. He needs to be exposed." Raven grinned, but there was little humor in the flash of teeth.

"It won't be cheap," Langdon said. "I charge thirty bucks an hour. Could get lucky and catch him right off in some improper indiscretion, but even that would need collaboration by the victim. Might take weeks. The money adds up."

Raven gave a tiny, shy smile that seemed more sincere. "Richam say you might consider doing it for free."

Of course he did, Langdon thought, wondering if perhaps he should start sending people down to the Wretched Lobster with the promise of a free meal on the owner.

"I just save' enough money to get out of the Tedfor' Shelter and into my own place," Raven said. "I got debt hanging over my head, but that don't mean I don't want to settle some past due accounts on this sleazeball preying on the women in his employ."

Langdon figured that Raven was about the same age as his daughter, Missouri, who currently lived in Brooklyn, the one in New York, not Maine. "I'll see what I can do," he said. Recently, Missouri had shared an incident with Langdon about the treatment she'd received from a boss, behavior that made Langdon's blood boil still. Missouri had quit and walked away rather than confront the bastard.

After Raven left, Langdon spent some time researching Annika Morin. She had few connections in Brunswick, according to her husband, Rudolph. She did have her own car, a beat-up old Corolla that he'd bought her so that she could grocery shop and do errands. They didn't socialize much as a couple. Langdon was willing to bet that Rudolph hung out with a crew of drinking buddies while the womenfolk were left home waiting for them. One thing that Ann did do was a yoga class three times a week.

Langdon had called the Yoga Bear Studio and was told that the owner would be in around 3:00, and thus, at 3:00 he found himself pulling his Jeep into the studio on Stanwood Street. The building was a one-story box affair next to the railroad tracks. Langdon wondered how that worked with the meditation piece of yoga—that is, to have the Amtrak train go rumbling by, to and from Boston five times a day. Perhaps it was soothing.

There was a foyer inside leading through an open archway to a larger room. To one side was a long counter, behind which stood two women who couldn't have weighed 200 pounds combined. The younger one had on a yoga bra that barely covered any part of the top half of her body, and Langdon hurriedly averted his eyes to look at the other lady, who was probably in her mid-thirties and wearing a tank top that at least didn't make him blush.

"Are you Diane?" he asked.

"That's me. What can I do for you?" Diane spoke in clipped tones like she was busy.

"My name's Langdon." He guessed that she always spoke like she was busy. "I was wondering if I might ask you a few questions about one of your members."

"We don't run a dating service here, bub."

"I'm a private investigator. Looking for a missing person."

"Missing person? Who?" Diane threw the words down like a challenge.

"Woman by the name of Ann Morin. Do you know her?"

Two women came in the door behind him and passed their membership keychain cards over a machine that beeped once, greeting Diane and the other lady enthusiastically, and disappeared through a doorway to the left. Langdon guessed it led to a locker room.

"I know Ann. You say she's missing?"

"Yes. Her husband came in and hired me this morning to find her. Said she up and disappeared four days ago." Langdon had gotten Rudolph to send him Ann's photo, which he'd cropped to just a headshot on his phone now, lest anyone think he was some kind of pervert. This he held up to Diane. "Is this the woman you know?"

"That's her. Looks like that was taken a few years back, but she hasn't changed much."

"When's the last time you saw her?"

"We've been closed to live classes since last March," Diane said. The door opened again and another woman in tight-fitting yoga pants and a sweatshirt came by with a big hello and disappeared through the small door. "We did some classes outside over the summer, but we've been strictly on Zoom for the past month."

"Has Ann been attending classes?" Langdon asked. He felt like Diane was being evasive, but he wasn't sure why. Maybe it had to do with the fact that she was blatantly breaking Covid restrictions and holding inside classes despite the regulations imposed by the state. "Outside or via Zoom?"

"What's that putz of a husband want with her, anyway?" the younger woman asked. "He didn't do anything but order her around. Tell her what she could do and couldn't do. I'd say she's better off gone."

"Suppose that depends on where she's gone to," Langdon said. "If she's safe and sound and doesn't want to return to him, nobody's going to make her." He wasn't sure this was quite true, as Chabal had so eloquently put it, 'fear does funny things to a person.'

"Haven't seen her for months," Diane said. "Not for some time now."

Langdon looked at the younger woman. "How about you?" He managed to maintain eye contact.

"Nope, Ann hasn't been around since spring. She used to come to my Core Awakening class, but I don't think I've seen her since at least June."

"Is she still a member?"

Diane pecked into the keyboard. "Yes."

A man and a woman came in and went through the smaller door.

"You have no idea where she could be?" Langdon asked. "Did she have any friends that you know of? Any interests outside of yoga?"

"You should ask her husband," Diane said.

Langdon walked back to his Jeep musing upon why the two women had been so unhelpful, almost to the point of antagonism. He figured it was most likely a protective contrariness, reflexively not sharing what they may or may not have known. And they'd obviously lied about not having any live classes, as the people streaming into the studio confirmed. Langdon was still going to the gym out behind his bookstore, so he knew that they were allowed to be open, but perhaps there was a capacity limit that Yoga Bear Studio was abusing and so the owner thought it best to pretend that live classes were not happening?

He should've brought dog in to soften them up, Langdon ruminated as he climbed into the Jeep and patted his canine sidekick on the head, turning to avoid being licked on the face. That was an idea—if not dog, perhaps Chabal would be up for some yoga. Most likely not, but maybe he could ask Jewell Denevieux, who was more into that sort of thing. Heck, it was possible that she was even a member or had previously attended Yoga Bear.

It wasn't like Langdon didn't exercise. He went to the gym four days a week. As a matter of fact, he'd considered the idea that stretching and yoga might be good for him, but he couldn't very well go undercover at Yoga Bear now that he'd been in asking questions. There were many contradictions in the life of Goff Langdon. He was an environmentalist as well as a red meat eater. He was a football fan and played golf, although he wasn't very good at the latter. He, like most Mainers, voted for Independents, sometimes Democrats, but never Republicans. He'd been known to carry a gun, but believed gun laws should be tightened. He offset his excessive drinking with daily workouts, ate abundantly sometimes, and forgot to even nibble at others.

Time to flip gears and pay Rick Strong a visit, Langdon thought as he pulled out onto the road. And he might as well have a beer while he was there. Brunswick Brew Pub was just outside of town on the Bath Road. When Langdon parked, he texted Chabal asking if she wanted to join him for dinner when she closed the store at 5:00. In normal times, the bookshop would be open until 8:00, but in Covid times, they had abbreviated hours.

Five was a bit early to eat, but a cocktail or two first would bring them into prime time, and another positive attribute to the brew pub was that they allowed dogs inside, supposedly on a leash. Langdon did not own a leash but knew from previous experience that he could most likely get away without it. He looked at the time and saw it was not quite 4:00.

The Brunswick Brew Pub was a new construction from about two years back. It looked to be a large barn other than the fact that the roof was comprised of solar panels with tall windows bedecking the façade. The bar was closed, and tables were socially-distanced hi-tops, each with four stools made of silver stainless steel. The place appeared to be rustling to life as the clock had passed 4:00 and was headed toward the happy hour of 5:00.

A waiter came over to get his order, and of the several IPAs on the menu, recommended the Cabot India Pale Ale, or CIPA, pronounced 'sipa,' the young man said with a smirk. "Like, why don't you go sip a beer." Dog implored Langdon to order some French fries as well.

There were maybe fifteen others scattered across the large space, but the door appeared busy with new arrivals. A fountain sprayed water upward in the middle of the room, giving the place an air of pretentiousness that rubbed Langdon the wrong way, or was it that he'd recently been informed that the owner was a sexual predator? Langdon had intended to make light conversation with the waitperson about Rick Strong just to get a vibe, but he hadn't considered that his server would be a male. Which, Langdon thought, was an entirely politically incorrect subconscious assumption that he needed to erase from the basement of his mind.

The young man came back with his CIPA, and Langdon gave it the ole college try anyway. "You worked here long?" he asked.

"Almost a year now," the young man said. He looked to be in his mid-twenties.

"What'd you say your name was?"

"Greg."

"My name's Langdon. How you like working here?" he asked.

"Reason I'm asking is my daughter is going to apply here, and I thought I'd check it out."

"Your daughter like you all mixed up in her business?" Greg asked.

Langdon laughed and took a drink. The beer was very good. "Not so much." They both knew that a tip hung in the balance. "My wife is meeting me here for dinner in a bit. We thought we'd check it out, on the sly, if you will."

"It's not so bad." Greg shrugged. "I was making a heckuva lot more money last February, but it could be worse."

"How's the boss? Rick, right? Is he easy to work for?"

Greg fidgeted slightly. "He's been pretty worked up on the whole mask mandate. Pretty steamed about the regulations and requirements. Look, I gotta get back to work."

Langdon went back to people-watching and sipping his beer. When his second beer arrived, he pried out of Greg that the best practices in regard to the Covid were not always followed at the Brunswick Brew Pub. He whispered that Rick Strong rarely wore a mask, and that the kitchen staff was not required to do so. Langdon eyed the French fries that had come with the CIPA and decided that dog would be happy but that dinner plans with Chabal would have to be changed.

As Greg went to wait upon another table, Langdon texted Chabal.

How about I get some takeout from Hog Heaven and bring it home?

Fine with me. She replied. Why the change of plans?

Tell you later.

Langdon looked up to see Rick Strong come in the door. He said hi to some people at a table, chatting and laughing with them about something, and then went back behind the counter to speak with the bartender.

He was probably about five-foot-eleven, but most likely told people that he was six-feet tall. His head was shaven clean, Langdon guessed to cover up that he was balding. His body looked like middle age might have added a few pounds, and his face was starting to get puffy around the edges, a combination of entering his forties and too much alcohol, Langdon figured. His eyes were blue and burned in his head with an intensity stoked by anger.

Hmmm. Might have to stick around for a bit, Langdon thought. He gave a small whistle for dog, which was promptly ignored, as the canine was working his beggarly magic on two young women, his eyes conveying years of starvation that could be resolved with just a bit of their sandwich, or maybe even a chip or two would do. Langdon tossed a fry on the ground, which managed to get dog's attention, as well as Rick Strong's.

The man came barreling around the bar as if the building were on fire. "Hey, that dog has to be on a leash," he said.

"Hi, Rick, how've you been?" Langdon said.

"Langdon." Rick nodded, having come to a standstill by the table. "Haven't I told you before that your dog has to be on a leash?"

"I thought you were kidding about that," Langdon said, grinning. "No. I was not."

Langdon didn't remember him being so unfriendly. "Sorry."

"You going to put a leash on him?"

"Don't have one."

Rick looked around the room and Langdon could almost hear him processing how much he needed Langdon's business. "Going to have to ask you to leave."

"Let me finish my beer. Can I buy you one?" Langdon raised his glass.

"No."

"This CIPA is outstanding."

"Thank you."

"How's business?"

Rick sighed. "Be better if the goddamn governor wouldn't go meddling in it."

"Seems to me our private liberties are being abused," Langdon said, goadingly. "She might as well have burned down my bookstore."

"Right?" Rick sat down. "Who's that bitch think she is."

Langdon hoped that he kept the wince off his face. He couldn't be sure. "That's what happens when you elect a woman to do a man's job."

"She sure as hell should know her place."

Langdon waved his empty glass at Greg as he walked by. "Another one of these bad boys," he said.

Rick looked at the glass, looked at Langdon, and gave a barely noticeable nod. "I'd think that reading would be big about now, with everybody staying home and all."

"When the governor closed us all down, everybody went to Amazon. Think they got used to it." This was a bald-faced lie, as Langdon's regulars had stuck with him through the thick and the thin of the pandemic. "Course, the big stores all got to stay open."

Greg brought the beer over. "This fellow was saying his daughter was going to apply to work here."

"That right?" Rick raised an eyebrow and turned back to Langdon. "Hard finding good help. Everybody wants a handout, but nobody wants to work for it. How old's your daughter?"

Langdon almost ruined the repartee with an angry retort before he remembered that none of this was true and that Missouri was not actually considering applying here, and what's more, was safely in Brooklyn. "Twenty-seven."

"Hmm. Send her in. We could use the help." Rick stood back up. "I got to get back to work. Next time bring a leash."

"You need anything?" Greg asked eyeballing Langdon's half-gone beer.

"You know a lady who used to work here named Raven Burke?"

"Yeah, sure. She was real nice." He licked his lips a bit when he said it. "Friendly."

"You know why she left?"

Greg looked around and then over to where Rick Strong was talking to the bartender. "Nah, man, think she just moved on."

"Suppose you can bring me my check," Langdon said, finishing his beer. "On second thought, you can run my card." He handed his Mastercard over.

"Thought you were meeting your wife for dinner?"

"That was before you told me the cooks don't wear masks," Langdon said.

When the check came out, Langdon did leave a twenty-dollar tip for three beers and French fries. He figured that there was more to be eased out of Greg, perhaps at a time when Rick Strong wasn't around.

Chapter 3

Friday, October 23rd

Dog woke Langdon at 6:00 a.m. to let him know that it was breakfast time. They'd long since banished him from the bedroom, but that didn't prevent him from clawing at the door. Langdon slid carefully from the bed, pausing for an appreciative glance at his wife and love, Chabal, who was softly snoring. He thought that perhaps he might feed the dog and sneak back into bed.

Langdon had no sooner poured a cup of food into dog's bowl when his phone buzzed on his desk, where he left it at night so as to not disturb them. Who would be bothering him at this time of the morning, he wondered? It might be best to ignore it if his idea of spooning with Chabal was actually going to come to fruition. If he didn't have a daughter, he would have disregarded it, but as it was, he had to know. It was a text from Bart. You up?

Was he up, Langdon wondered? It was not like Bart to text or call frivolously. The man was very spare with his words, even in conversation. It must be important. And Bart was a cop—and a friend. Langdon texted back. Yep.

The phone immediately rang. "What's up, Bart?" he asked.

"Missing kid. Out on Church Road. We're organizing a search out behind the house. Can you and Chabal join in?"

"For sure. How old?"

"Four."

"Give us half-an-hour."

"Can you call Richam and Jewell? And that hipster lawyer with the funny name?"

Langdon grinned. Bart and Jimmy 4 by Four fought like an old married couple. "Gotcha. What's the address?"

Bart told him and hung up without further ado.

Langdon crawled back into bed and lightly rubbed Chabal's back.

"Mmm. I was afraid you weren't coming back," she said pushing her butt into his midsection.

"Bart called. They're organizing a search for a missing kid on Church Road." Langdon said quickly, knowing that the point of no return was not far down this particular street if she kept wiggling into him. "Told him we'd be there ASAP."

Chabal rolled from bed and to her feet instantly. "How old?"

"Four."

She pulled the T-shirt that she'd worn to bed over her head, standing in just her panties as she grabbed a shirt to wear. Now in her mid-fifties, Chabal Langdon was still a beautiful woman. She was fit and healthy, even with a few extra pounds added to her midsection over the years. Blonde hair cascaded to her shoulders like a brook in the wilds, and her hazel eyes danced with perpetual mystery and mischief.

"Can you call Jewell and see if they can join in?" Langdon asked, his eyes riveted to her body.

"Sure. Let me get dressed first."

Langdon sighed and pulled a pair of pants on. He was pouring coffee into travel mugs while talking on the phone with 4 by Four when Chabal emerged looking as fresh as if she'd spent hours getting ready instead of five minutes. She was also on the phone. Dog was quite excited to be up and out so early in the morning, going so far as to try and claim the driver's seat of the Jeep.

Coming down Church Road it was obvious which house it was. Local and state police vehicles dotted the long driveway, forcing the volunteer searchers to park on the sides of the road. There had to be forty cars already gathered with more pulling in.

Bart came to meet them when they were halfway, or about fifty yards, up the drive. He was a huge bear of a man, five inches over six feet tall, and heading north of 350 pounds. He had on a brown suit jacket with several food stains on the lapels and a white shirt that was half-untucked with a red tie askew at the top. Sergeant Jeremiah Bartholomew and Langdon had been friends ever since the summer after Langdon's sophomore year of college. Bart, drunk, had come into the bar where Langdon was bouncing, and picked a fight with four drug dealers. Langdon jumping in to prevent Bart from being stabbed had cemented the friendship between him and the ill-tempered and gruff policeman.

"What's the deal?" Langdon asked.

"Dad woke up this morning, and his son was gone. We think he might've wandered off and got lost. That dog of yours any good at tracking?"

Langdon gave a small, wan smile. Bart knew that while dog aimed to please, he was pretty useless in terms of tracking, fetching, or hunting.

"No matter," Bart said. "There are two canine units out there now, but so far, nothing. I'm heading up a search team to follow behind them. We're going to spread out from Old Route 1 all the way across to Pleasant Hill Road and cover the area west to Highland Road."

Chabal had her phone out looking at the map. "Not much between here and there," she said.

"There's Bunganuc Stream and the old dump, but that's about it," Bart said.

There were a hundred people spread out over a distance of just about a mile. Dog thought it was great fun. Richam, Jewell, and 4 by Four walked along the line with Langdon and Chabal. Langdon thought it might be a good time to bring up Raven Burke with Richam and steered himself closer to his friend, the owner of the Wretched Lobster restaurant downtown.

Richam was a slim man with a military bearing even though he'd never served. He'd moved to Brunswick with his pregnant wife twenty-five years ago from a South American island nation when the politics of the country overflowed into violence. He wore thick-framed black glasses, had a narrow mustache, and was always impeccably dressed.

"Got a new client yesterday," Langdon said to his friend. "She said she works for you. Raven Burke."

"Is that right?" Richam didn't look at Langdon, keeping his gaze focused on the ground and in front of him. "Hired her a couple months back. Seems like a good sort."

"She said that she was sexually harassed by Rick Strong over at the Brunswick Brew Pub."

"Yes. She told me about that."

"Raven also said that you told her I'd handle her case pro bono."

Richam laughed. "I believe I told her that you, too, were a good sort and that you would treat her right."

"Raven also told me that you agreed to let me and Chabal eat at the Wretched Lobster free for a year. You know, as payment."

Richam stopped walking and looked over at Langdon. "Did she now? No, I don't think so. You are full of it."

Langdon chuckled. "No, she did no such thing, but it seems reasonable."

"Tell you what," Richam said. "Your next meal is free, and if you nail that bastard, I'll give you another free meal. And you can bring dog. All he can eat."

"You're convinced he did it, then?"

"I don't know. She told me the case was dismissed, and that gives her no real opportunity to seek any compensation. The courts would more than likely reject any suit she brought against Strong. Can't see why she would continue to pursue it if she can't collect any damages, not unless it was true."

Langdon mulled that over for a bit. "She said she has no tangible proof. She figures that she wasn't the first, the only, or the last one. Wants me to gather proof that he's making unwanted advances to other women that work for him now, maybe find those like her who used to work there but quit for the same reason."

Richam cursed and kicked a branch. "Never liked the man much."

"Why not?'

"Heard things. Small world, the restaurant business in Brunswick. Several people on my staff have worked at the Brew Pub in the past, and I hear snippets. Nothing tangible, mind you, just enough to know he is a disagreeable man."

"You sound pretty worked up about it."

"Tangerine quit her job down in Boston a few months back." Tangerine was his daughter. "Just admitted to me that her boss was always trying to get her to go out with him, and finally she just quit. She didn't want to make a scene. Figured it was easier to just leave."

"Same thing happened to Missouri last year. I almost went down to Brooklyn to rip the fucker's head off," Langdon said. "Thought better of it. Wish I hadn't."

"Men can be real dinks," Jewell said, having approached them to cross over a small stream, stepping over three stones situated well for her need.

Langdon had long thought that Jewell could be cast in a Quentin Tarantino film as a badass protagonist. She was tall and fit, had strong angular features, an afro exploding from her head in natural waves. "That they can be," he agreed. "Sorry to hear about Tangerine."

"Not that you're so innocent," Jimmy 4 by Four said, following them over the stream on the rocks.

"You talking to me?" Jewell demanded hotly.

4 by Four was a former New York City attorney turned hippie in the nineties and then hipster in the new century. He wore expensive clothes, had a carefully cultivated beard, and a man-bun atop his head. "Well, you neither," he said to Jewell with a chuckle. "But I was directing that at Langdon."

"What's that supposed to mean?" Langdon asked.

"You slept with your employee."

Jewell laughed. "He does have a point."

"I was the one targeted," Langdon said. "*She* was the one who took advantage of *me*."

Chabal leaped nimbly from rock to rock, her shorter legs finding the distance across the stream a little more difficult as she crossed and joined them where they'd paused for a break on the far side of the water. "Who took advantage of you?" she asked.

"You did," Langdon said. "You couldn't keep your hands off of me."

"Thought I'd at least get a raise," Chabal said.

"Must not have been that good," 4 by Four said.

"Not enough for a raise, that's for sure," Langdon agreed.

"But good enough that you've had me locked down for the past twenty years in an institution called marriage that makes Guantanamo look like a Boy Scout camp," Chabal said.

"Hmm," Langdon said. "Maybe tonight we can play-act that prison scenario you're so fond of."

"The one where I waterboard you?" Chabal asked.

"We should get back to looking for the missing boy," Richam said.

~ ~ ~ ~ ~

It was noon when Langdon, Chabal, and dog arrived home. The boy had not been found. They had to get something to eat, shower, and get into the bookshop to relieve Starling who'd opened that morning. Where could the boy have gone, Langdon wondered?

"You want to jump in the shower while I put something together to eat?" Langdon asked.

"I'm starving. How about we eat and then shower together?" she said.

Who was he to argue with that, Langdon thought? He made two eggs on English muffins with cheese that took all of four minutes, twice the time it took for Langdon to finish his plate. Chabal took longer to finish her food, but before long, they were off to the shower.

They were quite clean when they finally emerged and tumbled into bed together. Shower sex was not something that people in their fifties often engaged in, but it was a mighty fine place for foreplay, and sure beat showering alone. Plus, they were able to wash each other's backs.

"That was a waste of a shower," Chabal said afterward as she rolled from bed.

"I thought it was a mighty fine use of one, myself," Langdon said.

"Except I'm dirty again."

"Yes, you are."

"I just gotta dry my hair and we can skedaddle."

"Sounds good."

Langdon got up and flicked the television on as he got dressed. He glanced in the mirror, thinking it about time he got a trim, his red hair springing crazily from his head in various directions. There was a slight paunch to his stomach, which was not as flat and hard as it had been ten years ago, but not bad, he thought. His six-foot-four frame hid the bulge well enough. There were a few crinkles around his blue eyes that had also seemingly appeared out of nowhere. He figured that he'd earned them and left it at that.

He had clean jeans on and was buttoning up his Hawaiian shirt when a special report flashed across the screen. A news anchor came on, looking very serious. He said that they'd just received a video about a kidnapped boy in Brunswick, and that the message had been quite clear that the child would suffer if they didn't air it. Some of it was quite disturbing, the news anchor warned, and should not be watched if the viewer was squeamish.

"Chabal, you gotta come see this," Langdon called into the master bathroom, and she came out and stood next to him.

The image that came on was of fair quality, albeit with poor lighting. A man sat on a wooden chair underneath a dangling light bulb in an otherwise dark room. He had a mask over his face, not a Covid mask, but a plastic Halloween-style Salvador Dalí mask. The signature upturned horseshoe mustache rose pencil thin to just below his eyes, matching his eyebrows, all mimicking the long face of the Spanish surrealist artist. A red sweatshirt hoodie, pulled over his head, was zipped up to just below his neck. He had on khakis, and black gloves adorned his hands, making the only visible part of him his hazel eyes.

Next to him on a wooden chair sat the trembling figure of four-year-old Edward James Thomas, the very boy they'd spent the morning searching for. He also had on a red sweatshirt, but no mask, and he looked like he'd been crying. Nothing else could be made out other than the two figures underneath the dismal light bulb, and there was not a sound for approximately twenty seconds. Then the man began to speak.

"In the midst of the biggest hoax to ever grip our nation, and the false claims of death and sickness related to something called Covid-19, the governor of Maine has declared war on businesses, basic freedoms, and the American way of life in this United States. The coronavirus crisis has been contrived by radical left-wing anarchists who want to unseat the President from his throne and replace him with old, Black, communists. The governor has helped perpetrate this myth, going further than any other in infringing upon the freedom of the residents of Maine. There is no need for mask wearing. It is just the government trying to control our actions."

The man paused here, and Dalí himself would've been proud by the surreal effect projected by this unmoving mask under a red hoodie in the flickering light. Then he continued.

"If that basic infraction was not transgression enough, the governor has closed down businesses, taking away the rights of individuals to provide for themselves and their families. This has not been done equitably, though. While small, local businesses have been forced to close or limit the people inside to a number that is not sustainable, big-box stores and chains have not faced the same limitations. This offense is no longer tolerable. We the people are being ignored. Our government is no longer meeting our needs. A snowflake agenda has descended on our nation, on our state, and put a stranglehold on us within our very homes."

The man looked sideways at the boy and whispered something that couldn't be heard before turning back to face the camera. "I demand that this transgression be fixed. Governor, I call for you to open our economy back up and cease with the silly mask mandate. I give you eight days to accomplish that task. When you do so, the boy will be returned safely to his home. If by midnight on October 31st, All Hallows Eve, you have not complied, I will execute this child. The blood will be on your hands, Governor."

The screen went briefly black before the anchor reappeared.

Chapter 4

"Wow," Langdon said.

"That's pretty effed up, right there," Chabal said.

"These anti-maskers are getting pretty riled up."

"I don't think it's just the masks," Chabal said. "It's shutting things down, social distancing, restricting movement."

"All that's really closed now is bars and tasting rooms for indoor service." Langdon turned off the television. "That upsets a lot more people than just the owners."

"People are getting claustrophobic."

"Enough so to kidnap and execute a child?"

"There's a special place in Hell for that dude," Chabal said.

"For sure. Maybe Satan will put him in a room with Atilla the Hun and Hitler. That would do the trick."

"Or Vlad the Impaler?"

"Hannibal Lecter?" Langdon suggested.

"Is he a real person?"

"I think he was based on a real person. Speaking of real, was that a Salvador Dalí mask?"

"Yep. Kind of ironic, don't you think?" Chabal said.

"What?"

"That the dude was railing against having to wear a mask while wearing a mask."

Langdon gave a grim grunt that may have been an attempt at a chuckle. "Yeah. Sort of like the Klan. Don't want the government to tell you what to do while hiding your face."

"Think there's anything to the mask itself, that it's Sal Dalí?"

Langdon mused on that for a moment. "Don't know much about the man except he did those crazy paintings."

"Surrealist," Chabal said. "Might be worth looking up."

"I'm sure they're on top of it at the command post," Langdon said. "You ready to go? We should get to the bookshop before Star throws a hissy fit because we're late."

"Yep."

"Isn't the plan to move to the final phase and reopen places for indoor drinking, anyway?" Langdon asked as they climbed into the Jeep.

"Supposed to be, but there are rumors circulating that, with the new outbreak, the governor's going to hit the pause button. Again."

"Sal Dalí is doing his best to reverse that decision."

"Those poor people," Chabal said.

"Who?"

"The parents. What are their names?"

"Martin and Jill Thomas," Langdon said.

"Can you imagine if Missouri was kidnapped when she was four?"

"She was almost killed at that age," Langdon said grimly. "It wasn't pleasant."

"Sorry," Chabal said. "Sometimes the mouth forgets what the mind knows."

The afternoon was spent on bookstore business. In between waiting on customers and delivering curbside, Langdon and Chabal put together their December order of new mysteries, as well as customer requests, and took care of various other Coffee Dog Bookstore tasks like advertising, payroll, and making sure the bills got paid on time.

In between all of that, they discussed the horrific nature of the kidnapping, the lobsterman's 'stolen' wife, and Raven Burke's sexual harassment claim against Rick Strong.

Friday night they were open until 8:00, but shoppers coming through had dwindled to almost nil as they approached that hour. Langdon was just about to go lock the door when it opened and a couple walked in. The man had a long face, eyes that shifted from brown to green to gold depending on the light, all behind large round glasses, with a square chin. He was about thirty years old. The woman with him had brown eyes that matched her hair, was broad across her body, and appeared to be very fit.

They walked tentatively from the door to the counter where Langdon and Chabal stood, almost as if they were picking their way through a minefield. Langdon realized that their eyes were red, their faces were drawn, and that their body language bespoke some tragedy.

"We're looking for Goff Langdon," the man said when they reached the counter. His voice was a low whisper.

"I'm Langdon."

"We were wondering if you might help us out?"

"This is my wife and partner, Chabal. What can we help you with?"

"You're a private investigator."

Langdon hadn't thought that this distraught couple were looking for the most recent Kate Flora book. "I am."

"We'd like to hire you."

"Hold on. If you don't mind me locking us in, I should close up." Langdon stepped to the door, locking it and flipping the sign to *Closed*. "Would you mind coming back to my office?"

He led them back to his windowless office, motioning Chabal to join them. He figured that would save him on repeating everything.

"Please, have a seat," Langdon said, tapping one of the two leather wingback Clarke chairs as he went back behind his desk to sit down. Chabal sat next to him, the two desks side by side. "First, what are your names?"

"I'm Martin Thomas, and this is my wife, Jill."

"It was your boy who was kidnapped," Chabal said.

"Yes."

"I am very sorry," Chabal said.

"Can you help us?" Jill asked, a bit of a screech to her voice indicating the terrible stress she was under as did her restless eyes, darting around the room. "This can't be happening."

"We'll see what we can do," Langdon said soothingly.

"Some fucking maniac has my baby and says he's going to execute him in eight days," Jill stood up and slapped the desk. "What is this? The fucking Middle East? This is *Maine*. Shit like this doesn't happen here."

"Maybe we can start with what happened," Langdon said calmly.

Martin took her arm and eased her back into her seat. "I woke up this morning just before 5:00 and got my coffee. It wasn't for another twenty minutes or so that I thought it was strange that Eddie wasn't up yet. I went up to his room, and he wasn't there. I searched the house. I looked outside. He wasn't anywhere to be found. Nowhere. He wasn't there. He was just gone. Gone."

"Where is my boy?" Jill asked, her words anguished.

"His name is Eddie? Eddie Thomas? Do you have a photograph?" Langdon asked, trying to distract her with questions.

"Yes. Edward James Thomas," Martin said, taking out a cell phone. "I'll text you a recent picture."

"We have to find him before that whacko hurts him," Jill said, her voice rising along with her body as she again leaned over the desk.

"Tell me about last night," Langdon said. "Was there anything unusual?"

"No. We had dinner at 6:00. I helped him with his homework." Martin held his palms up in defeat. "We watched some TV. He went to bed at 8:30."

"Homework for a four-year-old?"

"We are trying to use this time at home wisely to advance his intelligence," Martin said. He took out a box of Chiclets and popped several of the multi-colored pieces of gum into his mouth. "Preparing him for kindergarten next year, you know?"

Langdon thought it a bit excessive for a preschooler. "Did you hear any noises during the night? Anything at all? Nothing is too small."

"No. Nothing." Martin shook his head.

Langdon looked over at Jill. "How about you, Mrs. Thomas?"

"I wasn't there," she said, sitting back down.

"You weren't home?"

"We're separated, okay. I don't live there anymore. I got my own place out on Brunswick Landing. Renting one of those converted townhomes."

Langdon wrote something on the pad in front of him, more to buy time than any other reason. This was definitely delicate but was indeed a topic that needed to be explored more deeply. He decided to come back to it. "Had Eddie slept in his bed?" he asked Martin instead.

"Yes, he was asleep when I left his room after reading him a book and lying with him for a bit." Martin stole a glance at Jill. "He's been a bit nervous about being alone since we split up."

"Was there anything out of place? Broken? The window open? Anything out of the ordinary?" Langdon asked.

"No. Nothing. He was just gone. Gone. Not there."

"I'd like to come out and see the room, once the police are done with it, of course," Langdon said.

"Does that mean you'll help us?" Jill asked.

"I'll do anything in my power to find your son," Langdon said. "How long have the two of you been separated?"

"About six months," Martin said. He took out the pack of Chiclets and popped two more into his mouth.

Langdon nodded. "And custody?"

"Right now, we share. Jill takes Eddie the nights she has off of work, and I have him the rest of the time."

Six months, Langdon thought. They'd made it about a month into the lockdown and realized that it was one thing to be married to somebody and another to be cooped up with them twenty-four/seven, or so would be his guess.

"Forgive me for asking," Langdon said, "but are you two working on your marriage? Or have you entered into divorce proceedings?"

"We have filed and have a hearing next month," Martin said.

"What does that have to do with anything?" Jill asked.

"He believes that we might be suspects," Martin said.

"What the fuck?" Jill asked.

"Not at all," Langdon said. "I just need to get all of the details straight." Of course, he thought, in most child abduction cases, it was one of the parents who did the abducting. This, though, was different. What with the video extortion of the government and all. "Did the kidnapper send you the video?"

"No," Martin said. "We saw it for the first time this morning, the same as everybody else. The policeman, Sergeant Bartholomew, was pissed. Said that TV station never had the right to show it before we could see it." The man shrugged. "They wanted to interview us. We said no."

Langdon could only imagine Bart's reaction. Not just at the kidnapper, but at the news station for playing the video without warning the family. "Do you know anybody who would want to harm either one of you?"

"You saw the video, Mr. Langdon?" Martin asked.

"Langdon will do. And yes, I saw it."

"It has nothing to do with us," Martin said. "Some sicko fanatic is using Eddie as some pawn against the government to get them to open up businesses and loosen the mask mandate."

"Why Eddie?" Jill said.

Exactly, Langdon thought. *Why Eddie?*

Chapter 5

Saturday, October 24th

Langdon and Chabal lived in a house in a Brunswick neighborhood that had the Town Commons as a backyard, a large tract of land with trails that dog loved to traverse. The trip into downtown was just about three miles and took about seven minutes. Coming into town they passed Bowdoin College on the right, slowing to yield as they came to the First Parish Church that was the gateway to downtown.

Spread out before and below them was downtown Brunswick, with Fort Andross on the Androscoggin River, the gateway to the north, a distance of less than a mile. It always gave Langdon a warm feeling to see his town spread out before him, inviting and welcoming, especially in late October when the leaf peepers had followed the summer people back to their homes in warmer climes.

This particular day was marred by a boisterous group on the Mall, which was a large grassy rectangle on the right as they drove into downtown. Langdon slowed the Jeep to get a better look. Often anti-war demonstrators congregated here, but not usually on the weekend, and not nearly as loudly. Over the summer, this had been the meeting point for several Black Lives Matter demonstrations, often followed by a march to the police station out on Pleasant Street.

Chabal suggested that they pull over, and he did, parking by *Burrito Borough,* one of the few food vendors still open as the temperatures drifted toward winter. It was a bit early for a burrito, Langdon thought, noting they weren't yet open, but it might not be a bad idea for lunch. There were about twenty people down by the new Veteran's Plaza on the far end of the Mall, and the first thing he noticed was that none of them were wearing masks. They got out of the Jeep and walked up the sidewalk, both wearing their masks, to pass in front of the protesters who were trying to get the attention of passing motorists.

Langdon next noted with a shake of his head that some of them were carrying AR-15-type semi-automatic rifles, either slung on their back, hanging from their neck in front, or held loosely in their hands. He figured that others had pistols on them, too, indeed becoming aware that several had holstered guns on their hips. Likely there were even more, but hidden, as Maine had no laws against concealed weapons, being an "open carry" state.

It was only then that Langdon started to actually take in the words they were all chanting, "Facts Not Fear, Facts Not Fear, Facts Not Fear," over and over again. Those not holding rifles flourished signs. THE GOVERNOR MUST GO. OUR BODIES OUR CHOICE. TRUMP 2020. THAT MASK IS AS USELESS AS OUR GOVERNOR. I WILL NOT BE MASKED, TESTED, TRACKED. FREEDOM IS UNMASKED. In the middle of the crowd were two men holding a banner with the words THIS IS WAR painted on it.

A middle-aged woman with a *Make America Great Again* hat and dark glasses spotted them and started yelling, "Take off that mask, take off that mask, take off that mask!" The others picked up the chant, all of them shouting at Langdon and Chabal as they walked past. A man in camouflage with a rifle hanging from his neck stepped in front of them, blocking their passage.

"Move," Langdon said.

"You're a sheep," Camo Man said. "Don't follow blindly."

"Those masks are your shackles," a woman said, pushing in from the side. "Take them off and be free!"

An unshaven man with whiskey breath lurched in front of them. "The fear is the virus," he yelled.

Langdon shoved him, sending him stumbling back and then falling off the curb into an empty parking space on the edge of the street. Camo Man with the rifle grasped the stock of his weapon, not pointing, but in what Langdon took to be a threatening manner, and so he punched him in the face. A fist crashed into the side of his head, and he heard Chabal gasp beside him.

A police siren chirped next to them, and everybody froze. Bart emerged from the driver's seat of a cop car stopped in the middle of the street. "What's going on here?"

"This guy and his broad attacked us out of nowhere," Camo Man said.

"Government stooges!" a woman yelled.

"Sheep to the slaughter. Sheep to the slaughter. Sheep to the slaughter."

"Is that right?" Bart asked. He stepped forward until he was face to face with Langdon. "Is that your Jeep back there, sir?"

"Yes. Yes, it is," Langdon said through compressed lips.

"I suggest you go back and get in it and get out of here." Bart turned his back on him and faced Camo Man. "I'm going to need you to stay off the sidewalk and not block pedestrian traffic."

Chabal took Langdon's arm and pulled him backward. He allowed it, grudgingly, knowing that it was the wise choice. Even Bart knew how volatile the situation was, and that his standing as a cop held little sway in front of this angry crowd. If push came to shove, he was outnumbered and outgunned. As they reached the Jeep, several speakers began blaring out the song, "We're Not Gonna Take It."

Langdon backed into Maine Street and drove slowly around the police cruiser. He stopped at the light and watched in his rearview mirror to make sure that Bart got back in before he continued on, taking the left to swing around behind the building that housed the Coffee Dog Bookstore. It was an old department store that now

housed five small shops on the main floor, multiple office spaces in
the basement, and apartments upstairs. Langdon pulled up next to
the rear entrance to the building.

"What was that all about?" Chabal asked.

"I think Brunswick just became Minneapolis, Seattle, Portland,
and New York City all rolled into one," Langdon said.

"Our little town?"

"Yep."

"Who were all those people?"

"I'm betting a fair number of them are from away. Rabble-rousers
traveling around looking to stoke the anger of hatred, and feeling
good when something like what just happened happens."

"Our fucking education system fails us again," Chabal said.

"People who get their news from Twitter," Langdon agreed. "You'll
be okay opening the bookshop on your own today?"

"Aren't you coming in?" Chabal asked.

"Didn't I tell you? I have a 9:00 with 4 by Four and Raven Burke."

"Where? Jimmy's office?"

"Yep." Langdon was still seething from the altercation. He took
a deep breath. "Sorry. Must've slipped my mind. I should be back
in an hour, two tops."

"That the lady who hired you a couple days back?"

"That's the one. 'Hired' might be the wrong word."

"What do you mean?"

Langdon took another breath. "Means she's not paying us."

Chabal looked at him for a moment. "She's a good-looking woman.
Young woman."

Langdon smiled. "I didn't notice. Richam suggested I might take
the case pro bono."

"What'd she hire… engage your services for? Don't believe you
mentioned it."

"Sexual harassment, which you're bordering on right now,"
Langdon said.

"No wonder you're keeping your comments to yourself. I'll see you in a bit." Chabal got out of the Jeep and walked off. She stopped and turned around, and Langdon put the passenger window down. "Don't you go back and mess with those meatheads, or you'll really learn the meaning of sexual harassment, as in, ain't gettin' none," she said.

Langdon was still grinning as he pulled into the parking lot out behind Fort Andross. It was a huge old mill building back when mills drove American industry, always on water, in this case, the Androscoggin River, for it was the water that originally drove the machinery until most converted to electric power, itself generated by small hydro plants. The building had since been converted into a wide range of businesses. There was a flea market with tables set up every Saturday, storage units, restaurants, and various businesses. Jimmy 4 by Four's legal office was on the third floor overlooking the river. It'd been a tough choice picking between this and a view of the downtown, but the inner hippie who'd escaped the pressures of a corporate New York City law office won out, and he chose the river cascading down over the dam for his daily perspective.

"Morning, Rachel," Langdon said to the receptionist as he walked in, dog on his heels.

"Langdon," she nodded. "He's waiting for you." Rachel set about the business of rubbing dog's head, which he put up with because he'd already eyeballed the piece of donut on her desk.

Langdon had arrived a bit early to go over some ground rules with 4 by Four. The lawyer was sitting behind his expansive walnut desk with his feet up on it as Langdon walked in. There was a large picture window to the side that he was gazing out, taking in the river, or perhaps lost in thought.

The reason that Langdon had come early was that 4 by Four thought of himself as a lady's man. The lawyer had never been in a relationship that lasted longer than a few months, moving from woman to woman like the hands of a clock ticking steadily onward, and never pausing to take a breath. He dressed in expensive clothes, wore a $5,000 Chopard watch on his wrist, had a diamond stud in his ear, and carefully cultivated his appearance right down to his weekly mani-pedi from one of the gals at the day spa in Topsham.

Other than this character flaw in pursuing and dumping women, he was a fascinating person, loyal friend, and he took on many pro bono cases for good causes. He was honest to a fault, and never made a promise he couldn't keep, nor did he mislead women about his intentions and commitment.

"Did you bring me a paying customer for once?" 4 by Four asked.

"You can blame Richam," Langdon said. "He sent her to me and said I'd take her case for no charge."

"Couple of suckers, we are."

"For sure."

"You're early," 4 by Four said.

"Wanted to talk to you alone before Raven gets here."

"Go ahead."

Langdon sat down in one of two chairs across from 4 by Four. "Raven Burke is pursuing her employer at the Brunswick Brew Pub for sexual harassment."

4 by Four nodded. "So you said. Rick Strong."

"She's about thirty and quite good-looking."

"I don't think it appropriate for you to be profiling her."

"Fair enough. But you neither," Langdon said. "Keep your thoughts in your head and your actions to yourself in the solitude of your abode."

4 by Four grinned. "When have you ever known me to be inappropriate?"

"Whenever a female comes within your sphere of noticeability, for starters," Langdon said. "Past that, I wouldn't know."

"Duly noted, my married friend. I will be the perfect gentleman."

"Plus, she's about thirty and you're—what are you, sixty?"

"Not yet, but I don't know what age should have to do with compatibility."

There was a knock at the door and Rachel stuck her head in. "Raven Burke is here."

"Send her in," 4 by Four said and winked at Langdon.

Raven came in and sat next to Langdon. She proceeded to share the details of Rick Strong touching her, even letting his hand slide down to her ass on two occasions. How he'd asked her if she liked the cowgirl position or was more of a missionary kind of gal. Strong had asked her whether or not she had a boyfriend, and when she said no, had asked when the last time she got laid was, and then proceeded to ask her out for drinks. He was persistent and relentless.

As far as she knew, nobody else had witnessed any of it, but she couldn't be sure, as, when she threatened to report him, Strong had fired her then and there on the spot. She hadn't spoken with any of her co-workers since. At first, she'd been busy looking for another job. Then Covid hit and there was no work to be found, and she didn't even qualify for unemployment because, Strong claimed, she had quit when he'd confronted her, supposedly for theft and drinking on the job.

"But you did file a claim with the Maine Human Rights Commission?" 4 by Four asked.

"Ya. But it was dismiss' because they couldn't get ahol' of me."

"Because you'd been evicted and lost everything?"

"Ya." Raven hung her head, but then looked back up, eyes flashing. "Because of that scumbag."

"I could probably get the case reopened," 4 by Four said. "But it'd sure help to have some more information. Maybe somebody who saw or heard something?"

"Nobody saw nothing."

"Not saying and not seeing are two different things."

"What do you want me to do?" Raven asked.

"Make a list of everybody you remember that worked with you, and write down every incident that occurred with a date to the best of your ability to recollect, and get it to Langdon," 4 by Four said. "He will dig into the personnel there and try to get corroboration. While he's doing that, he'll keep his eyes and ears peeled for any indiscretions currently taking place, or perhaps will unearth other women who may have faced his unwanted sexual advances."

"You're telling me I have to hang around in a bar for work purposes?" Langdon asked. "Can you put that in writing for me to share with Chabal?"

~ ~ ~ ~ ~

Chabal made a pot of coffee behind the counter and then set about the process of preparing to open the bookshop. Normally, they'd have coffee out on a table for customers to help themselves, but this had had to go during the pandemic, so now they had to hide it. She checked to make sure there was starting cash in the register, even though it was her the night before who'd put it there. A knock at the door caused her to look up. It was Jewell.

"Sorry, ma'am, we don't open for another ten minutes," Chabal said as she unlocked the door and cracked it just about six inches.

"Oh, I don't want to buy a book. I'm the new cleaning lady your husband hired," Jewell said pushing past Chabal.

Chabal considered re-locking the door behind her, shrugged, and pushed the sign to open and flicked the lights on. "What brings you to my place of business if you're not interested in a book?"

"Oh, I'll probably buy a damn book. But I wanted to get your thoughts on that kidnapped boy. That is some messed up shit."

"Yep. Parents came in last night and hired us to investigate. Didn't seem to have a whole lot of faith in the police."

"If my boy goes missing, I'm going to do every damn thing I can to find him, make sure he's safe, then torture the bastard who took him."

Chabal cast her best quizzical glance at her friend. "Something bothering you?"

Jewell took a deep breath. "Just don't know what's wrong with some people, is all."

Chabal wondered who she might mean by *some people*. It sounded like more than just the kidnapper. "Parents' names are Martin and Jill Thomas," she said.

"Were they all tore up?"

"Yeah. Been crying. Martin was pretty calm, but Jill looked like she was about to lose it."

"You can bet your ass I'd be climbing the walls if they took my son."

"Will can take care of himself now. How's he doing?"

"He's good. Living with a girl. Working. Remember when that foppish guy came to my house and threatened my kids?" Jewell asked.

Chabal fingered the small scar where that same man had pressed a knife blade into her face. "Yep."

"Now that, *that* was some messed up shit. What's the deal with this kid?"

"Boy's name is Edward James," Chabal said.

"People suck."

"Not all people."

"I think Richam is cheating on me," Jewell blurted out.

"*What*?" Chabal froze in shock.

"He's been texting more than usual and coming home from work later than normal."

"That's a hell of a long way from he's cheating on you."

"We been married a long time. I know when something's up, and something's definitely up."

"There's no way in the world that he'd cheat on you. He loves you."

Jewell sighed. "He changed the password on his phone."

"You think Richam is having sex with another woman because he changed the password on his phone? I can't believe that."

"I don't know. I just don't know. But something is up, that I'm sure of."

Chapter 6

Annika knew that it had been the carelessness of the oafish brute, Rudolph, that had led to the death of her perfect baby. James would be four going on five now, if not for the ogre of a man she was technically still married to. He'd been drinking that night. She knew that because he drank every night. His drinking on that night had been enough that he'd not bothered to paw at her and demand his rights to her body as a husband.

More than likely, he'd gone in and lay the boy face down, too drunk to know which way was up. Her first fairy tale had ended when Taras had forced her to have sex with his friend. The second had come crashing down when her husband killed her baby.

Her mistake had been relying on men. And that she was still doing, but no longer blindly. She was going to become the shaper of her own destiny. The game had begun. She had picked out the *chelovek* she wanted. A chiseled and intelligent man with a kindness Taras had never shown and a beauty Rudolph had probably only had as a youth. The man stood no chance against her advances. Annika was certain that the third time would be the charm.

Her child would be all the more beautiful with this man. They would raise him to be smart, kind and caring—especially to women. Her James would be the envy of the boys, but he wouldn't lord it over them. He'd draw the admiration of the girls, even though he wouldn't flaunt this.

She would have her castle in the sky and live happily ever after. It was coming. Soon.

~ ~ ~ ~ ~

Langdon drove out to Brunswick Landing after meeting with 4 by Four and Raven. He went the back way, avoiding the Bath Road traffic, and entered the old military base, repurposed for commercial enterprises and an executive airport, through the nine-hole golf course. This former Naval Air Station was now host to a multitude of businesses including college classrooms, health care facilities, a recreation center, restaurants, breweries, and housing.

This was where Jill Thomas had been renting a townhouse for the past five months. Langdon parked across the street from her place in what looked to be visitor spaces, five of them. He told dog that he needed to stay in the Jeep, and went up and rang the bell. Jill answered the door almost immediately, her eyes going past Langdon to the Jeep. "Hello, and please bring your dog in. I love dogs."

Langdon complied. Dog was happy. Happier when she shared a piece of apple with him, nestling close to her on the couch with an attentive look, hoping for more, as Langdon sat across the living room in an armchair. The townhome had been old military housing, showing some of its age and abuse over the years, matching the downtrodden furniture. But the room was neat and clean, even if cluttered with pictures and things.

Jill had kind eyes, currently puffy and red-rimmed. She wore a purple blouse and jeans. "Can I get you coffee or something else to drink?" she asked.

"No, I'm fine," Langdon said. "Is there any news about Edward?"

"No. What did you want to see me about?"

"I thought it'd be helpful to get to know you better." Langdon didn't mention that he also wanted to get a feel for whether or not she thought her husband could be responsible for the kidnapping. "Are you from Maine originally?"

Jill, originally Deering, now Thomas, grew up in Bowdoinham, just about fifteen minutes north of Brunswick. She'd gone to UMaine up in Orono where she'd majored in art history and also met Martin Thomas. They'd dated through their senior year in college and moved to Brunswick upon graduating. After four years they got married, and three years later, Edward James Thomas was born. Jill had worked as a waitress until she stopped to stay home with her son.

"Are you working now?" Langdon knew that Edward stayed with her on the nights she didn't work, but hadn't gotten what occupation that was.

"Yes. I work at the Brunswick Brew Pub."

Small world, Langdon thought. "How long you been there?"

"About a year now."

"Did you know a woman named Raven Burke?"

"What does this have to do with anything?" Jill's genial smile was gone from her face.

"Sorry, just a friend that was employed there for a little bit, back in January."

"No, I didn't know her."

"How about Rick Strong? I was just chatting with him the other day. He seems like a good guy to work for."

Jill's weary grin returned. "Rick's a great boss. Very understanding. Told me to take as much time as I needed. Even offered any help he or his business could provide."

"I have to ask you something, and I don't want you to get upset," Langdon said. "It's something that is unpleasant but which I have to know to do a full investigation, okay?"

"Go ahead."

"Do you think it possible that Martin is the kidnapper?"

"No. Absolutely not. Why would he do that?" Dog jumped down from the couch, startled at her vehemence.

"In many cases of child abduction in a situation where the parents are no longer together, it is often one parent or the other who is responsible."

"Martin loves Eddie."

"That may be the reason that he has taken him, so that he doesn't have to share him with you. What are the long-range plans for custody of Edward?"

"We are going to split it down the week. Half and half. I'm setting up my schedule with Rick so that I work Thursday to Sunday. I'll get Eddie Monday morning through Thursday afternoon."

"And Eddie will be with Martin the rest of the time."

"Yes. Martin works during the week. I don't know what he plans for Friday, but I suppose that's none of my business, is it?"

"Where does Martin work?"

"At the Bowdoin College art museum."

"Was he an art history major as well?" Langdon asked.

"Yes. As a matter of fact, we both applied for the job as assistant curator when we graduated. He got the job. I didn't. We moved here. I became a waitress."

Langdon reflected on the twisting path of life. "Has the museum been shut down due to the pandemic?"

"Yes. But Martin is still getting paid. He works from home setting up online events and whatnot." Jill looked down at her phone in her hand, a smile creasing her face.

"What are your feelings about the governor?" Langdon asked.

"And by that you're actually asking if I'm so upset by Covid restrictions that I'd kidnap and threaten to kill my own child?" Jill's eyes, the color of almonds, glinted in anger.

"Do you know of anybody who'd want to harm you, Martin, or Eddie?"

"No. Why would they? You don't think that freak will actually kill Eddie if the governor doesn't give in to his demands, do you?"

"I think it best if we find him before midnight on October 31st,"

Langdon said. "Is there anything—nothing is too small or too inconsequential—that you haven't told me or the police?"

Jill shook her head, tears now streaming down her cheeks. "No. Please, I just want to know where my boy is."

Once back in the Jeep, Langdon checked the time. Close enough to get some lunch. "What say you, dog, should we go to Hog Heaven?" This was the drive-in restaurant on the way back into town on the Bath Road. Dog seemed to think that it was a grand idea, so Langdon texted Chabal asking if she wanted anything. She replied almost immediately, something silly about having a yogurt and apple for lunch.

Langdon was thinking about her diet when he ordered only two McDonny burgers and one order of fries to share with dog. And a coffee shake. He asked for the order to go as he was supposed to be at Martin Thomas's house twenty minutes later. The only downside of Hog Heaven was that the wait staff didn't wear roller skates, an idea that Langdon would implement immediately if he were to ever buy the place. All the better if they didn't know how to roller skate.

Somehow dog managed to get an entire McDonny burger instead of the half that Langdon had planned for him, and all of the fries because he drooled into the carton. At least he had the coffee shake all to himself, Langdon thought, as he drove across the bridge from Brunswick to Topsham. Martin Thomas was staying with a friend on the Middlesex Road in a small development as his house was currently being scoured for evidence. The friend lived in a small cape with an attached garage with maybe a half-acre of yard around it. The car in the driveway was a bronze-orange Toyota Prius.

Langdon was concerned that dog might have to drop a poop after eating an entire burger and carton of fries, so he let him out in the driveway. Dog hadn't yet worked anything through when Martin Thomas opened the door.

"Langdon, come on in." Martin paused momentarily when he noticed dog sniffing around his garage.

"Mind if my dog comes in?" Langdon asked.

"Sorry, but I'd prefer that he didn't. Not my house, you know."

"No problem," Langdon called dog back to the Jeep. He was, of course, soundly ignored. He shrugged and followed Martin inside, leaving dog wandering around the yard.

The living room was a little prim for Langdon's taste. A sofa and chairs designed for aesthetic appeal rather than comfort. Books on a shelf that looked like they'd been chosen for the pleasing colors of their spines rather than what was between the covers. He did like several of the paintings on the walls, one of which may have been a nude woman cavorting in a field of daisies, though he couldn't be sure.

"Have you found out anything about Eddie yet?" Martin asked without preamble.

"No." *Was the man hoping for miracles?* Langdon thought, and then figured that, yes, he was wishing that God himself would reach down from the sky and restore his son to him. "I was hoping to get some background information from you to help me with my investigation."

"Go ahead, if you think that will help." Martin sat perched on the edge of the sofa, his foot tapping the carpet, a gathering angst emanating from him.

"Are you from the area, originally?"

Martin gave Langdon an exasperated look. "No. I grew up in Oregon."

"I understand you went to UMO. What brought you all the way across the country?"

"Hockey."

"You played hockey for the Black Bears?"

"Yes."

Langdon was surprised but wasn't sure why. Martin Thomas seemed fit enough, even if not very big. Hockey was often more about agility than size. Perhaps it was because the man seemed to have all of his teeth. "You got family back in Oregon?"

"No. My parents recently died. Covid."

"I'm sorry to hear that."

"I wasn't allowed to see them," Martin said. "They passed within hours of each other."

"No siblings?"

"Sister who lives in Florida. We don't keep up."

Langdon nodded. "Were you close with Jill's family?"

"We got along fair enough, I suppose." Martin stood up and walked to the front window. "Not so much since we split up."

"How is Jill with splitting custody of Eddie?"

"You mean, like, would she kidnap him so that she could have him all the time?"

"I'm sorry," Langdon said. "But I do have to ask. Check all the boxes, you know."

Martin flinched. "You don't fuck around, do you? Not much of a segue. Aren't private investigators supposed to be subtle?"

Langdon waited him out. If nothing else, he was patient, an invaluable trait in his line of work. Nobody liked silence.

"No," Martin said eventually. "Why would Jill kidnap her son and threaten to kill him? That makes no sense."

"What happened between the two of you?" Langdon asked, seeing as he was no longer considered subtle.

Martin licked his lips. "I don't know. She went back to waitressing. Was working nights over at the Brunswick Brew Pub. I suppose we just started to drift apart, you know? Two ships passing in the night. We lived together but pretty much only saw each other to hand off Eddie at shift change, kinda."

"So, your split was a mutual agreement?"

"Well, uh, I suppose so."

Langdon had his doubts. The man was hiding something. "She seems to be a good woman. Sorry I had to ask about whether she might've taken Eddie."

"She is the salt of the earth," Martin said. "I've never known anybody with a heart as big as hers. She'd do anything for anybody."

"I sense that from her. That she is good people," Langdon agreed.

"The best." Martin shook his head as if to ward off mosquitoes that didn't exist.

"No big fights? No other issues?"

"Oh, we had our squabbles. I presume all couples do. The largest wedge in our relationship was our differing view on the pandemic. Jill believes that the entire thing is a hoax, created by the media to take down the president."

Langdon could see how that might be a problem in a marriage. "I take it you disagree with that assessment?" he asked.

"I just told you that my parents were killed by Covid," Martin said angrily. "How can anybody believe this fucking thing is a hoax?"

Chapter 7

Langdon interviewed Martin Thomas for another twenty minutes. The sum total of what he learned was that Martin was intelligent and seemed to have few friends, a sister he didn't get along with, a wife who had left him, and recently deceased parents out in Oregon. That, coupled with his kidnapped son, gave him a bristling anger never too far from the surface. He liked his job and loved his son. He'd certainly had more than his fair share of grief over the past year.

Langdon assured the man he'd do everything in his power to find his boy, pausing to lay his hand on Martin's shoulder as he left. When he opened the door, he found dog patiently waiting. He was happy to hop back in the Jeep. It seemed that being alone outside was not high on his agenda. Langdon thought about Martin and then asked dog if he had any insight, but the canine merely looked at him like he'd gone crazy.

Langdon hit Bart's name in the favorites' menu of his cell phone, put it on speaker, and pulled out of the driveway. He thought that the police might have more input than dog on the kidnapping.

"What?" Bart barked into the phone after eight rings.

"And good afternoon to you, too," Langdon replied.

"I'm kind of busy."

"Was wondering if I might pick your brain on the kidnapping case. You still on it?"

"The chief made me crime scene team leader. In conjunction with the State Police, of course."

"Congratulations."

"I think he just gave it to me because the case is so fucked up that it's likely to destroy whoever is in charge. That's his way of staying out of it and getting rid of me in one fell swoop."

"Can you give me twenty minutes?"

There was a long pause on the phone. "Haven't eaten anything since yesterday. Buy me lunch at the Wretched Lobster in half an hour."

"You got it." If Bart hadn't eaten since yesterday, he truly must've been busy, and it was most certainly going to cost Langdon a pretty penny.

Langdon parked behind the Coffee Dog Bookstore in the all-day lot, stopping to check in with Chabal and Star before leaving dog behind with them. He got a high-top table in the downstairs bar and texted to let Bart know where he was.

The first-floor restaurant had lace tablecloths and was the kind of place where the music was muted soft rock, but the downstairs was much more comfortable. The bar itself was made of Brazilian cherry, polished to a fine sheen, with plush padded stools, and shelves crowded with every liquor imaginable. Postcards sent from patrons on vacation around the world were pinned, taped, and tacked to every inch of available wall space. Lanterns with brass bases bolstered dim, recessed lighting along the bar, smaller lanterns deployed on the seven or eight high tables scattered across the room. A dartboard took up one corner, while two pool tables sat on display, silent and inviting at this time of day.

Langdon got a Baxter Stowaway, a fine IPA from Maine. His beer arrived at the same time as Bart, who immediately asked for two Natural Lights, a steak and cheese *and* a Reuben, onion rings, and a piece of blueberry pie. It took a lot of fuel to keep his svelte figure filled out at 350 pounds, or so Langdon figured.

"Why you want to know about the kidnapping case?" Bart asked.

"The parents, Martin and Jill Thomas, hired me last night to find the boy, Eddie."

"Didn't happen to mention that fact to me."

"Probably didn't want to offend your delicate sensitivities." Bart was well known for his gruff and grumpy exterior, but Langdon knew of a softer side of the man that loved children, kittens, and even wrote poetry on occasion, not that he ever planned on sharing that aloud with anyone.

"Guess it wouldn't hurt to have you nosing around, seeing what you can dig up. The media spotlight is on the case and me. The FBI is in town, supposedly supporting our actions, but looking every bit like they're taking the whole thing over. I mean, if you got a Child Abduction and Serial Killer Unit out at Quantico, you most likely want to use it, don't you think?"

"They might not want the mess any more than the chief does," Langdon said.

"Pass the fucking buck, is what it is," Bart said.

"Seems to make sense," Langdon said. "That's our Department of Justice hard at work."

"Yeah, whatever. Anyway, I got to watch my Ps and Qs on this or I'm gonna get fucked. You, on the other hand, can do the dirty stuff that usually solves crimes like this. Meanwhile, I'll be acting like Martha fucking Stewart."

"She is an ex-con, now—you do know that, right?"

"Look, I haven't slept for thirty-four hours. This is what we know so far. All family members have been interviewed and seem to be unlikely suspects. Of course, with the video sent to the news station, it's pretty clear what the motivation behind the kidnapping is, which most closely falls into the ransom category. But this time, not for money, but to coerce the governor into action. We are chasing down leads on several cars seen driving slowly down the street the night and morning of the abduction, as well as a jogger, but my guess would be nothing is gonna come from any of it."

The waitress brought over the two cans of beer for Bart who opened the first one and drank it down, burping loudly when he was done.

"There is no previous history of disappearances," Bart continued. "No prior incidents with family. No other attempted abductions in town. No perverts in white vans trying to lure kids inside."

"How about Ann Morin?" Langdon asked.

"Rudolph's missing wife?" Bart barked a sharp laugh. "What do you know about that?"

"He hired me to find her."

"You've been a busy little beaver, haven't you?" Bart asked. "Well, I'll solve that one for you. She didn't get taken. She left his sorry ass. You met the man, right?"

"He was a little worse for wear," Langdon said.

"With a beautiful mail-order bride, twenty-five years younger, no less. She got her permanent residency, a ticket to citizenship, and then she moved on to greener pastures, surprise, surprise."

"No surprise, I agree, but I still gotta find that greener pasture. I could use the money."

"You do what you gotta do."

"To be clear," Langdon said, "the police are not looking for Ann Morin?"

"No, we're don't get into the business of cheating spouses unless somebody shoots somebody else."

"It seems clear that the kidnapper is trying to hold the governor hostage to get the state opened up. You been looking at anti-maskers?" Langdon thought he might as well get a second beer if he was going to sit through Bart eating an entire buffet right in front of him.

"Yeah, we're putting together a list. The staties and FBI have been real helpful in that."

"Anything stick out so far?"

"Well, just about every small business in the state has been hurt by the restrictions. It's not a small list."

The food, two more beers for Bart, and a second for Langdon were delivered by the waitress. Langdon had an inkling that little more conversation would occur until Bart plowed through the plates arranged in front of him. He was right. Luckily, it didn't take very long before Bart was down to pie crust crumbs.

"What's your angle?" Bart asked, burping again.

"I think the key is Edward James Thomas," Langdon said.

"What do you mean?"

"Why him?"

Bart nodded. "Of all people, why him? You might have a good point there. I'll get a couple of the computer geeks to run that down and a couple of foot soldiers to ask around."

The waitress came over, and Langdon handed her his credit card. "We're all set," he said, hoping that Bart wasn't going to go for round two.

"I gotta get back," Bart said. He stood up. "You know how to get ahold of me."

Langdon settled up and went up the stairs. He decided to check in and see if Richam was in the restaurant on the first floor. Just inside the door was the hostess station, or was it the host station? Langdon wasn't sure if there was a correct term that was gender neutral, and made a mental note to just not call it anything.

There was nobody there at this midafternoon hour, and he drifted past the station toward the rear of the establishment where the small upstairs bar was located. A couple of tables were occupied but the space was mostly empty. Richam was at the end of the bar in close conversation with a woman, and as Langdon walked up, she turned around. It was Raven Burke.

"Langdon, what brings you in?" Richam was the first to speak.

"Just had to buy lunch for your cop friend," Langdon said with a grin.

"Oof," Richam said. "At least it's cheaper down than up."

"Long time no see," Raven said.

Richam gave her a curious look.

"We met with 4 by Four today to go over some things," Langdon said.

"Ah, right," Richam said. "Did I see that Bart is running the kidnapping case?"

"That he is," Langdon said. "Do you know Martin or Jill Thomas?"

"And they are…?" Richam asked.

"They're the parents of the boy who was taken."

"Jill Thomas was at the pub when I work there," Raven said. "She was a… she was difficult to work with."

"What do you mean?" Langdon asked.

"Oh, I don't know," Raven said. "She seem' to have a stick up her ass. Don't think she like' me much, is all."

Funny that Jill Thomas didn't remember Raven, Langdon thought, not that she'd said as much. "What can you tell me about her?"

"Not much. She seem' smart and was friendly enough to people, just not me. Talk' about her little boy Eddie nonstop."

"Martin Thomas have a long face with big round glasses?" Richam asked.

"Sounds about right," Langdon said. He pulled out his phone and did a search. Martin having been in the news recently, a picture popped up immediately. "This is him."

"Yes, I believe I've seen him in here a few times, with a woman."

Langdon scrolled down to a picture of Jill Thomas and showed it to Richam. "This the woman?"

Richam shook his head. "No. She was a blonde. About the same age and height, though."

"Women dye their hair all the time." Langdon cast a nervous glance at Raven, wondering if that was a fair enough statement. "Could it be her?"

Richam shifted his feet and pursed his lips. "Nope."

"Why not?"

"The woman he was with," Richam looked over at Raven, "she, uh, had much larger breasts."

Raven gave him a disgusted look and walked off.

Richam shrugged, looked at Langdon. "What?"

~ ~

It was almost four when Langdon walked into the bookshop. There were a few customers in the store. Star was talking with one of them across the way. Chabal was at the computer behind the counter.

"Glad you could make it in," Chabal said as he walked over. "Almost closing time, but here you are."

"My nap was longer than planned," he said.

"Smells like it might've included a couple of beers."

"Had to watch Bart eat. I needed a support system."

"Find out anything?"

Langdon shared his conversations with Raven, 4 by Four, Jill, Martin, Bart, Richam, and Raven again. "But enough about me, I got you a present."

"You did? What'd you get me?"

Langdon lay a twenty-dollar bill on the counter. "A yoga class."

"You shouldn't have," Chabal said.

"Not a problem."

"No, you really shouldn't have. I *hate* yoga."

"Class is at 5:00 if you need to run home and get some... yoga pants and a tank top." Langdon stepped away and out of reach.

"Why don't *you* go and do fucking yoga?" Chabal asked.

"I was already over there asking about Ann Morin. They were fairly cold to my inquiries."

"You give 'em your name? The one that happens to be attached to my back end?"

Langdon mentally kicked himself. "You'll just have to give them a fake name."

"Or you could send somebody else."

"Send them where?" Star asked, walking over.

Langdon and Chabal both looked at him with appraising glances, immediately putting him on the defensive. Star put his hands up. "No. Whatever it is, no."

"How do you feel about yoga?" Langdon asked.

"I said no."

"Lots of good-looking women, I'm betting," Langdon said.

Star grabbed his jacket from behind the counter, said "no" one more time, and walked out the door.

Chabal laughed. "Think we scared him a tad. Do you think it was exercise, stretching, or women in yoga pants that got his panties all in a bundle?"

"I'd say it was a trifecta," Langdon said.

"You're paying for Jewell to go with me," Chabal said.

Langdon put another twenty on the counter.

"And we're going to have drinks at Goldilocks afterward."

Langdon put another twenty on the counter.

"I said drinks, not *a* drink."

Chapter 8

Saturday

"We heard that you have a Core Awakening class at 5:00." Chabal and Jewell stood in the foyer of the Yoga Bear Studio. "We were wondering if we might try it out?"

The woman, who'd said her name was Diane, looked at Chabal's baggy sweatpants and too-large T-shirt. "We only offer classes via Zoom."

Another woman came in and went behind the desk and put her purse down. She wore yoga pants and a tank top and couldn't have weighed more than eighty pounds. Two other women came in and flashed their member keychains in front of a scanner and went through a doorway.

"I heard that you've been doing in-person classes," Jewell said. She had on yoga pants sculpted to her legs and a matching T-shirt.

"Where'd you hear that?" Diane asked.

"A friend of ours comes here," Chabal said.

"Who's that?" Diane asked.

"Ann Morin. I've been meaning to come take a class for months, but with Covid and all..." Chabal shrugged. "But a girl's gotta get out of the house, am I right?"

Diane glared at her, but the second woman looked up. "Ah, go ahead Diane, let 'em in. I don't think they're the Corona police or the governor's private Gestapo."

"I suppose that we might have room in the Core Awakening class," Diane said. She slapped two pieces of paper down on the counter. "Please fill these out, and it'll be fifteen apiece."

Chabal and Jewell filled out the liability waiver and handed it back. Diane looked at Chabal's form and wrinkled her nose. "Do you have your driver's license with you, Mrs. Daniels?"

Chabal grimaced. "Sorry, I didn't know I'd need it."

"Not to worry. Just bring it next time."

Chabal and Jewell followed the other woman into the locker room. "Thanks for the good word out there," Chabal said.

"Not a problem," she said with a peppiness that was somehow tiring. "Diane can be too much of a hardass, but I suppose it is her business."

"I'm Chabal, and this is Jewell."

"Karen." She mimed an elbow bump. "You say you're friends with Ann?"

"We're in a book club together," Chabal said. "How long has Ann been coming here?"

"Few years now, I guess," Karen said. "Ever since the incident. A way of healing, I guess."

Chabal bit her lip to stop from asking 'what incident?' "That was a tough one," she said.

"Can't imagine losing a child," Karen said. "You seen her lately?"

"Nah, not since summer. We were meeting outside, but when September rolled around, we had to cancel. How about you?"

"I don't think I've seen her since June or July."

"That's odd. Just last week she told me she was coming here three times a week."

Karen closed her locker. "I thought you hadn't seen each other since summer?"

Chabal frowned. "We spoke on the phone. Could've sworn she said she was coming in on a regular basis. That's why we're here, 'cause she spoke so highly of Core Awakening."

"Well, I'm the instructor, and I haven't seen her for at least three months."

"I bet it's that fellow she's been seeing," Jewell said. "Probably tells her husband that she's coming here and goes to meet up with him. Was she at home when you spoke with her?" Jewell looked at Chabal.

"Could've been, I guess."

"That'd be it, then, I suppose," Jewell said. "She was probably standing right next to him when you asked her about class. Least she could've done is called you back and told you the truth."

"I thought there might be a man in her life," Karen said excitedly. "One day, I was out in the parking lot, and that husband of hers, the awful fellow, dropped her off. As I was getting out of my car, I saw Ann walk to the door, but as soon as her husband drove off, she went and got in another car."

"Maybe she was just meeting a friend?" Chabal asked.

"She was all herky-jerky and jittery," Karen said. "And it wasn't like I was spying or anything, but I think she leaned over and kissed the driver."

"Ooh, the mystery man revealed," Jewell said. "Ann won't tell us his name. What'd he look like?"

"Was he handsome?" Chabal asked.

"I couldn't really see as the sun was shining off the windshield," Karen said.

"Was it a nice car?"

Karen shrugged. "Nice enough, I guess. Thought I might've seen it here before. Tiny thing. Shiny. Certainly no sports car or anything like that." She headed for the door. "You two hurry up, I got to get class started."

Chabal kept herself fairly fit. She no longer worked out at the gym with Langdon, but did walk almost every day, did some stretching, and watched what she ate. This in no way prepared her for yoga, which she thought involved a lot of lying around and meditating. The hour-long class seemed to stretch into the following day until, finally, blissfully, it was over, and she found herself sitting on the floor next to Jewell, who looked no better than Chabal.

"You want to get a drink?" Chabal asked.

"Hell, yes," Jewell said.

They peeled themselves off the floor. In the foyer, Diane was talking with Karen. They didn't feel like following up with either the grumpy owner or the Nazi instructor and left without a wave. Chabal got to Goldilocks Pub first and got them an outside table. There wouldn't be too many more times when it would be possible to sit outside with winter coming, and even now it was getting chilly.

Jewell came around the corner and through the gate to the table and sat down. "You going to tell me the rest of what is going on?"

Chabal hadn't gotten a chance to tell Jewell anything but the most basic information about why they were taking the yoga class, other than for the healing aspects of it, of course. "We've been hired to find a missing woman, Ann Morin."

A waiter came by and took their drink orders. Jewell went with a margarita and Chabal got a twisted tea, having missed her afternoon coffee.

"And?" Jewell prompted.

Chabal made a face. "First of all, the husband's name is Rudolph, and he has a very red nose."

Jewell laughed. "I take it we don't like this fellow very much."

"For starters, he said his wife was *stolen*. Not kidnapped. Not having an affair. 'She was stolen,' like somebody might've taken his boat."

"If my body wasn't so exhausted, we'd be going to teach Rudolph some manners right now."

"As far as Rudolph knows, Ann has been going to that yoga class three times a week, every week."

"And ole miss prissy pants hasn't seen her in class for at least three months," Jewell said slowly. "Sounds like Ann was having an affair and decided to make it a more permanent thing. Why are we looking for the poor girl?"

"To make sure she is safe, first of all," Chabal said. "What if Rudolph found out about the affair and killed her, then hired us as part of covering up what he did?"

"Perhaps people who have affairs should pay the price for their infidelities," Jewell said.

Chabal had a sneaking suspicion they were no longer talking about Rudolph and Ann Morin. "I don't believe for a minute that Richam would sleep with another woman," she said. "That man loves you." The waiter came by with two more drinks. Chabal wondered how the first one had gone down so quickly.

"What does love have to do with getting naked with another woman?" Jewell asked.

"Commitment?"

Jewell snorted. "Men? More like fear of losing what they got. If you let them, they'd be drooling around every young thing out there."

"I don't know if I agree," Chabal said. "But either way, I don't think Richam is having an affair on you."

"What do you think constitutes cheating?" Jewell took a sip of the fresh cocktail.

"What are you asking?"

"Does an affair have to be physical? Or is he a moonlighting two-faced bastard by having an emotional affair?"

Chabal took a gulp of her second drink, having moved on to a Mike's Lemonade. "That might be worse," she agreed.

"He's been pulling away, growing distant."

"Life can sure get busy at times."

"We haven't been laughing together so much," Jewell said. "There's some sort of divide, something out there keeping us apart."

"Not much goes on in a man's mind," Chabal observed. "Money? Sports? Kids?"

"And fucking women."

"You don't know that! Slow your roll, woman."

"And he's on his goddamn phone all the time, doing who knows what, texting or social media or some such thing. Then I discover he's changed his password."

Chabal didn't ask why Jewell was trying to access Richam's phone. Now was the time to be supportive, not necessarily rational. "Men can be assholes."

"Drink to that," Jewell said, raising her glass. They clinked and drank.

"You should talk to him," Chabal said. "Ask him directly."

"Not sure I want to hear his answer."

"What can I do?"

"You just did it. When I got enough to tar and feather the bastard, I want you carrying one end of the pole."

"Fair enough." The waiter came by and Chabal ordered a pizza to go, half loaded, half spinach and mushroom.

"You guys are back to being empty-nesters, so I hear," Jewell said.

"Yeah, my boy moved down to Portland to live with Tug." Tug had been a client of Langdon's earlier in the year, and her son and him had hit it off, finding a similar interest in computer technology.

Two men came over and sat down at their table, uninvited. "Hello, ladies. I'm Michael and this is my friend Donald."

"Tell me, Michael," Jewell said sweetly. "Are you into anal?"

"What's that?" he asked, startled.

"Meaning, if you don't take your motherfuckin' friend and leave, I'm going to stick my foot all the way up your asshole."

Chabal was still grinning as she walked into the house. Langdon was on the computer in the living room, but dog greeted her enthusiastically. She'd like to think that he would've done the same even if she didn't have a pizza. Then Langdon came into the kitchen and gave her a kiss. Any way you looked at it, her life was pretty darn good.

"You and Jewell have a good time?" he asked.

"Once we were done with that horrible yoga class, yes we had fun," she said.

Langdon laughed. "It couldn't have been that bad."

"It was worse."

"Find out anything?"

Chabal told him about Karen, and the man who picked up Ann one day. "She couldn't see him at all and the only thing she seems to remember about the car was that it was bright, or shiny, or something like that."

"Sounds like she's definitely having an affair and most likely ran off with the guy," Langdon said. "Which sure beats swimming with the fishes at the bottom of Mackerel Cove."

"Just because she was seen being picked up by a man doesn't mean she's having an affair," Chabal said, then rethought the statement. "The yoga teacher did say Ann leaned in the car window and kissed him…"

"Either way, we need to find her, make sure she's safe."

"Karen said that Ann started going to Yoga Bear Studio after 'the incident,' and then something about it being terrible to lose a child."

"Losing a child, huh?" Langdon rolled the words slowly off his lips. "Rudolph didn't mention that. Something to look into."

"I'll do some digging into the background of Ann *and* Rudolph more tomorrow," Chabal said. "What've you been up to?"

"I've been watching the video posted by Sal Dalí," Langdon said. "Trying to pick up some clue or nugget of information that might help find Eddie."

"Any luck?"

"Nope."

"You still working, or do you want to chill out?"

Langdon pulled her into a tight hug, and then turned her chin upward and kissed her firmly. They watched a movie on Netflix, sharing the pizza and a few glasses from a box of wine, before moving to the bedroom where they got naked.

Chapter 9

Langdon was reading the *Maine Sunday Telegram*, a cup of joe on the table next to him, not yet out of the pajamas he'd pulled on this morning. He was wondering about making a breakfast of potatoes with assorted leftovers, bacon, and eggs. Dog was sleeping noisily between him and Chabal on the couch, fairly certain that nothing exciting was bound to happen for some time now. The television was on, and Chabal was flicking through her phone while she half-paid attention.

That's when the phone buzzed, an unusual Sunday morning event. Even telemarketers seemed to hold back, considering this time period as sacred. Perhaps it was Starling, who was opening the bookstore this morning, with a question. Or maybe Missouri, not that she'd be up this early on a Sunday. None of the above, Langdon thought, looking at the name 'Bart' on his screen.

"Turn on the news, your friend is back on in two minutes," Bart said and hung up. He was not very fond of texting, although his phone conversations had the same abbreviated, curt, sometimes abrupt quality.

"Believe we have another message from Sal Dalí coming on," Langdon said drily to Chabal. She put her phone down.

The anchor of the local Portland news affiliate appeared behind a desk. Across the bottom of the screen in bold letters, the chyron scrolled WHERE IS THE BOY?

The anchor seemed to gather her breath before beginning to speak. "It is not usually the task of this station to do the bidding of criminals seeking ransom or with other demands. This particular story demands special handling, as it involves the kidnapping of a four-year-old boy. His captor has threatened to begin sending fingers if we do not televise his segment. The local, state, and federal authorities have given us the go-ahead." Her voice belied the words, as she certainly seemed very excited to be presenting this riveting drama to the television audience.

The same image as before came on. A flickering light with two wooden chairs. Eddie Thomas sat next to a person with a plastic Salvador Dalí mask on his face, the mustache turned up and almost reaching the eyes, and the same red hoodie zipped up to his neck. Then the boy pulled on a second Dalí mask, the two of them sitting there quietly for a few seconds, each clones of the other, disparate only in size.

"Welcome to you sinners who have chosen not to attend church on this morning. My condolences to those who were turned away because of the totalitarian rule of the governor. Six days," Salvador Dalí said in his oddly-modulated, almost monotone voice, which had been obviously filtered to hide his identity. "There has been no word issued from the Blaine House. There have been no executive orders promulgated. The legislature has not been called back into session. There are no signs that the governor has any concerns for the life of this child at my side."

The man stood and stepped out of the picture and returned with an axe. He sat back down, the wicked-looking weapon propped casually in front of him.

"My body. My choice. Free my face. Liberate. The snowflakes of the left do not rule me, nor will they ever. The coronavirus is not to be feared. We cannot let it dominate us. Don't be afraid of it. We *are* going to beat it. We will not let it take over our lives. We will fight back. We will stand up and be proud.

"We are ready for the final phase of reopening our state. Do not falter. The fool who has not the sense to discriminate between what is good and what is bad is well-nigh as dangerous as the man who does discriminate and yet chooses the bad. There is nothing more distressing to every good patriot, to every good American, than the cynical, scoffing spirit which treats the allegation of dishonesty in a public man as a cause for laughter. We, who know the truth, must speak up.

"I demand that this transgression be fixed. Governor, I call for you to open our economy back up and cease with the silly mask mandate. I give you six more days to accomplish that task. When you do so, the boy will be returned safely to his home. If by midnight on October 31st, All Hallows Eve, you have not complied, I will execute this child. Make no mistake. His innocent blood will be on your hands, Governor."

The screen went black before returning to the news anchor.

"That sort of puts a damper on a lazy Sunday morning," Langdon said.

"Where are you with the investigation?" Chabal asked.

"Nowhere. Still circling around the question of, why that boy in particular? Bart and I were throwing it around, and he agrees."

"Suspects?"

"None."

"Tell me about the parents," Chabal said.

"Jill grew up locally, went to UMO, got married, had a kid. She moved out six months back or so, and they're in the process of getting a divorce. She's been working at the Brunswick Brew Pub for the past year." Langdon stood up to get another cup of coffee.

"What'd she go to college for?"

"Art history."

"Good career path for an art history major," Chabal said.

"Martin was art history, too. That's how they met. Now he works at the Bowdoin Museum."

"Ouch. That's tough. He gets a dream job, and she works in a brew pub?"

"Yeah, she did seem a bit disgruntled about that, even though she says she likes working there. Says Rick Strong is a good boss."

"Is that the reason for their... marital discord?"

Langdon thought back to the interviews. "No, Martin said that Jill thought that the coronavirus was a hoax. He seemed quite angry with that."

"I can understand why."

"Especially seeing as his parents died from the Covid," Langdon said.

"Whoever took little Eddie is an anti-masker," Chabal said. "That much seems to be clear."

"Who is threatening to kill the boy," Langdon said. "I can't believe for a second that Jill Thomas would do that, no matter how strongly she believes the pandemic is a government or media conspiracy. And who's the man in the videos, then?"

"I imagine she travels in circles with like-minded people," Chabal said. "That's how these things tend to work. Who are her friends? Associates? Some radical whack-job who came over to her house for tea one day and saw Eddie and had an inspiration?"

"Could be," Langdon said. "It's at least a better lead to follow than anything else I got right now."

~ ~ ~ ~ ~

Langdon was at the police station. He hadn't been allowed into the command post room, but was in a conference room with Bart, Martin, and Jill. The room was bright and airy and much improved from days of old. There were two large windows along one wall, a table that would seat twelve, comfortable chairs, and a pitcher of water with glasses. Langdon thought back to the old station conference rooms that were windowless, with concrete blocks for walls that seemed to seep a musty smell like old gym shorts.

Martin sat next to Langdon wearing striped pants, a white shirt with bright red suspenders that matched his bow tie, and ankle boots. The whites around his hazel eyes were streaked with red, matching his suspenders. Bart sat at the head of the table, seemingly wearing the same clothes he had the day before, although with a few more stains. Jill was across from Langdon, tears streaking her face, a loose T-shirt hanging down over her jeans.

"Our techs have confirmed that he's most likely using an AlterSpeak voice changer to hide his identity," Bart said. "As well as the mask and hoodie, of course."

"How can they tell that?" Langdon asked.

"Quality of sound, the fact that it is prerecorded, and a bunch of other stuff I don't have the foggiest clue about," Bart said.

"It was prerecorded?"

"Yeah, I didn't catch that at first," Bart said, "because of the mask covering his mouth. If you look closely, his head movements and eyes don't match the words. He most likely recorded it, filmed it, and then mixed in the sound with the visual."

"That would take a certain level of expertise, wouldn't it?" Langdon asked.

"Some, but most millennials have that expertise, especially if they're gamers."

"Or that new generation, what is called, Gen Z?"

Bart shuffled some papers. "Based on his vocabulary, size, mannerisms, and a host of other things, our experts believe that he is twenty-five to thirty-five years of age, putting him firmly in the millennial camp."

"He's our age," Jill said in a voice so quiet it was barely audible.

"I wanted to ask you about that," Langdon said. "The question I keep coming back to is, 'why Eddie?'"

"What do you mean?" Martin asked.

Langdon took a sip of the water. "It would seem that your son,

Eddie, is being used as a pawn in a deadly game, but why choose Eddie? Why not somebody related to the governor? You're not celebrities, nor are you rich and powerful people, no insult intended. Why'd the kidnapper take Eddie? It seems so random, when it shouldn't be, in other words."

"Opportunity?" Bart said tentatively.

"It could be random opportunity," Langdon said, "but plucked from your house in the middle of the night suggests otherwise. So many things could have gone wrong. But they didn't."

"What are you saying?" Jill asked.

"I am thinking that the kidnapper is somebody you know. A friend, neighbor, workmate, acquaintance—somebody who knows you, even tangentially; where you live, how to get into the house."

"The downstairs bathroom window was broken," Martin said.

Langdon stared at him, thinking that it was hard to believe that the man hadn't heard a breaking window. That somebody then crept up the stairs to his son's room and abducted him, leaving through the front door, without Martin Thomas hearing a thing. "If that is truly how they accessed the house, they must've known where Eddie's room is, right? Or did they just get lucky?" he asked.

"What do you mean, *if* that is true?" Martin asked, his voice rising.

"We believe that the perpetrator came through the bathroom window, but we can't be sure," Bart said. "There were no fingerprints. No hairs left behind. No clothing fibers like you might find if an adult body squeezed through a window that small."

"How else would they have gotten in?" Martin asked. "All the doors were locked."

"You said that you keep a spare key in the birdhouse on the side of the house," Bart said.

"Nobody knows about that except Jill and me."

"Maybe you retrieved it once with a friend or a neighbor saw you, or you told the cleaning lady about it?" Langdon said.

"I've covered this too many times to count with the police already,"

Martin said. "Nobody knew about the key. Why else would the window be broken?"

"Why do you suppose you didn't hear the window being broken that night?" Langdon asked. "I mean, I'm a deep sleeper, but if somebody breaks a window in my house, I'm gonna hear it, and then as I'm lying there wondering what woke me up, the stairs are going to creak, and at first I'm going to tell myself I'm paranoid, but at that point, there is no way that a kidnapper is going to slip away with my child before I go check with a baseball bat in hand."

"You were drunk!" Jill said the words with such impact, it was as if she had slammed the table with both hands. "You bastard. You were passed out while our boy was taken, weren't you?"

"I... wasn't... I didn't have that—"

"You asshole," Jill said. "You can get drunk when Eddie's with me. What kind of father are you?"

"Oh, like I'm not doing most of the care-giving for our child after you went and moved out. Don't you dare point your fucking finger at me," Martin said.

"Maybe I moved out because I was sick of you getting drunk every night."

"And maybe I had to get drunk every night to put up with you."

Bart spread his enormous arms out as if to separate the two of them. "Let's all just take a deep breath," he said soothingly. "One thing at a time. Were you drinking, Mr. Thomas, the night that Eddie was abducted?"

Martin looked sullenly at the table. "I had a few."

"By that, he means he drank an entire fucking bottle," Jill said.

"Like you're some kind of goddamn saint," Martin replied. "Like I don't know you're sleeping with your boss, that high frickin' muckamuck, Rick Strong."

"You're a shit," Jill said.

"Rick Strong?" Langdon asked. "You're... in a relationship with Rick Strong?"

"No," Jill said. "I work for Rick, and that's it."

"You're a lying bitch," Martin said. "I was on to you and your shenanigans months before you told me you thought we needed some space. What's the problem? He didn't leave *his* wife?"

Langdon left the conference room with his thoughts in turmoil. Martin had a drinking problem. Jill, or so Martin thought, was sleeping with Rick Strong, who was married. Raven Burke had hired Langdon to prove that Rick Strong sexually harassed his employees. Jill worked for Rick.

Langdon thought back to his recent visit to the brew pub. His waiter—Greg was it?—told him that the kitchen staff didn't wear face masks. That would only happen with the support of the boss, in this case, the owner. Greg had said that Rick was pretty upset over the mask mandate and business restrictions.

Then Rick himself had said that business would be better if the governor didn't go meddling in it. It would be fair to say that Rick Strong was opposed to mask-wearing and governmental restrictions on his business. It might even be legitimate to suggest that he was an anti-masker.

Under Langdon's latest theory, it was most likely somebody who knew the Thomases well who had taken Eddie. It would seem that Rick knew Jill very well indeed, perhaps had even met her son. It was possible that he could've put a finger to his lips when he woke Eddie up, saying something like they were playing a game, and then walked out with him.

Jill had undoubtedly gone to the house to pick up things, or even to check up on Martin when he wasn't home, and had more than likely used the spare key hidden in the birdhouse to access the house, as she claimed to have given her key back to Martin. It was quite possible, Langdon thought, that Rick had been along one of those times. A known anti-masker with a grudge against the governor, he knew the boy, perhaps knew how to access the house, and had the motive that fitted the profile of the kidnapper.

But the part that his mind couldn't let go of was that Strong had sexually harassed Raven and fired her when she refused his advances. The man had then moved on to another, perhaps more fragile, woman, who had accepted his indecent proposal, in turn, ripping her family apart. These were things that steamed Langdon all on their own, but his daughter's recent revelations of why, exactly, she'd left her last job—the boss' inappropriate advances—was causing the kettle to whistle.

Missouri Langdon had probably been over-served on the scotch when she broke down and told her father about her treatment by a former boss at the literary agency. A couple of years back she'd dabbled with the idea of becoming a book agent and managed to procure a job as the executive assistant to the founder of a well-known agency in the city. This was a glorified way of saying she was this man's gopher. But Langdon had understood the need to work your way up and dutifully supported his daughter.

His encouraging words might have been more nuanced if he'd understood that his daughter's growing dissatisfaction with the job had less to do with the menial aspects of the position and more to do with the uncomfortable position her boss was increasingly putting her in. He'd started with crude jokes. When she didn't tell him to stop, he went further. When he went too far, she snapped at him. The next day, she was out of a job. At the time, Missouri had told Langdon simply that she didn't think the literary agent field was her thing.

There was a tear in her eye when she told Langdon about this abuse by a man in New York City, a man that Langdon had never even met. She blamed herself for letting it go too far. Figured that it was somehow her fault. That she had *allowed* it. The next morning, Langdon had driven as far as the highway on his way to New York City to pay the man a visit when he'd decided that perhaps it was best to let sleeping dogs lie. Every day since he'd regretted that decision.

The man had victimized his daughter and gotten away with it—worse, he'd made her feel like it was her fault.

What was it with some men, Langdon wondered? His ire was spiraling upward at a dangerous rate. It wasn't even the sex they were interested in. It was power. Dominance. And at the very base, insecurity. Their self-doubt turned them into monsters preying upon women. Look at that film producer, Harvey Weinstein. Just another vulture seeking weakness to exploit to make himself feel potent. Langdon knew that this had happened with Chabal, who in turn, claimed that most of the women she knew had been violated by men in one manner or another, usually more than once throughout their lives.

And what did people do to stop it, Langdon thought? They drove as far as the highway and turned around, telling themselves not to stir the pot. Don't drag your daughter into the muck. Move on. But where did it stop? Who would be the next victim?

It was time to pay Rick Strong another visit.

Chapter 10

Chabal looked at the time on her phone. She had about an hour until she needed to be at the bookshop. Dog was looking at her askance, hoping that a walk was in his future. She grabbed her tennis shoes, a light jacket, and went out the back door, dog bursting past her with excitement. The backyard led into the Town Commons, and over the years, they'd worn a path that led to the marked trail.

She pulled up the favorites on her phone. Her son, Jack, had just recently moved out, down to Portland, where he worked for a company that developed promotional online commercials for businesses. Jack lived with Tugiramhoro Mduwimana, a recent immigrant from Burundi, who'd helped out this past summer in tracking down the men who'd framed him.

Both Jack and Tug were computer-savvy, more so than the average millennial or even Gen-Zer, and certainly more so than a Gen-Xer like Chabal. She tapped his name and put the phone on speaker and walked into the woods.

"Hey, Mom."

His voice always sent a warm rush of love through her body. "Morning. Not calling too early, am I?"

"Nope."

"You holding up okay?"

"Yep."

Jack was not a very talkative young man. Never had been. "Got any Halloween plans?"

"Turn off the lights like the rest of America and hide in my room."

"Have you been following the kidnapped boy?"

"Just watched the new video."

"The parents hired us to find the kid. I was wondering if you and Tug might help out."

"Sure. What do you need?"

Chabal veered to the left onto the loop trail that swooped through the large tract of conservation land out behind her house. Dog was barreling through the woods ahead of her, hot on the trail of something, most likely a squirrel. "Can you take a closer look at the video? See if you can pick up anything of interest?"

"Like what?"

"I don't know. That's why I'm asking you."

"Okay."

"Thanks."

"That all?"

"Yep. Talk to you later."

Chabal put the phone back in her pocket. Her heart was swollen with sympathetic pain for the poor parents of the boy. Martin and Jill Thomas must be, by turns, devastated and in torment that their precious child had been taken and might be killed. She couldn't imagine what that would be like, but just picturing her own son in that situation made her insides melt. *Where is the boy*, she thought?

~ ~ ~ ~ ~

Langdon walked into the Brunswick Brew Pub a seething mass of anger. He tried to dampen it down, tried to walk away and come back another time, but something in his ancient Viking heritage said no, that this had to be dealt with here and now.

Raven Burke had come to him with a tale of sexual harassment she'd faced at the hands of Rick Strong. How he'd talked dirty to her, propositioned her, asked questions about her sexual preferences, and then fired her when she'd refused his advances.

Was it only three days ago, Langdon mused through the shadows of the burgeoning rage, that Langdon had stopped in and discovered that the man was an anti-masker who didn't require his kitchen staff to mask up? And then Langdon had made small talk with the man of an offensive nature towards the governor and women in general, all to sidle up and learn more about him, an experience that had left him feeling dirty.

And now to discover that Rick Strong was carrying on an affair with Jill Thomas, a liaison that may have wrecked her marriage, and one his wife most certainly didn't know about. All the while, he was her employer. Had he coerced her into the relationship with the threat of firing her?

At the back of Langdon's mind was the harassment that Missouri had been put through and which he, her father, had done nothing about.

Langdon had no plan. His only thought was to attack the issue head-on. He pushed open the door of the brew pub and entered. A hostess led him to a high-top table, and he ordered a CIPA, the IPA he'd had last time. He was hoping to have the same waiter, Greg, but a young woman brought him his beverage. She looked strangely at him when he thanked her, and he wondered if his voice had come out as sharp-edged and brittle as it sounded inside his head.

Rick Strong was over behind the bar and Langdon watched him, trying to understand the man. Langdon was not hiding the fact that he was staring at Rick, and after a bit, the man looked up, saw him, and came around the bar and over to his table.

"Langdon, looks like you left the mutt at home," Rick sat down across from Langdon. "Appreciate that."

"No worries. How's business?"

"Could be better. Could be a lot worse if the governor shuts us down in November."

"You think that's gonna happen?"

Rick shrugged. "People got their panties all in a wad about this coronavirus hoax."

"You don't believe Covid is real? I mean, exaggerated, sure, but you think it's a complete hoax?"

"Oh, there might be a virus, but it ain't no worse than the flu."

"What about all the deaths? Quarter-million and counting."

"You know same as I do that those numbers are inflated. The government's doling out funding left and right if you report more cases and deaths. Some guy dies from cancer, and the hospital chalks it up to the coronavirus so they can get more handouts."

"You don't think that anybody actually dies from the virus?" Langdon was unable to keep the incredulity out of his voice, but Rick didn't seem to pay any mind.

"Oh sure, old people, but you know, herd mentality and all that."

The waitress came over with another CIPA for Langdon, and a glass that might've been just tonic—but most likely also had a hit of gin or vodka in it—for Rick. As she walked away, Rick's eyes crawled over her rear-end as he licked his lips.

"She's a good-looking, young woman," Langdon said.

"She sure is," Rick said.

"You married?"

"Yep. Got two kids in high school. Doing fucking hybrid learning. Stuck at home half the time. No sports. No activities. Busy getting addicted to video games."

"They must almost be as old as that waitress," Langdon said.

Rick peeled his eyes from the backside of the waitress and looked at Langdon. "What's that supposed to mean?"

"Just thought she might be a little bit young for you."

"A guy can still look at a pretty girl, can't he? An ass is an ass. Or is that politically incorrect?"

"Do you remember a woman by the name of Raven Burke?"

"Yeah, what of it?" Rick's eyes had grown wary, an animosity starting to rise to the surface like a no-longer dormant volcano with the dawning realization that Langdon was not the person he'd thought him to be.

"She's the age of my daughter," Langdon said.

"What the fuck are you going on about?"

"Does your constant trolling ever lead to success?"

Rick stood up and laid his forearms on the round tabletop, his eyes inches from Langdon's. "Are you drunk?"

"Did you, or did you not, proposition Raven Burke for sex?"

"That bitch," Rick fumed. "She wishes."

"I understand that Jill Thomas works for you," Langdon said.

"Jill?"

"You know, the one whose son was just kidnapped?"

"Yeah, I know Jill. What of it?"

"Terrible thing, about her boy, Eddie."

"Yes. Yes it is. Even if the cause is right, that's no way to go about it."

"If the *cause* is right?" Langdon stood up, his face right smack in the middle of Rick Strong's face. "What are you saying?"

"I ain't saying nothing, you fucking lunatic."

"Does your wife know that you're sleeping with Jill?" Langdon asked.

"Where do you get off?" Rick rolled his shoulder so that it made contact with Langdon, pushing him back a couple of inches. "Coming into my place of business with your fake allegations."

"Tell me, Rick, did you kidnap Eddie Thomas?"

"What?"

"Did your insidious mind come to rest on that little boy one day when you were locked away in the bedroom with his mother, and he was napping in his room?" Langdon asked, no longer aware of his own thoughts, his own emotions, barely controlled now by his fury.

"Get out of my bar."

"Tell me. Did you take Eddie? Where is the boy?"

"Get out!" Rick shoved Langdon with both hands, pushing him backwards and almost knocking him over his chair.

Langdon righted his balance, stepped forward, and bulldozed Rick backward with his body. "Tell me," he said, propelling Rick abaft across the room.

Rick locked his left arm around Langdon's back and drove a punch up under his chin, his rearward momentum diminishing any real power to the blow. Langdon cupped his hand behind Rick's head and brought his own forehead crashing into the shorter man's face with a barbaric ferocity. The man crumpled to his knees, a stunned look on his face, and then toppled sideways to the floor.

~ ~ ~ ~ ~

"Star," Chabal said into the phone. "Are you okay at the shop alone for a bit more? I have to go bail my husband out of jail."

Chapter 11

"Rick Strong isn't going to press charges," Bart said. He, Langdon, Chabal, and 4 by Four were in an interview room at the police station. Not the conference room that Langdon had been in the day before discussing the kidnapping case.

"That's lucky," 4 by Four said. "There was no way you were going to beat an assault charge, even with the best lawyer in all of New England in your corner."

"I was going to use *you* for my defense," Langdon said.

"And that sarcasm is why I would've let you rot in jail," 4 by Four said.

"But I didn't figure he'd want me in a courtroom detailing why I headbutted his ass," Langdon said. "So I didn't need the best lawyer."

"And so why did you try to cave in a local business owner's face with your noggin?" Bart asked.

"I have a client who faced daily sexual harassment while working for the creep, and when she wouldn't put out and asked him to stop, he fired her."

"She hired you four days ago," Chabal said. "Seems you're a bit slow on processing things."

"Yeah, I guess I am," Langdon said. "I'm still married to you."

"You're not going to headbutt me when you realize your mistake, are you?" Chabal asked.

Langdon laughed and took her hand, closing his eyes wearily. It'd been a long night on an uncomfortable cot in a jail cell.

"Seems to me you went over there right after finding out that Jill Thomas is having an affair with Rick Strong," Bart said.

"What?" Chabal asked.

"Is that the woman whose son was kidnapped?" 4 by Four asked.

"I've also been hired to find Eddie Thomas," Langdon said. "The big sticking point seems to be why him. It doesn't seem to have been a random grab of opportunity, but a carefully planned snatch in the middle of the night from his home. Why go to all the trouble?"

"Meaning you figured that it was somebody they knew?" 4 by Four asked.

"Yes. Knew them. Knew their house. Perhaps even knew that Martin would be passed out drunk."

"Rick Strong," Chabal said. "Isn't he pretty worked up by the governmental rules on business operations?"

"Extremely so," Langdon said. "I believe, if given the opportunity, he'd shoot the governor, he's so pissed off."

"And this is the man who's having an affair with the mother, Jill?" 4 by Four asked.

Langdon nodded. "Martin and Jill had a little spat during our interview, and it came out. Motivation plus opportunity. I figure him for the kidnapper."

Bart shook his head to the negative. "Instead of rushing over there and picking a fight with a suspect, I actually did police work. That is, once Rick Strong was released from the ER, I interviewed him. He took the wife and kids to their cottage out to Small Point. Wife verified that they played board games until almost midnight and went to bed."

"Did you happen to mention that her husband is having an affair? She might've decided not to lie for him if she knew that," Langdon said.

"Not my place," Bart said. "Of course, if that'd gotten out, then Rick wouldn't have any reason to refuse to press charges, now, would he?"

"It wouldn't be unbelievable for a wife to lie to protect her husband," 4 by Four said.

"Perhaps I should say that Langdon was with me and couldn't have been the one who smashed Rick Strong's face in with his head," Chabal said. "I could say we were in the sack together."

"They could be lying," Bart admitted. "This is where it is good to have a PI on the case who doesn't necessarily have to follow protocol."

"I need a shower," Langdon said. "Am I free to go?"

"You just have to sign some paperwork, and you're out of here," Bart said. "Next time you get that temper up, perhaps you should take a breath. If Strong is the bad guy, you've put him on alert."

"Seems to me that the day we met, you showed up drunk at the bar I was working and attacked four drug dealers," Langdon said dryly. "Kind of the pot calling the kettle black, don't you think?"

"Wiser with age, my friend, I've grown wiser with age," Bart said, steepling his fingers in a faux solemn gesture.

4 by Four snorted. "Wilier, maybe, but certainly not wiser."

~ ~ ~ ~ ~

Richam was supposed to be at work by noontime but often went in earlier to catch up on things, being the boss and owner after all. As a result, it was no surprise to Jewell when he went out the door a bit before 10:00 in the morning. At least he'd be home for dinner, as long as nobody called in sick at the last moment. He'd considered closing the restaurant down on Monday nights, but needed all the business he could get. As it was, he was pulling double shifts Thursday through Sunday.

The reason for leaving home early was not to go in and catch up on paperwork, though. Truth be told, he could do that at home. The Denevieuxs lived in a ranch with a view of Maquoit Bay, and Richam took a moment to appreciate it before pulling down the winding driveway to the road. The kids were grown up and moved out, and he indeed missed their infectious personalities. He hoped they'd be able to come home for the holidays, but Covid might play a hand in that. It wasn't bad having his wife to himself, and more than one afternoon had turned passionate, now that they were empty-nesters.

And Richam loved Jewell deeply. His wife was the rock of his existence and kept him steady throughout this tumultuous journey of life. It was for this reason that he silently cussed himself as he drove down the road toward downtown. Richam knew that he should've told Jewell what he was doing. The time for that seemed to have come and gone, though, and now he'd be remiss, and he did fear her wrath, especially when it was righteous.

The protesters were out early this morning on the town mall. And in force. Richam realized that there was a second group, over at the near end, by the gazebo, all dressed in black with likewise colored umbrellas, even though it wasn't raining. There were about twelve of them, and they were chanting something, so he slowed to hear. "We shouldn't have to ask. Wear a mask." There were four police officers in position between them and about thirty anti-maskers on the other end near the new Veterans monument.

Richam drove on into the center of downtown. There was public parking a block back from the businesses on the east side. He took the turn just after Goldilocks Pub onto Center Street, and then immediately to the left into the lot. There were several businesses in the block of buildings facing Maine Street, including the Lenin Stop Coffee Shop, with apartments up above. Richam parked, pulling his bowler low on his face, and got out. He turned up the collar of his peacoat and strode briskly around the front of the building. The entrance to the apartments could only be accessed from Maine Street, and he knew too many people in town.

He pulled open the door and went up the stairs two at a time, not having seen anybody he recognized. His thoughts again turned to his wife, Jewell, and he knew that he needed to sit down and have a conversation with her. Soon. Real soon. They'd come to the United States together twenty-six years ago, already a married couple, raised two children, and built a life with each other that left no place for sin of omission.

The hallway was empty. Richam took a deep breath and knocked on the door.

Raven Burke opened the door with a smile. "Come in."

~ ~ ~ ~ ~

Chabal drove Langdon to get his Jeep from the Brunswick Brew Pub. It was gone. Of course, Langdon thought, Rick Strong had made sure to have the vehicle towed. It took forty-five minutes to find the lot it'd been brought to, and $150 to get it back. Chabal then went off to open the bookshop, while he and dog went home to freshen up. While dog chewed his nails, Langdon took a shower and shaved.

He was hungry and had an idea of killing two birds with one stone. Langdon had read that the phrase originated from the story of Daedalus and Icarus from Greek mythology. Daedalus killed two birds with one stone in order to get the feathers of the birds and make the wings. That was much better than just a hunting metaphor, he thought, for it led to the ability to fly, even if the tale didn't end so well. Icarus, having had the hubris to believe he could fly to the sun, flew up until that sun melted the wax holding the wings to his body, and he plunged to the earth. Greatly he failed, Langdon mused, but greatly he had dared.

With a whistle for dog, Langdon went into the garage, started the Jeep, and drove to the diner. Rosie's Diner had been around since before Langdon was born, passed down from Momma Rosie to the current Rosie. There were twelve round stools with padded red tops along the counter of the diner, every other one blocked off with a variety of hats for Covid social distancing purposes. Langdon picked up one, settling the beret on his own head, tilting the brim down low on his face.

"Don't you owe me money," he said to the man on his right.

"Langdon," the man said, a broad grin creasing his wide face. "I think you got that backwards."

Danny T. was about five inches over five feet and weighed a minimum of 300 pounds. His hair was greasy and his clothes dirty, but Langdon was well aware that nobody had a pulse on the town of Brunswick like the former fisherman, blackballed from the Gulf of Maine waterfront for having made the choice to cut through a net full of herring to save a buddy's arm. The man had spent the last thirty years clerking at various establishments until his slovenly appearance and utter lack of personal hygiene got him fired.

"How's that?" Langdon asked.

"Your Vikings got splattered by the Falcons last week. *You* owe *me* a fin."

Langdon already had the five spot in his hand and now handed it over. "Yeah, that was a tough one," he said. "But I thought we had money on the Pats, as well."

"I told you I wasn't betting on them this year," Danny T. said. "No Brady, the best players on defense leaving or sitting out for Covid. Heck, I don't think I can even name two of their receivers. So, no, we did not bet on the Pats."

Rosie came over and lay her massive forearms on the countertop. She was five inches shorter than Danny T. but every bit as wide. Her face glistened from perspiration even though it was cool in the diner. Her normally smiling face was set to a grimace. "What the hell you think you're doing?" she asked. "Those hats are there for Covid purposes. We're supposed to be spaced out at the counter, every other one."

"I believe that exceptions are made for family who live together," Langdon said.

"You and Danny T. are family now?" Rosie asked.

"Brothers. Just discovered it. He's my brother from another mother."

Rosie cackled. Langdon was about a foot taller than Danny T., and while carrying a trace of mid-life extra padding about the middle, still thin, with red hair that in no way resembled the other man's receding black hair. "I knew both of your mothers," she said. "And both of your fathers."

Langdon had known Rosie for over thirty years, and she'd appeared to be about sixty-five for all of that time. "We just found out about it ourselves," he said, shaking his head. "Danny's dad was shacking up with my mom after my own pa up and disappeared."

"I believe Danny T. is older than you, Goff Langdon," Rosie said. "Would you tell your dog to not bother the other customers?"

Dog was currently standing at a booth with his chin resting on the table, his brown eyes imploring the young couple sitting there to feed him, as he if he were starving. As Langdon looked, the woman gave him a piece of bacon.

"He's providing a valuable dietary service for your establishment, tableside waste disposal, and you have the nerve to complain?" Langdon said. "Now I've heard everything."

Rosie cackled again. "You eating or ya just sitting?" Rosie asked.

"I'll take the Lumberjack Special," Langdon said. "And coffee would be great."

"Eggs over easy," Rosie said. It was not a question. She well knew what he liked. "Hey, dog," she called out and threw a piece of bacon across the counter which he snatched out of midair with the grace of an alligator plucking a bird from the banks of a swamp. "Brothers from another mother," she mumbled, shaking her head, as she went back into the kitchen.

"You working today?" Langdon asked Danny T.

"Nah. Got downsized at Cumbies."

"Stimulus check running a little low?"

"Could say that."

"Wanna make a little extra money?"

Danny T. sipped his coffee, studiously staring at the counter. "No."

"You haven't heard my offer."

"Every time you want my help, I almost die."

"This is different. You like the food out to the Brunswick Brew Pub?"

"Little pricey for me."

Langdon knew full well that the way to Danny T.'s heart was through his stomach. "How about I give you fifty bucks to go hang out there, until, say, eight o'clock tonight?"

Danny T. looked up with hungry eyes. "And do what?"

"Eat. Drink. Talk."

"Talk about what?"

This was the delicate part; Langdon had Danny T. on the hook, and now he had to finagle him into the boat without losing him. "Perhaps ask some questions about the owner."

"Rick Strong?" Danny T. asked.

"Guy's a prick. Thinks his own shit don't stink," a voice from down the counter said.

Langdon looked to his left. "What do you know about Strong, Phil?"

Phil was old, gnarled, and had shocking white hair. "Not much. Kicked me out of there for no reason."

Langdon nodded. "That's too bad."

"Some fellow came in with no mask and was table hopping between his buddies and a group of young ladies. I told him he was a punk and to put a goddamn mask on. He got up in my face, spreading his virus all over, and then Strong comes over and kicks *me* out."

Langdon's food arrived. French toast, pancakes, two eggs, bacon, sausage, and toast. He went to work on it.

"Is that what you want me to find out about him?" Danny T. said, snatching a piece of bacon from Langdon's plate. "Whether he's an anti-masker or whatchamacallit, Covid denier?"

"In a roundabout sort of way," Langdon said, his mouth full.

"I suppose I could do that," Danny T. said. "You gotta pay me up front."

Langdon had no doubt that the man would wade his way through the money by eight o'clock. He wasn't much of a drinker, but eating his way through that much pub food would be a real treat. He pulled the single bill from his pocket, courtesy of Rudolph Morin's retainer, and handed it over.

It wasn't until they were back in the Jeep on their way to the brew pub that Langdon finished detailing the task. "You been following the kidnapped boy?" he asked.

"Yeah, sure, I don't live in a hole in the ground."

"What do you know about it?"

"Some weirdo in a plastic mask took the kid to get the governor to ease up on the business and mask restrictions." Danny T.'s eyes widened. "You think it has something to do with Strong?"

"He fits the model. Vehement anti-masker. Business that is more tap room than restaurant, which might put it on the short list to be shut down if the virus numbers keep expanding." Langdon pulled up to the light at the end of Pleasant Street and took a right on Maine Street. Two groups were on the mall, spaced apart by a good hundred yards, but chanting back and forth, blue-uniformed cops in between. "Plus, it has come to my attention that he might sexually harass his employees."

"Is that all?" Danny T. asked.

Langdon drove past the protesters and swung to the left behind the First Parish Church onto the Bath Road. "Oh, and he's sleeping with the mother of the kidnapped boy."

"I've changed my mind. You can have your money back."

"Have you tried the bacon cheeseburger there?" Langdon asked.

It was only after he'd dropped Danny T. off with a few further instructions that Langdon remembered Greg the waiter whispering to him that the kitchen staff didn't even wear masks while preparing the food. This thought made him feel a tad guilty, but there truly was nobody better than Danny T. at ferreting information out of unexpected hiding places. It was probably due to the fact that there was absolutely nothing intimidating about the man, his gentle nature, unimposing appearance, and self-deprecation somehow making people want to share gossip and their darkest secrets.

The next stop was back toward Brunswick on Boody Street where Jonathan Starling lived. Star had the day off from the bookshop, this thought causing Langdon to check the time, knowing that he had to get into the store soon so Chabal could have a bathroom break. If he knew what was good for him, Langdon should probably bring her some lunch, too.

Star lived in a three-bedroom ranch toward the end of a dead-end street. His turquoise 1966 Ford F100 Ranger Styleside was parked in the driveway, suggesting he was indeed home. Where else would he be, Langdon wondered? Even in the best of times, this former lawyer almost destroyed by alcohol had few pursuits that took him away from home. He'd restored the truck, read incessantly, watched old movies on television, and did crossword puzzles. He often came into the Coffee Dog to help out even when he wasn't on shift.

"Langdon, you missing me?" Star said as he opened the door.

"Star. Morning." He looked at his phone. "Afternoon, I guess."

"Come on in," Star said. "Heard you been making new friends." He led the way back to his small living room and sat down.

Langdon closed the door and followed him. The room was sparse, pared down to just the essentials, no clutter, much like the man. "Leaned in a bit too quick to give the guy a kiss on the cheek, is all," he said. He chose a worn armchair facing Star.

"Never did fancy that European cheek-kissing stuff," Star said.

"You got plans today?"

"You need me at the shop?"

Langdon shook his head. "Nah. Had something else in mind."

"Got a crossword puzzle needs doing."

"Perfect. I imagine you'll have plenty of time to do both."

"Care to share?"

"Thought maybe you could keep an eye on Rick Strong," Langdon said. "Figure he's at home mending his face, but if he *is* the kidnapper, I reckon he might try and sneak out."

"You think he's the one who abducted the little boy?"

Langdon told him about Rick being an anti-masker and carrying on an affair with Jill Thomas. "His wife claims he was with her at their summer cottage out to Small Point the entire night the boy was taken."

"Wouldn't be the first wife to lie for her husband," Star said.

"No."

"But the evidence is pretty thin."

Langdon could tell that Star had mentally put on his old lawyer's cap. "That's where you come in."

"I suppose I can do that. Finally, a job I can do from home."

Langdon stood up and walked to the window. The Strongs lived across the street in a white colonial. "You ever talk to them?"

"Yeah, the wife seems a nice enough sort. A little weary looking. The boys seem to be good, far as I can tell."

"Is that Mustang Rick's?" The license plate said: MYRITES.

"Sure is. Washes and waxes it monthly. Drives a little too fast."

"Do you suppose he knows he spelled RITES wrong?"

"Ha," Star said. "Although he may be smarter than you think. A rite can be a religious ceremony, but it can also be a tradition that is followed."

"Like the rite of not following the rules?" Langdon asked.

Star shrugged. "He is an entitled asshole."

"That fits the guy I know."

"What do you want me to do?"

"If he goes out, follow him. If anybody stops by, keep an eye and get their license plate. Other than that?" Langdon shrugged. "Sit here in the window and do your crossword."

Chapter 12

Langdon climbed back into the Jeep and texted Chabal. Need food? He backed into the street and drove slowly past the Strong household. There were no signs of life, other than several lights on.

His phone buzzed with a reply from Chabal. All set. Found some crackers in your office.

Langdon stared at the phone. He had the distinct impression that she was being sarcastic, but where did that leave him. You sure?

LOL. I ordered a sandwich from Darlings if you want to swing by and get it for me.

Langdon went left on upper Maine Street to the market and deli and picked up the sandwich and a bag of chips. For good measure, he grabbed a chocolate bar.

As he drove by the Mall, he noticed that the protesters had grown in number. By the gazebo there were about twenty-five people chanting, "Just wear the damn mask." About a dozen of them were dressed all in black, with black umbrellas unfurled. They all wore masks and seemed to be making an effort to socially distance, but still appeared to be awfully close together for Langdon's comfort.

He slowed to see if he recognized anybody and realized that Jewell Denevieux was with the pro-mask group. Her tall, slender form, along with the afro, helped her to stand out. She held a sign that said: PROTECT AMERICA. WEAR IT FOR YOUR MOTHER.

On the far side of the Mall, by the not-yet-dedicated Veterans Monument, was a group of about fifty people, twice as loud—

bordering on the raucous, really—as the smaller group by the gazebo. They were not masked, or so Langdon thought at first, and then he realized that seven or eight of them wore the plastic Salvador Dalí mask that the kidnapper had worn in the two videos.

What has Brunswick turned into, Langdon wondered? The threat of violence was a palpable presence, as evidenced by the blue-uniformed cops settled into no-man's land between the two opposing armies. And armies they were, Langdon thought. The abductor of a four-year-old boy was being elevated to the status of cult hero by a part of the population who felt their rights were being infringed upon by a callous government.

He supposed that it was just human nature to have expectations, feelings of entitlement, the desire to be free of the control of others, especially those you hadn't voted for, yet at the same time, desire, too, to be provided for and protected. After all, wasn't that what the birth of this great nation had been all about, Langdon mused? The fledgling colonies had wanted to retain the benefits of Great Britain, mutinying against the seemingly arbitrary imposition of taxes they had no say in passing, though they might support those very same safeguards and assurances. As had been the Civil War that almost turned the nation into two countries instead of one, all because of a difference of opinion of what the rights of the individual actually meant.

And now, Langdon thought, here we are on the cusp of another battle for the morality and the soul of the country. A conflict looking for a common ground between freedom and safety, science and business, empathy and indifference. The enduring wounds of that war which had freed the slaves were still raw, festering, and their healing unresolved. The failure of Reconstruction still lingered, needing to either be fixed once and for all, or promising the death of the American Dream which only existed, more and more, for a very few, mostly elite at the very top.

These were his thoughts as he parked in the back of the bookshop. Dog jumped out in hot pursuit of a squirrel, the rodent quickly disappearing up a tree. That was the way with people, too, Langdon thought, always chasing the squirrel but often not sure what they'd do if they caught it.

The Coffee Dog Bookstore was vacant except for Chabal sitting on a stool behind the counter reading a book. "'Bout time," she said, hopping down and heading out the doorway to the bathroom.

A man came through the door and straight to the counter. "I'm looking for a book called *Trojan Horse*," he said.

"You know which one?" Langdon asked. "There's a lot of Trojan Horses out there." That there was, he thought. Things were never quite as innocent as they seemed, and free gifts, especially from strangers, should be considered carefully.

"This one has a descendant of Vlad the Impaler as the bad guy," the man said.

"Ah, you want the one by S. Lee Manning," Langdon said, leading him over to a shelf. "In this case, it's a digital virus."

"What's that?"

"Trojan Horses come in many varieties. This one is… never mind, I won't spoil it for you. Excellent book."

The man paid and passed by Chabal as she was returning. Making sure the shop was empty, she turned her attention to Langdon. "You going to tell me what yesterday was about?"

"Rick Strong needed his face cracked in." Langdon shrugged. "I did what needed to be done."

"Because he's cheating on his wife?"

Langdon looked upward as if the answer might be nestled in a crack in the ceiling. Technically, he and Chabal had both still been married to other people when they'd had a single tryst that grew into twenty years of their own marriage. "Probably more that he propositions and, at the very least, verbally abuses his female employees from his position of power as owner."

"Are we talking about Raven Burke?"

"Yes. And others."

"Others?"

"There are always others. We think we're lucky when we nail some prick like Weinstein or Epstein when we get the chance, but what we're usually seeing is just the tip of the iceberg. We comfort ourselves that Weinstein went away for twenty-three years and Epstein hanged himself in prison, and we think, hey, problem solved, justice served. Meanwhile, the danger lays hidden, and is more times than not, enormous, just like the body of that berg invisible to the eye."

Chabal gave him a look. *The* look. "What are you talking about?"

Langdon fidgeted. "I think," he admitted almost bashfully, "I think that it was the thing with Missouri that got my gears grinding. That I didn't do anything about it when it happened."

Chabal stepped over and kissed him. "Don't get me wrong. Assholes need their faces cracked. That's why I love you."

"Because I'm an asshole crack...er?"

Chabal laughed. "Anything going on out in the world?" she asked. "Since I bailed you out of jail and came to work?"

"Well, for one, our streets seem to be getting increasingly cluttered with protesters," Langdon replied.

"Yeah, a guy came in earlier and said he got an earful walking past them. Little louder than the war protesters were."

"Saw Jewell out there with the pro-maskers. With a bunch of people all in black and with black umbrellas."

"Jewell told me they were coming into town. Didn't see them when I came by to bail your ass out of jail this morning."

"They?"

"Some group who call themselves VAIN. Voices Against Ignorant Notions. How many were out there?"

"About a dozen."

"Jewell said they expect to get more than a hundred of them in over the next few days. They travel around countering the far-right rhetoric. Think they were out in Seattle and have been down in D.C. the last couple of days outside the White House but decided to come to Brunswick and oppose the anti-maskers flocking here to support some fucking psycho kidnapper." There'd been a day when f-bombs dropped from Chabal's mouth like rain from a thunder cloud but that had been tempered as of late.

"There's a lot of angst out there, that's for sure," Langdon said.

"This is just the topper to what's been one shit year."

"You want to get involved in some way?"

Chabal's eyes were blazing, and she started to reply, stopped, and took a breath. "I suppose the best way we can help out is to find this sick... Sally Dalí and lock his ass in jail. Then these protesters can all go away, we can win the election, create a vaccine, and end world hunger."

"How about one step at a time?"

"Okay, let's start with Sally Dalí. What do you got so far?"

Langdon pursed his lips. What *did* he have so far, he wondered? "We know that Rick Strong has been accused of sexual harassment and is an anti-masker."

"Sexual harassment makes him an asshole but doesn't really add up to him being the kidnapper," Chabal said.

"Gotta be an asshole to abduct a four-year-old boy," Langdon said.

"Fair enough."

"Then it comes out that he's sleeping with Jill Thomas. All a bit too coincidental for me."

"You probably shouldn't have gone and tipped him off that you were onto him," Chabal said.

"I wanted to rattle his cage a bit."

"You sure did that."

"Shake him up a bit and hope he makes a mistake."

"Sure you didn't just lose your temper?"

Langdon shrugged. "Could be."

"What's the play?"

"I got Danny T. down to the brew pub with his ear to the ground, and Star watching out his front window."

"His front window?"

"Funny enough, the Strongs live just down and across from him on Boody."

"And what are you doing?"

Langdon looked at the computer screen to check the time. "Actually, I got to get out to Bailey Island. I'm supposed to have a chat with Rudolph Morin when he gets off his boat. Said he'd be into the wharf about 2:00. Afterward, I'm going to canvass the neighborhood and see if anybody knows anything."

"Ask about a guy in a shiny car. That's what the lady at the yoga studio said."

"What color?"

"She just said shiny."

The drive out to Harpswell was calming, once Langdon got past the protesters and headed out ME-123. He passed Bowdoin College on the right, and then the Town Commons, which his house was just on the other side of, before going by the golf course and Brunswick Landing. Maine has almost 3,500 miles of coastline—more than the state of California—and Harpswell is twenty or so of those spectacular miles, endless jagged rips of land extending into bays, harbors, inlets, and the Atlantic Ocean.

Rudolph was offloading his lobster catch at the wharf when Langdon arrived in Mackerel Cove. He wore Grunden oil pants and jacket, muck boots, and had traded out the warmer hat he most likely wore out on the water for a red MAGA baseball cap. Langdon guessed that he probably wore Carhartt pants, shirt, and sweatshirts underneath everything. It got chilly out on the water in October in Maine.

This chill on the water, Langdon knew from experience, having gone to work on a lobster boat when he was just eight, soon after his father disappeared and finances at home became tight. He'd been taken on by a man named Goldilocks, the original owner of the downtown restaurant, who'd become his mentor and a father-figure to him. Although Langdon didn't believe in God, at least not in any traditional sense, he felt that he should cross himself when thinking of Goldilocks, but wasn't sure how to do so and thus, skipped it. *Rest in peace,* he said under his breath, and went on down to the dock. He still blamed himself for Goldilocks' violent death at the hands of a man Langdon had been tracking some twenty years earlier.

Rudolph had already drained the lobster tank on the boat and placed the crustaceans into crates, which he was handing up to two young men who were bringing them onshore to release into their own lobster tanks. This holding area was refrigerated sea water that was circulated and aerated. The water was kept at about thirty-nine degrees to slow down the lobsters' metabolism. This made them easier to handle and reduced the chance of injury. Each of the crates was marked to show that they belonged to Rudolph and would be pulled out later to be weighed so that he could be paid. At that point, the majority of the lobsters would be wholesaled and delivered to another lobster dealer, or to restaurants and fish markets. In the summer, there was also a lobster pound on the street-side so locals could come buy their dinner directly from the boat, so to speak.

Rudolph paused as Langdon walked up. "You find my damn wife?" he asked. It seemed to be a scant catch, but there wasn't that big of a market in October, now that all the tourists were gone. No sense catching more than you can sell.

"No. Not yet." Langdon knew better than to be pleasant with the man, as Rudolph would just take it as him being weak, a snowflake of politeness. "Got some things to ask you."

"Gotta go moor my boat." Rudolph stepped back onto the lobster boat. Maine lobster boats were often referred to as the pick-up trucks of the coast, with a front cab and a long bed in back to house the pots, or traps.

Langdon followed him onto the boat, noting that it was called the *Annika.* Perhaps the man did have more than a gruff fondness for his missing wife, he thought. "That's a beautiful wooden wheel," he said, pointing at the antique steering wheel in the cabin of the boat. It was decorative, its four spokes crossing through a small circle in the center and a larger one outside. "How old is it?"

Rudolph seemed to soften just slightly. "Been in my family for over 200 years. My ancestor, Captain Raymond Morin, took it with him when the British sank his ship off of Castine during the war of 1812."

"That's a real beaut," Langdon said. "This thing built-down?"

Rudolph shot him an appraising glance. "Couldn't have a skeg-built out where I go," he said. "What do you know about lobster boats?"

Skegs were more stable with large loads, Langdon knew, faster and generally lighter, with bottoms that are much flatter with a sharp entry into the keel. With this you get more speed with less horsepower, a more stable platform on the drift, more room per foot, the trade-off being that you lose some comfort in the ride in heavy seas because of the wider beam. Built-down boats were designed to carry loads in a heavy sea, giving up some room for seaworthiness and maneuverability. Their bottoms are more tapered than the flatter skeg design, kind of like a wine glass.

"Grew up on one," Langdon said. "Started going out when I was eight."

Rudolph pulled up to his mooring, and Langdon secured the boat. "Figured you for a college boy," he said. "Thought you might even be from away."

"We Langdons have been around long as anybody can remember," Langdon said. He did *not* mention that he *had* gone to college.

"What you wanting to ask me?"

"You said your wife's been going to yoga three times a week? Even through the..." Langdon almost said pandemic, thought better of it, "the government shut-down?"

"She wouldn't miss it. Sometimes it makes her late to make my dinner."

"Is it possible that's she's been meeting with someone instead?"

"T'aint likely. She knows better than to lie to me."

"The yoga studio said that she hasn't been there in at least three months, maybe longer."

Rudolph stopped cleaning up the boat and turned and glared at Langdon. "Whatcha talking about? They been taking that monthly fee out of my bank account like clockwork."

Langdon didn't say anything. The worst thing one could do with a good ole' Maine boy was to talk too much, run on at the mouth. Much better to keep a tight lip.

"Who done and told you she ain't been going?" Rudolph asked after a long pause.

"We talked to the owner and one of the instructors," Langdon said. "She hasn't been in since June."

"What are you saying?"

"It would sure help me out if you can think of any friends she might have?"

"She don't have no friends."

"How about neighbors? Anybody she was close to?" Langdon followed Rudolph into the dinghy.

"You might try Betsy Boudreau. That woman got her nose in everything."

"She live close by to you?"

"Two houses past on the left."

"I might go have a chat with her," Langdon said, stepping onto the dock. "Can you think of anything else that might be helpful?"

"You think there's been foul play?"

"Heard you lost a boy a few years back," Langdon said. "Sorry about that."

"Shit happens," Rudolph said. "We done here?"

Five minutes later, Langdon pulled into the driveway of Betsy Boudreau. He got out of the Jeep and looked out over the ocean.

Closer up, the Giant Stairs were visible out behind her house, a couple walking their dog along the path that creased the very edge of the coastline, beyond tumbling down into jumbled piles of rock, then into the sea. He took a moment to enjoy the view of several sailboats, fishing boats, and even a large transport ship way off in the distance. Seagulls floated on the wind, looking for crabs on the rocky shore, and waves crashed upon the rocks.

Not a bad place, Langdon thought, looking back down the road to where he could see Rudolph Morin's bungalow, which had the same view. Obviously, summer residents hadn't bought up the entire area, and rising taxes hadn't driven out all of the locals, not here on Bailey Island, anyway. Of course, give it a month, and the wind swooping in off the ocean would cut through these homes like an air strike.

The woman who answered the door was perhaps seventy, tight white curls encasing her aged and weather-beaten features. She might've been a few inches over five-feet tall and couldn't have weighed more than the hundred-pound punching bag Langdon used at the gym.

"Can I help you, young man?"

Langdon couldn't remember the last time he'd been called 'young man.' He wasn't exactly old at fifty-three, but young? "Hello, Mrs. Boudreau. I was wondering if I could ask you some questions about Ann Morin?"

"What about?" Sudden suspicion clouded her pale features.

"Do you think I might come inside?"

The woman didn't want to let him in, that he could tell, but an ingrained sense of polite hospitality wouldn't allow her to decline. That did not extend so far as an offer of something to drink or to take his jacket. He was ushered into the kitchen where they sat down at a small round table. The only decoration was a book-size picture of Jesus on the cross.

"What's this about?" she asked again.

"Have you seen Ann in the last two weeks, Mrs. Boudreau?"

She looked, if anything, even warier, drawing back in her chair. "No. No, I haven't."

"My name is Langdon. I've been hired to find Ann by her husband. She seems to be missing."

"Rudolph Morin? He and his family are bad apples. Have been so for generations. They've been in and out of jail for as long as I can remember."

Langdon had done his research and come to the same conclusion. At the same time, their problems with the law were usually of a petty nature. Drunk and disorderly. Fishing without the correct license. Rudolph had been found with some stolen fishing equipment about twelve years back. That sort of thing.

"Ask what you want."

"I understand they lost a baby," Langdon said. "That must've been hard on them."

"Crib death." She coughed. "Nothing anybody can do about that. Some babies just die. Way it is."

"Did she seem to be depressed?"

"Wouldn't know."

"Do you think it possible that Rudolph would harm Ann?" he asked.

"Thought you said he'd hired you."

It wouldn't be the first time he'd been hired by the culprit, Langdon thought. "I have. I just want to cross off possibilities, Mrs. Boudreau, before I get to finding her."

She sighed. "No. He adored the ground she walked on. Talked gruff and all, but she had him wound around her little pinky, that she did."

"How about if she threatened to leave him? Do you think he'd physically try to stop her?"

"She was up to something, for sure she was." Mrs. Boudreau stood up, seeming to have made the decision to trust him. "Would you like something to drink, Mr. Langdon?"

"Glass of water would be nice," he said. "What do you mean, she was up to something?"

Mrs. Boudreau filled a glass of water from a jug in the fridge and brought it over and sat back down. "She asked me once to tell Rudolph if he asked that she'd been here visiting one day around noon. That she'd had lunch with me."

"And she didn't have lunch with you?"

"I don't much like lying." Mrs. Boudreau squirmed in her chair. "But he's such an awful man and much too old for such a pretty young lady like Ann."

"Do you know who Ann was with when she was supposedly having lunch with you?"

She shook her head. "No. Ann didn't tell me, and I didn't ask. None of my business."

Langdon took a drink. "She didn't talk to you about seeing a man?"

"No. What are you thinking happened to her?"

"I don't know."

"Do you think she's okay?" The words were spoken with concern, which had replaced the older woman's initial suspicion.

If things had gone south between Rudolph and Ann, Langdon thought, and he'd killed her, either on purpose or accidentally, it wasn't exactly a stretch for him to take her out to sea on his boat and dump her into Davy Jones' locker, never to be found again. "That's what I'm trying to figure out, Mrs. Boudreau. Were there other people who visited with Ann? Neighbors? Did she tell you about any of her friends?"

"She told me once she was going to the yoga studio downtown, but never mentioned any names."

Langdon handed her a card. "If you remember anything, Mrs. Boudreau, can you please give me a call?"

She took the card. "I don't know if this is anything or not, but about two weeks back, there was a car I didn't recognize parked out front of her house on the road."

There had been lots of cars parked on the sides of the small winding road as Langdon had wended his way here. "Something special about the car you remember?"

"It's just, well, it didn't fit in. Stuck out like a red bowl in a cupboard of blue dinnerware, it did."

"Why's that?"

"It was too shiny and bright."

Langdon's best lead was a clean car, he thought with an ironic inward grin. "What do you mean bright?"

"It was orange. Bright orange. Who in tarnation would buy an orange car?"

Chapter 13

Langdon decided to swing into Brunswick Landing on his way home and pay Jill Thomas a visit. He thought about calling to make sure she'd be home but decided against, thinking that the element of surprise might be beneficial. She, after all, was in a relationship with a married man who was an anti-masker. Was it possible that she was involved with the kidnapping of her own son, Langdon wondered? To what purpose?

Had Rick Strong and Jill Thomas concocted this whole scheme together? Langdon could see it possibly being used as a strong-arm technique to loosen business restrictions in the state, but even that was a long shot. Was the governor really going to rescind business closings and give in to a kidnapper's demands? It might possibly affect the decision, a judgment still being debated, whether to go ahead with phase four of reopening in the face of a fresh surge in coronavirus cases.

The governor had promised that a verdict would be coming soon, no later than November first. This, then, dovetailed with the kidnappers' demands to be met by midnight on Halloween, or the boy would be killed. If the governor was on the fence, this might be the impetus to push her to keep restaurants fully open, rather than a return to limited seating. Langdon had checked, and the Brunswick Brew Pub did indeed have a restaurant license, as opposed to one for just a bar or tasting room—two types of business not yet cleared for reopening.

How did Jill Thomas fit in? There were three options. She was a willing participant, she was pressured into being involved, or she had no idea at all. Langdon thought it more than likely that Rick was the abductor. But proving it would be harder. Langdon was willing to bet that if either of the first two choices were accurate, that the boy was in no real danger—for what mother would allow her son to be killed like that?

Langdon parked in the visitor spaces and walked across the road to Jill's townhome, noting that her car was in the drive, an old Volvo station wagon, almost an antique. He had to knock twice before she opened the door a crack.

"Are you here to beat me up, too?" she asked.

"No. I need to ask you some questions."

"I'm not sure I want to speak with you."

"You've hired me to find your son," Langdon said. "That will be pretty tough if you refuse to talk to me."

"I'm not sure I still want your services."

"I believe that you and Martin both hired me. It'll take two to fire me."

"Martin didn't want to hire you in the first place," Jill said. "He thought you would just muck things up. He may have been right, for once."

"Can I please come in so we can talk about this?"

Jill seemed to contemplate the question, and then opened the door wide, stepping aside. "I suppose it can't hurt."

The living room was immediately to the left as Langdon entered, and this is where Jill motioned for him to sit, not offering a beverage. He could've used a beer. Maybe he'd swing by the Brew Pub afterward and see if Danny T. had dug up anything. He chose the sofa.

"What is it that you want?" Jill asked, sitting down in the armchair kitty corner to him.

"I want to find your son."

"Why did you beat up Rick?"

"Why didn't you tell me you were having an affair with him?"

"I kind of figured it was none of your business."

Langdon settled back into the sofa. It was actually quite comfortable. The room was cluttered, filled with pictures, many of little Eddie, of herself, a woman who looked like she might've been Jill's sister. There were no pictures of Martin.

"I believe it was only two days ago that I was here, and the last thing I said was that there was no detail too small to omit. I'm kind of thinking you having an affair might fit into that category," he said.

"What does my sex life have to do with anything?" Jill asked.

"Are you aware that Rick Strong is an outspoken critic of the governor and her restrictions on businesses and mask policy?"

"He would never put Eddie in harm."

"The person who took your son is trying to extort the government into going ahead with the reopening in spite of this second wave of Covid, or continuation of the first wave, or whatever it is. It seems to me that Rick is a prime candidate for being the kidnapper."

Jill stared across the room at the blank television set. A tear coursed its way down her right cheek, and then another. "He wouldn't do that. He's a good man."

"Would you say he's a good *family* man?" he asked gently.

"He doesn't love his wife. He stays with her for the sake of the kids. He loves his children."

Langdon wasn't sure how many times he'd heard that before. Too often his job as a PI required listening to tales of misunderstood men and women who took the moral high ground in talk while traversing a path through the murk at the bottom of the bog.

"How long have you been seeing him?"

Jill leaned over and pulled a tissue from a box on a side table. She wiped her cheeks, blew her nose, and tossed it into a wastebasket that looked like it had been brought out for that express purpose.

"About eight months now."

"Is that why you and Martin got separated?"

"I left Martin because he's an ass."

"Has Rick been around Eddie?"

"What are you asking?"

"Do they know each other? Is there a bond between them?"

"No. We keep our meetings a secret."

"Has Rick been here when Eddie was here?"

Jill grabbed another tissue. Wiped. Blew. Tossed. "Yes. Only when Eddie's been asleep, though."

"Has Rick ever been to Martin's house?"

She looked away from him, not answering. "You're married, aren't you, Mr. Langdon?" she asked finally.

"I am."

"It's not always a bed of roses, is it?" Jill had a pleading note to her voice. "I mean, it can be awful tough. You marry somebody, and then they change. Or you change."

"Could you answer my question?"

"Which was what?"

"Has Rick ever been inside Martin's house?"

Jill took a deep breath. "I started seeing Rick back in February. He'd come over when Eddie was at school and Martin was at work. When the Covid rolled in and sent everybody home, he wasn't able to come over anymore. That's why I decided to move out."

Langdon nodded. Covid had certainly disrupted life in many mysterious—and certainly unexpected—ways.

~ ~ ~ ~ ~

Danny T. had been sitting at the round high-top at the Brunswick Brew Pub for almost five hours. Not much of a drinker, he was just on his second Budweiser. He had, however, consumed a turkey club, an everything nachos, twelve wings, and was currently contemplating a further order. Langdon had said the bacon cheeseburger was good. That would hit the spot. Danny T. licked his lips. He realized that the money that Langdon had given him was quickly dissipating with each plate, but Danny T. didn't care. It was not often that he got to eat this way.

So far, his intel had been minimal. He'd stood outside with a guy he knew who was having a smoke break from washing dishes, and learned that the kitchen staff was not required to wear masks. They were required to have them around their ears, but could be pushed down under the chin, ready to be affixed if inspectors came in. They'd even had several drills, practicing for that eventuality. The guy knew nothing about sexual harassment, but did say some really hot chicks worked there—as a matter of fact, they were all pretty smoking hot.

Danny T.'s waiter was a young fellow named Greg. He let on that Rick Strong was a likeable fellow, even if a strict boss, and that most everybody liked him. He might've put an emphasis on the word *most*, but Danny T. couldn't be sure. When Danny T. commented that all the waitresses were pretty hot, Greg had nodded with a small smile creasing the corners of his mouth and had agreed that the women of the Brunswick Brew Pub deserved to be on a calendar.

It'd just gotten dark outside, all of a sudden, like somebody flipped a switch, when a group of a dozen or so men came in. Several of them wore camouflage, as well as Salvador Dalí masks pushed up onto the top of their heads. All but two had beards, and those two were pretty scruffy. None of them wore face masks. They came in boisterously, pushing several rectangular tables together without asking, and sitting down, talking loudly. Danny T. guessed that they'd already been drinking for some time.

Danny T. figured them for the anti-maskers who'd been out protesting on the Mall today. He didn't recognize any of them, which was odd, because he knew most people's faces from one place or another. He'd been here all his life. What's more, they didn't look like Brunswick people. Maybe Harpswell, or out to Durham, or further afield in the rural areas. Their waiter brought them a round of shots.

Danny T. sensed trouble, and considered leaving, but Langdon had asked him to stay until around 8:00, plus he was still hungry. He went ahead and ordered the bacon cheeseburger with onion rings on the side.

He was lost in thought about the burger being grilled in the kitchen, one of his favorite things being fantasizing about the preparation of the food that he was going to soon consume, when a man sat down opposite him, snapping his fingers.

"You awake in there?" the man asked.

It was Jimmy 4 by Four. Danny T. shook his head, sorry to banish the sizzling beef and bacon from his mind. "Hey, 4 by Four, what's up?"

"Thought I'd come in and have myself a happy hour cocktail, even if it is Monday," 4 by Four said. "How about you? First time I've seen you in here."

"Doing a job for Langdon," Danny T. said.

"Is that right?" 4 by Four waved to Greg and asked for Ketel One vodka on the rocks with two limes.

Danny T. added a second bacon cheeseburger to the order. "Yep."

"Langdon paying you to eat? Pretty good gig, that there."

"I'm on a stakeout."

4 by Four sized him up. "You finding out anything?"

"I'm not at liberty to talk about the case," Danny T. said.

"So, no, you don't know if Rick Strong is a sexual harasser or a kidnapper?"

Danny T. was flummoxed. It seemed that this glib-talking lawyer friend of Langdon's knew his business. He figured it couldn't hurt, then, to share. "You know that Langdon thinks Strong is the kidnapper?" he asked.

"Came in here yesterday and broke the man's nose with the crown of his head," 4 by Four said. "Can't imagine he did that for no reason."

Langdon hadn't mentioned the physical altercation to him, Danny T. thought. He was saved a reply as two women came in and sat down a few tables away. They instantly drew 4 by Four's attention.

"Well, lookie, lookie," 4 by Four said. "What do we have here?"

"What do you know about all this?" Danny T. asked.

Greg brought over 4 by Four's vodka. He took a sip, his eyes never leaving the two women. "Not much. I only know Langdon was hired to investigate Rick Strong for sexually harassing his employees," he said.

Danny T. had little interest in women. That ship had sailed long ago. He had no female friends. Not that he had many people he could call his friend of any gender. "How about the kidnapping of that little boy?"

Two men from the boisterous crowd approached the two women 4 by Four had been eyeing. The one on the right had a wild and unkempt beard that hid capacious cheeks but did little for his broad nose. The other fellow was four inches short of six feet with a carefully trimmed beard, a black skull cap, mournful eyes, and wearing a T-shirt with an eagle encased in an elaborate Q. Above it was the slogan, TRUST THE PLAN.

"You ladies look like you might need some company," Q said.

"We're fine."

"Maybe we can buy you a drink?" Q asked.

"Look, we're not interested. Can you leave us alone?"

"Perhaps you don't know who we are," Q asked. "We're Good Citizens."

"Aren't we all," the woman with short brown hair said. "Can you please leave us alone?"

"You're a feisty one," Q said. "I like my women feisty."

"Get lost."

"I could get lost between your legs for an entire night," Q said.

4 by Four cursed audibly, stood up, and walked over. "How about you leave them alone?" he said.

"How about you fuck off?" Q said.

"They've asked you nicely to leave. Just go back to your table."

Danny T. wasn't sure if he was supposed to be backing 4 by Four's play, but ten men rising from the table and walking over convinced him to stay put.

Q stepped into 4 by Four's space, the two men about equal height, and surveyed him from head to foot. His eyes were a hot hazel. "You look like one of them snowflakes that fill the landscape up here in New England," he said.

"Look, I don't want any trouble. I just think you should respect the wishes of these two ladies and go back to your table and leave them alone."

"You one of those Satan-worshipping pedophiles, ain't you?" Q asked.

"What?"

"Us Good Citizens are onto you."

"Good Citizens?"

"The storm is coming. You best not be out in it," Q said.

"What storm?" 4 by Four asked. He edged backward a step.

"Where we go one, we go all."

"Just go back to your table."

"Do you know the Great Awakening is coming?" Q asked.

"Where are you from?" 4 by Four asked with a perplexed look.

"Q plus sent me," Q said, and punched 4 by Four, the blow glancing off his jaw and into his neck.

He followed it up with a sweeping left hook that crashed into the side of 4 by Four's head, and then a right to the nose, sending the lawyer crashing to the floor.

Danny T. stood up, but a ring of Q's followers had formed, and he was unable to get past, not that he tried very hard.

Q kicked 4 by Four in the side, and an audible whoosh of air expelled from his lungs followed by a grunt of pain.

Several bouncers rushed over to break it up but couldn't get through the ring of men surrounding the altercation. A swirling wrestling match ensued.

Q grabbed 4 by Four by the bun on top of his head, lifting him a foot off the floor by the hair, and sent a punch crashing into his jaw. "Your part of the cabal, aren't you?" Q yelled as he straddled 4 by Four and began raining blows into his face. "You'll never molest another child!"

~ ~ ~ ~ ~

Langdon was back at the bookshop helping Chabal close down when his phone rang. It was Danny T. "Hey, Danny, what's up?"

"They killed him," Danny T.'s trembling voice echoed through the phone. "I think they killed him."

"Who? What?"

"He just started hitting him and didn't stop."

"What's going on?" Langdon barked into the phone.

"They're taking him out on a stretcher right now."

"Who? Goddamn it, Danny, who?"

"4 by Four. I think he's dead."

Chapter 14

It was five miles to Mid Coast Hospital via Route 1. Langdon pushed the Jeep up to eighty miles an hour. Chabal, for her part, didn't say a word, but did brace her hands against the dashboard. Dog, for a change, sat quietly in back. They came off the exit at Cook's Corner and took the left on a red light, coming up behind an ambulance, more than likely the one carrying 4 by Four. It was going considerably slower than the Jeep had been, and Langdon was forced to ease off the accelerator and tap the brakes.

Medical Drive was a winding road that forced them to a crawl and caused Langdon to curse the engineers who had planned such a twisting approach to a hospital. he followed the ambulance past the hospital and through the parking lot, another poor design choice for the quickest way to reach the emergency entrance, he thought, before finally arriving at the back of the hospital. Langdon was out of the Jeep and waiting as the ambulance doors were opened and a broken-looking 4 by Four was wheeled from the back of the vehicle.

"Is he okay?" Langdon asked, his voice hard in his throat.

"Please step aside, sir."

4 by Four was white as a fresh blanket of snow, although red splotches dotted his face still. He was frighteningly still, like a store mannequin, his body fragile under the sheet covering him, his eyes closed, though whether he was unconscious, sedated, or simply in shock, it was impossible to tell.

"I'm coming in with you," Langdon said.

"Come back tomorrow during visiting hours."

They swiped the card and wheeled 4 by Four through the open doors, a security guard staring down Langdon as they closed behind him. Langdon and Chabal went back around to the front, but were told the same thing—that now, during Covid times, visitors were limited to one at a time, and only between 10:30 and 12:00, or 4:30 and 6:00. There was nothing more to be done.

"What happened to him?" Chabal asked as they climbed back into the Jeep, the first words they'd exchanged since the bookstore.

"Don't know," Langdon said. "Danny T. said something about, 'he started hitting him,' and 'they killed him'—that's all I know."

"Where was he?"

"I had Danny T. prying around out to the brew pub," Langdon said. "I'm thinking that's where they were."

"That where we're going now?"

"Yep."

"He'll be alright," Chabal said. "If we know anything about Jimmy, he can take a punch."

Langdon cracked a grim smile. "That he can. He does have a habit of getting beat up, doesn't he?"

"I imagine he was defending some woman's honor," Chabal said. "He's always willing to risk physical pain for the possibility of physical pleasure."

Langdon's phone buzzed. He wrestled it out of his pocket, accepted the call from Star, put it on speaker, and lay it on his lap. "Star. What do you got?"

"Strong is on the move."

"You following him?"

"Yep. He's going left on Upper Maine Street."

"I figure we're going to the same place," Langdon said.

"What's that?"

"4 by Four just got beat up out to the brew pub. I figure Strong has been called in."

"Is 4 by Four okay?"

"Don't know. They wouldn't let us in the door at the hospital."

Star cursed. "You with Chabal?"

"Yep."

"Yeah, he's turning right on the Bath Road, alright," Star said.

"We should get there about the same time," Langdon said. "Call me back if he goes someplace else, otherwise I'll see you in a minute."

Langdon saw the flashing blue lights first. There were two cop cars in the expansive parking lot that was otherwise mostly empty. One of the cars had somebody in the back seat, the officer in the front filling out some sort of paperwork. A few people stood off to the side, smoking cigarettes.

A red Mustang pulled into the lot, soon followed by a turquoise Ranger Styleside. Rick Strong jumped out of the sports car and walked hurriedly into the brew pub. Star got out of the truck that he'd parked next to the Jeep.

"What's the plan, boss?" he said through the window.

"Why don't you and Chabal go inside and see what you can find out?" Langdon said. "Can't imagine I'd be very welcome."

"Gotcha," Chabal said and started to get out.

"Hey," Langdon said. "If Danny T. is still there, send him out."

"Sure thing, boss."

Langdon shook his head. He'd just been called boss by both Star and his wife. He watched them go through the door and then called Bart.

"What?" the burly cop answered the phone.

"You hear about 4 by Four?" Langdon asked.

"What about that bun-headed pretty boy now?"

"He got himself beat up pretty bad out to the Brunswick Brew Pub."

"What happened?" Bart's tone eased in gruffness.

"Was hoping you could tell me that. You being the cop and all."

"Pretty busy with the kidnapping of a young boy. You'd be

surprised how many people have seen a suspicious man with a little kid. Of course, they all turn out to be the father. Seems a man with a child is suspect, while a woman with one is just normal, or so thinks the population of the greater Brunswick area."

"I saw them cart 4 by Four into the emergency room. He didn't look very good," Langdon said.

There was a pause on the line. "Where you at now?"

"Sitting in the parking lot at the brew pub. Chabal and Star went inside to ask around. Didn't figure Rick would be too happy to see my face."

"I'll check with dispatch, see who's on it. Give you a call in a bit."

Langdon hung up the phone as the passenger door opened. Langdon shooed dog into the back and Danny T. hoisted his short but bulky body up into the Jeep.

"What'd you get me into now?" Danny T. asked in a quavering voice.

"Tell me what happened."

"There was these two women—"

"Of course there were," Langdon said. "Was it their boyfriends who beat up 4 by Four?"

"No, nothing like that." Danny T. sniffled. "There was this group of guys came in. I think they were from that group on the Mall. You know? The ones protesting business restrictions and masking regulations?"

"Yeah? Why you think that?"

"Couple of them had those plastic masks pushed up on their head. You know, with the weird mustache?"

"You mean Salvador Dalí?"

Danny T. shrugged. "Don't know who that is."

Langdon nodded. "Go ahead, tell me what happened."

Danny T. proceeded to tell Langdon about how 4 by Four had confronted the men being rude to the women, and how the one just kept on beating him, savagely punching and kicking him while he was on the ground.

"And nobody tried to break it up?" Langdon asked. "Stop him?"

Danny T. sniffled louder. "I tried, but the others, they wouldn't let anybody get close."

"You said it was a group of them?"

"Probably a dozen of them. All pretty rugged."

"Are they still in there?"

"No." Danny T. started to blubber, small slurping sounds belching from his mouth. "When the guy was done kicking 4 by Four, they all just turned and walked out."

"You recognize any of them?"

"No. Don't think they're from around here. They had that 'from away' thing about them."

Chabal and Star came out the front door and walked over, so Langdon climbed out of the Jeep. Danny T. stayed inside.

"Get anything?" Langdon asked.

"Sounds like one guy kicked 4 by Four around while a bunch of other guys prevented anybody from breaking it up," Chabal said. "Probably same thing Danny T. told you."

"Nobody knew any of them?"

"Rick Strong was kicking everybody out. Shutting down for the night. One waiter guy told us what happened. That's about it."

"Star, can you give Danny T. a ride home?" Langdon asked.

"Sure."

"What are we doing?" Chabal asked.

"Thought we'd keep an eye on Rick. Chances are he'll just go home, but you never know."

It was a half-hour until Rick came out and climbed into his Mustang. It was interesting that he turned right instead of left toward home, but that was quickly answered as he took another right into Brunswick Landing. They passed the plane that served as a monument from when this had been a Naval Air Station and took the left toward the townhome where Jill Thomas lived. Langdon parked at the head of the short street that ended in a cul-de-sac.

"Is that whose place I think it is?" Chabal asked as Rick went up to the door. There was no need of an answer as Jill opened the door, and they immediately kissed, a lustful lingering kiss, before Rick pushed his way inside, and the door closed behind them. "Somebody should probably tell his wife."

"She seems like a good sort," Langdon said. "Jill, that is. Don't know the wife. I can't quite figure out why they're together."

"People get lonely, I suppose," Chabal said.

"How about Rick? He's married. How's he lonely?"

"I suppose not all marriages are all that... bonding. Nothing so lonely as a loveless marriage." Chabal sighed and leaned her head back, and dog licked the side of her face from the back seat. "But in Rick's case, I think he's probably just an ass. Can't keep it in his pants even if he does have a loving wife at home. Some men like the conquest better than the sex."

"Speaking of cheating spouses, it sounds like Ann Morin was having an affair on her husband as well."

"That's what it sounds like," Chabal agreed.

"Seems like everybody in town is cheating on their spouse."

"Rudolph? Can you blame her?"

"Because he's older and uglier than her?" Langdon asked.

"No, because he's an ass."

"Seems to me that as far as you're concerned it doesn't matter who cheats, the guy is the ass," Langdon said.

Chabal snickered. "That *is* generally the case, yes."

"Neighbor said she saw Anna being visited by some guy in a shiny orange car."

"Not red?"

"Red?"

"Like a red Mustang driven by a known ass?"

It was Langdon's turn to laugh. "That, coupled with what the yoga instructor told you, seems to point to some sort of hanky-panky anyway. And it's been going on for some time, as Rudolph thought Anna was going to yoga for the last four or five months, and she was not."

"You think they ran off, or are they still around town?"

"Kind of hard to run off in a pandemic," Langdon said.

"Unless the guy was planning on moving already," Chabal said. "Causing Ann to make her choice. Go with him or stay with the ass."

"Good point. Maybe you can check in with Nancy Gleason in the morning." She was a local realtor who Chabal was friends with. "See if she can provide you with a list of recent home sales, and any forwarding information for the seller."

"She can access rental turnover as well. How big a loop you think we should cover?"

Langdon drummed the steering wheel. "Cumberland, Sagadahoc, and Androscoggin counties should do the trick."

"Your dog hasn't eaten his dinner yet," Chabal said.

"*My* dog?"

"Your wife is hungry as well."

"I suppose I could run you home and get back before Strong is done with what he's doing." Langdon turned the Jeep on, continuing down the road toward the back entrance to Brunswick Landing.

"Not sure what's in the air, but Jewell thinks something is up with Richam."

"Up?"

Chabal took a deep breath. "She thinks he's hiding something from her."

"Like what?"

"A woman."

Langdon thought about how Raven Burke had hired him on Richam's recommendation. And then how he'd seen them at the Wretched Lobster looking more intimate than owner and waitress should be. "I can't believe that Richam would ever cheat on Jewell," he said.

"Is thinking about cheating, cheating?"

Langdon wondered if withholding information from one's spouse was lying. "Kind of like watching porn without your spouse is cheating?"

"I was thinking more about flirting with intention."

This was most certainly a delicate subject, Langdon thought, as he pulled into their driveway. Of course, if he mentioned his concerns to Chabal, she would be obligated to say something to Jewell. He didn't want to put her in that position. "Want me to talk to him?"

"No," Chabal said. "Jewell told me this in confidence. You coming inside?"

"Thought I'd go back and see if Strong goes home to the wife and kids or goes elsewhere?"

"Elsewhere?"

"Like maybe to where he is holding a kid hostage to force the governor's hand."

Dog began whining in the backseat, a communication that most definitely meant that somebody should open his door, take him inside, and feed him his dinner.

"You going to be out late?"

"Doubt it. Rick's wife will probably hear the brew pub shut down early and will wonder where Mr. Wonderful is if he stays out too late. Of course, if he leads me to a kidnapped boy, I might be gone for a bit."

"Okay. When you're done with the cheaters, come on home to me. I promise to make it worth your while."

Chapter 15

Tuesday, October 27th

Martin Thomas had taken a leave of absence from the Bowdoin Museum. He doubted he'd ever go back, he mused, as he drove out to his buddy's cottage. He was considering going home, to Oregon, and his hometown of Cannon Beach. Not that he knew anybody there. The year his parents moved there, Martin's sixth grade year, coincided with him being shipped off to private school in Portland.

Come to think of it, Martin thought, he didn't really have many close connections in life at all. He had no real friends at the exclusive private school he'd gone to, and while he got along with his teammates from both the school and travel teams, that rapport was confined to the ice. Martin had always been a loner, a tendency perhaps instilled in him by his parents' arm's-length relationship with him even before he'd gone away to school.

Percival and Bernice Thomas both came from money, and Martin could still picture how they literally looked down their noses at others. He hated them for that. Still, it had devastated him this past summer when they both died of Covid-19. This, coming so soon after Jill moved out, had been a calamitous incident that had rocked the foundation of his being.

Martin had flown to Portland, Oregon, rented a car and driven to Seaside Hospital, where he hadn't even been allowed to see Percival and Bernice. While he spent his days in the nearby hotel bar, the virus had slowly worked its way down their respiratory tree and into their chests. As he tipped back gin and tonics, the alveoli in his parents' lungs began to lose the battle of exchanging fresh oxygen for the used carbon dioxide.

He imagined them turning blue, their breathing labored, the ventilator trying to force their bodies to process the intake of good air and the expulsion of bad. Their frantic bodies sending chemicals to all parts of the body to ward off this alien invasion, pushed to DEFCON-1 by this unforeseen attack, fighting back valiantly and uselessly, until they could fight no more.

Martin had taken care of the funeral arrangements, closed up the house overlooking Haystack Rock—the geological formation rising out of the Pacific Ocean—hired a caretaker, and had the family lawyer begin processing the will, before returning to Maine. His sister never bothered to make the trip from Florida, she perhaps having a worse relationship with their mother and father than Martin did.

Jill had been sympathetic, but had already moved out by his return, happy with her affair with the brew pub asshole. Martin thought that he'd been a good husband and father. He worked and brought in the bulk of the money, shared the duties of being a parent, and contributed to chores around the house. What more could Jill ask of him? He knew that he sometimes had trouble sharing his emotions. But he did love his wife. As a matter of fact, he'd do anything for her and would take her back in a heartbeat if she showed the slightest sign of desiring him again.

Back in the fall of his senior year in college, Jill had shown up with a friend at SigEp for a private party, and Martin had fallen in love immediately. He'd seen her around before, taken classes with her, even talked together, but that night, something had clicked. She was transformed from a mere mortal into his shining light. What should have been his crowning season of a solid hockey career no longer seemed important, his enthusiasm had dwindled, as had his time on the ice. He literally pined for Jill when he was away from her.

Graduation, dream job, marriage, a son—everything they had built together seemed to have been dashed on the rocks that day in March when Jill told him that she was moving out. At first, she refused to tell him why, but he'd worn her down. Finally, she admitted that there was somebody else. It'd been up to him to discover who that somebody was. The third day after she'd moved to Brunswick Landing, Martin stopped by to drop off a jacket she'd left behind—really just an excuse to see her, maybe convince her to come back to him—and had run into Rick Strong leaving.

Strong was her boss, so perhaps he'd just come by to drop off her check, which is what Jill claimed. If that was the case, he did the same thing the next three days in a row, even when Eddie was there. Strong would arrive at ten minutes past noon and stay for one hour. The fourth day, Martin waited for the man to leave, and then confronted his estranged wife.

Martin pressed her into confessing that she'd been fucking her boss, who happened to be a married man. He told Jill that he did not much care to be a cuckold. She told him that being a cuckold was the least of his problems. Jill said that Martin should be more concerned about being an alcoholic, emotionally distant asshole.

For some time after that, Martin and Jill didn't speak, even when dropping off Eddie. It was then that Martin had met somebody new. It was at the Yoga Bear Studio. She was voluptuous, exotic, and erotic. That she was shapely in all the right places he had realized the first class he took. That she had a foreign allure become apparent on the third class when he managed to strike up a conversation with her and become captivated by her Russian accent. The sensual, sexual side of her was exposed soon after as they skipped class and went to his house and did crazy things in the bedroom that he'd never before experienced.

Yet, it was still less than the love he felt for Jill. Maybe this is why he hadn't originally shared with the PI that Jill had strayed into an affair with Rick Strong. Because it was still too raw. Too painful.

If he didn't say it out loud, it wasn't true—or something like that.

As he pulled down the drive to his buddy's cottage, Martin reflected on the strange twists of fate that had brought him to this place. His friend from college was an artist who also had a place in Central America somewhere where he spent the winters. Martin believed that he came from money, and that it was not art alone that allowed him this perk in life. For the past few years, Martin had watched over the cottage for him through the winter. He and Jill had even used it like a getaway bed and breakfast a few times.

Thus far, Ann had refused to move into Martin's home, as she was afraid her husband would find her there, and she was very much afraid of him. But when Martin presented this unknown secluded cottage on the water as a steppingstone, she had agreed to leave her husband. Martin very much thought it was for the best to keep their relationship on the down low, and had only stayed with her at the cabin when Eddie was with Jill.

And then came the kidnapping, Martin thought with a sad and sardonic smile, as he stepped out of the Prius. The abduction of his son had brought Jill back into his life, and with that, the realization that she was the true love of his life, even if Ann was his passion. If there was even the slightest chance he could go back to Jill, start their life over again, Martin felt certain that he'd do so in a heartbeat.

Would the kidnapping of his son win him back the affections of his wife, Martin wondered? He stepped through the door of the cottage and directly into the embrace of Ann Morin, who attacked him like a lioness in heat, temporarily banishing thoughts of wandering wives and missing boys.

~ ~ ~ ~ ~

Four days from Halloween, Langdon thought grimly, and there were no leads on the kidnapped boy. It was early yet, and he was sipping coffee at his desk in the office at the back of the Coffee Dog

Bookstore, which wouldn't open for another three hours. He got out a blank piece of paper and a pen.

He wrote the name Rick Strong. This was his main suspect. The man definitely had motive in wanting the governor to loosen, rather than tighten, Covid restrictions for businesses such as his. Not enforcing mask-wearing for his kitchen staff certainly led Langdon to believe that he either didn't think the virus was real, or he didn't believe that masks and social distancing provided any true protection. Of course, the short conversation they'd had a few days back had bolstered that notion.

And now, knowing that Rick had been having an affair with Jill Thomas, mother of the kidnapped boy, for some time—well, the means to taking Eddie had been provided. He knew the house and quite possibly knew where the hidden key was. He probably also knew that Martin Thomas had a drinking problem. A thought niggled at the corner of Langdon's mind. What if Martin had gone into the brew pub earlier, perhaps with his son, to have dinner, and Rick had witnessed him getting lit and realized that opportunity was presenting itself? He made a note to double-check with Martin, who'd claimed to have eaten at home that night—but what drunk wanted to admit they were doing so while driving their young son around?

Of course, this theory that Rick Strong was the kidnapper had one flaw. Where was the boy? Rick was at work or home or with Jill, as far as Langdon could tell. Last night, he'd gone back to keep watch, and at eleven o'clock, Rick had come out of Jill's townhouse and driven straight home where, half an hour later, the last of the lights had clicked off. Langdon had given it another fifteen minutes and gone on home to his own wife.

Strong's wife and two kids had verified to the police that he was with them at their cottage out to Small Point the night of the kidnapping. Perhaps that was a lie, but teenagers and honest women aren't usually able to hoodwink the police. Plus, who was watching

Eddie? It seemed to suggest an accomplice. Perhaps Strong had hired somebody else to do the actual kidnapping while he created an iron-clad alibi, and that person was feeding and caring for the abducted boy at some unknown location.

Either way, it seemed important to keep tabs on Strong. It'd be best to shut the bookstore down for the next few days to have all hands on deck. A boy's life was at stake, after all. That way, Star would be available to keep an eye on Strong. It would also free up Chabal as well as Langdon.

Chabal might have better luck digging into Jill Thomas. If Rick Strong was behind the abduction, then there seemed a fair to middling chance that Jill knew something about it. Why would she knowingly be involved in taking her own son and threatening to execute him? Langdon texted Chabal. You want to tail Jill Thomas around today?

The reply came back immediately. Sure. You were up and out early today.

We have just four days to save that boy's life.

What about the bookshop? Supposed to open it today.

Closing it down.

Where you at now?

Office.

You eat?

No.

I'll bring a breakfast sandwich on my way over to JT's.

Langdon answered with a smiley face emoji.

The next text was to Star. Closing shop for a few days. Can you keep an eye on Strong?

No problem, boss. Car's still in the driveway. Got in a little after 11 last night. Saw you drive by.

Thanks. Keep me updated on where he goes.

A smiling emoji that faintly resembled Star came back with a huge thumbs-up.

For Langdon, that left Martin Thomas as the only other person associated with the kidnapping. He had, after all, been the one from whose care little Eddie had been plucked. What motive could the man have? He seemed angry about Jill leaving him. Could it be related to that in some way? Was he trying to hurt her by hurting their son?

Langdon heard the outer door to the bookshop unlock and a few seconds later Chabal came through the door with a bag. "Gotcha a bacon, egg, and cheese on an English muffin." She tossed him the sandwich, grabbed a cup of coffee from the pot, and plunked herself down on the worn couch.

"Morning, babe," Langdon said.

"Did you come home last night?" Chabal asked. "Because some man came into my bedroom after I went to sleep and did naughty things to me and then was gone before I woke up this morning."

Langdon smiled. "Nope. Came straight here after I followed Rick Strong home."

"I thought it was bigger than normal." Chabal cracked with a bawdy snicker. "How soon should I get out to Jill's place?"

"Right off, as soon as you finish your coffee, I guess. Don't want to miss her." Langdon picked up his phone. "Hold on, let me check in with Bart." He hit the cop's name on his phone and called instead of texting, knowing that the man hated texting, probably because his thumbs were the size of a baby's feet.

"What?" Bart answered.

Langdon clicked the speaker icon so Chabal could hear. "Morning, sunshine. You didn't call me back last night about 4 by Four."

"Bit too busy to be your errand boy."

"You find out anything?"

"I stopped by the hospital and saw him. Guy messed him up pretty good. Broke two ribs. Busted his nose. Left eye is swollen shut."

Langdon could hear the barely contained anger in his friend's voice. "You talk to him?"

"He was out the whole time I was there. Doctor said he'd be able to talk today. Daigle and Dean are over there now seeing if they can get a statement."

It wasn't so long ago that officer Harry Daigle had been chasing Langdon through the streets of Brunswick. "Any leads on the guy who did it?"

"One of the anti-maskers from the Mall, we think. Nobody recognized him, so we don't believe he's local. Just here to stir shit up. Daigle and Dean will be out on the Mall when the protesters arrive, which has been around 10:00 the last few days. They got a picture of the guy from the cameras. If he shows, they'll nab him."

"You got a picture of the guy?" Langdon wondered if this might somehow be connected to the kidnapping case. If Strong was really behind it all, and had an accomplice, what better person than somebody from away who believed strongly that requiring masks and placing restrictions on businesses was infringing upon the rights of Americans?

"Yep. I'll send it to you. Daigle and Dean were out hoofing it around the hotels and motels last night, but so far, no luck."

"Running it through facial recognition?"

"Don't be cop-splaining to me," Bart said.

"Cop-splaining?"

"Yeah, you know, talking to me like I don't know shit." Bart belched.

Langdon chuckled. "So you did?"

"The Feds have all that fancy technology. They're hot on the trail."

"Any progress on the Thomas case?"

"Not a goddamn thing."

"You think the guy who beat up 4 by Four, or one of that group, could be responsible for the kidnapping?"

"I haven't a clue. Sounds like you don't either. You done taking up my time?"

"How much do you see of Martin and Jill?"

"I try to personally brief them three times a day."

"They come to you?"

"Yep. Be here at 10:00."

"Thanks."

Bart ended the connection abruptly.

"We should go visit Jimmy," Chabal said, "when visiting hours come around."

"Only one visitor allowed at a time. Maybe Richam or Jewell can visit him this morning and one of us can go this afternoon?"

"I'll call Jewell," Chabal said, standing up. "You don't really think Jill Thomas abducted her own kid, do you?"

"No, but we have to cover all the bases. I'm going to go check on Martin, so I guess I'll probably see you in the police station parking lot at 10:00."

~ ~ ~ ~ ~

Martin had wanted to get a second helping, Annika thought with a smile, but she'd left him wanting more. That was the trick. Plus, the first time should've been enough for any fellow. Taras had trained her in the ways to please a man—skills she'd put to good use in escaping his clutches and surviving on the streets. Rudolph had bought the cow, so to speak, but that didn't necessarily mean the sweet cream was his alone.

Annika was certain that she'd rocked Martin Thomas's world more so than any woman ever had, and certainly to a greater extent than that blocky wife of his. Men liked women who were adventurous in the sack. Nice ladies who moaned and were so overcome with pleasure that they pinched and scratched and bit. Men wanted their sexual mates to be at once innocent but with a touch of the naughty, seemingly naive but skilled. Gushing praise of his incredible sexual prowess was always welcome. And by promising to provide yet more exotic and forbidden fruit at some point in the near future, well, she had the man stuck like a tuna on a hook. Annika smiled.

He was a good man, Martin Thomas was, and Annika was more than willing to exchange the security he offered her for the pleasure she brought him. Who knows, perhaps with time he would come to provide her with pleasure as well, and maybe she'd be able to complement their finances from her own labors. She had always dreamed of being an artist, and with a husband who had a degree in art and a job as a curator, those fantasies might just be realized.

Annika stretched her naked body luxuriously as if she were already lounging in the satin sheets of some feather bed in a castle high on the cliffs. In her mind, Martin was in the kitchen making them breakfast, or perhaps letting a manservant do that while he sat in a rocker on the screened porch reading the newspaper. James was just down the hallway, sleeping in, about to wake and go clattering down to his playroom, or perhaps to watch the wide screen television. Martin would bring her a cup of coffee when it was ready, and she'd put on a silk robe, giving him a glimpse of her *pizda*, the soft blonde fur that controlled him. She'd turn and sway, arching her back to emphasize the swell of her creamy breasts, her nipples jutting through the fabric, and...

There was a rustle in the hallway, and Annika hastily stood up and dressed. The fairy tale was still a breathing beast within her, but it would have to wait. There was the now to attend to.

Chapter 16

Martin Thomas had been allowed back into his home by the crime scene people, but he was not there when Langdon swung by. No bright orange Toyota Prius to be seen anywhere. This is when it clicked in. *Son-of-a-gun*, Langdon said to himself. Could it be? The mysterious orange car that Mr. Boudreau had mentioned. Martin Thomas. Ann Morin. Maybe. Just maybe.

No lights on. Pretty clearly not home. Langdon called the Bowdoin Museum, but it went straight to the answering machine, which informed him that the museum was not currently open to the public. It was possible that Martin had gone in to work on something, so Langdon trolled the parking lots of the college, again to no avail. He'd just have to pick him up after his briefing at the police station at 10:00.

The theme music to *Halloween*, the movie, interrupted Langdon's search. This was the ringtone assigned to his wife. "Hey, babe," he said. "You got eyes on Jill?"

"I do. She's sitting in her living room reading a book," Chabal said. "How about Martin?"

"Nowhere to be found. I'll have to pick him up at the police station. You get ahold of Jewell?"

"I did. She said no-can-do to visiting Jimmy this morning. Has a Zoom call for work."

"How about Richam?"

"That's why I'm calling. I gave him a ring. No answer. Texted.

Nothing. Called Jewell back, and she said he was at work. Called the Wretched Lobster and was told he wasn't there and wasn't on the schedule until 11:00."

Langdon didn't know quite what to say. "You tell Jewell he wasn't there?"

"No. You think I should?"

"She already thinks he's hiding something from her."

"Yes."

"Let me talk to him first. We don't want to send Jewell into a tirade because Richam had a meeting over at the Lenin Stop Coffee Shop."

"Okay. See you at the fuzz headquarters at 10:00." Chabal disconnected the call.

Langdon checked the time. He had an hour to kill. Was worth a shot, he figured, and pulled the Jeep onto upper Maine Street, heading back toward his office at the bookshop. He drove by the Town Mall, serene and silent at this time of day, so much so that he found it hard to believe that in an hour it would be filled with protesters and anti-protesters waving signs and trying to drown each other out chanting their slogans.

There was a man reading the closed sign that Langdon had put on the door. It was Al Jenkins, a bank manager and good customer.

"You're not going to make me order from Amazon, are you?" Al asked.

Langdon laughed. "Closed down until November 1st. But I gotta grab something out back if you wanted to pick out a book."

"You got that Crosby book? *Blacktop Wasteland*?"

"Cosby, S.A. Cosby," Langdon said unlocking the door. "It's over on the 'New' shelf, Al."

Langdon went in the back and looked at the paperwork he'd gotten Raven Burke to fill out. She lived just down and across the street in one of the upstairs apartments. Number three, to be exact. No time like the present to go see if his suspicions were correct, Langdon thought, walking back through the bookstore.

"Looks great," Al said. "How much do I owe you?"

"How about next time you come in we settle up?" Langdon said. "Everything's shut down."

"Fair enough."

Langdon locked the door behind them and followed Al out onto the street where the banker went to the right and he to the left.

The apartments were located above a Greek restaurant and a running-shoe store. The door to the staircase that led to the upstairs apartments was located between the two businesses with mailboxes at the bottom. The stairs were wooden and had seen better days. Number three was to the right, a faded painted numeral on the heavy oak door. As Langdon was about to knock, it swung open, revealing Raven Burke and Richam Denevieux.

"Mr. Langdon?" Raven was the first to react. "What are you doing here?"

"I wanted to give you an update on your sexual harassment case against Rick Strong," Langdon said.

Richam gave him a knowing look that suggested he knew that wasn't the truth.

"I was just going out. Why didn't you call first?" Raven said.

"Spur of the moment. I was walking by and thought I'd just pop in. Maybe we can talk on the phone later?" Langdon said.

"Ya. I work until 8:00," Raven said.

"How about you, Richam?" Langdon asked. "You free to grab a cup of coffee?"

"Raven, you know my car," Richam said. "It's in the short-term parking out back. Unlocked. I'll be right down."

Raven locked the door and went down the stairs, leaving Richam and Langdon standing in the hallway.

"You want to tell me what's going on?" Langdon asked.

"It is not what it looks like."

"Jewell told Chabal she thinks you got another woman in your life. I said no way. Was I wrong?"

"She's half my age. I love my wife."

"Exactly my point," Langdon said. "What the hell are you doing? I mean, I warned 4 by Four to keep his mitts off her, but didn't think I had to tell *you* that."

"How is 4 by Four?"

"Don't know. Was hoping you could go over during visiting hours between 10:30 and noon today. That's why I was looking for you."

"I got this thing I have to go do now."

"You going to tell me what is going on?"

Richam exhaled a huge breath. "No. Not yet."

"Jewell doesn't deserve this."

"Don't worry. I'll tell her everything."

"When?" Langdon stepped closer to his friend, his face just inches away. "I don't like keeping things from *my* wife, Richam, and this seems to be a thing that I am going to have to keep from her."

Richam held his stare. "I will tell her everything by this Friday. I just have to work out a few things first."

~ ~ ~ ~ ~

Working the bookshop was easily a hundred times more fun than tailing a suspect, Chabal thought. Jill Thomas had left her rental unit exactly three times all day, each time to go to the police station and get updated. As there was nothing really going on in the case, these visits were no more than thirty minutes long. At least Chabal was able to slide into the Jeep with her husband while they waited, even if he was acting strange about something.

Chabal couldn't imagine what Jill Thomas must be going through right now. She thought back to when her own children were little Eddie's age and tried to envision what her emotions might be. She would've absolutely been a basket case. And then to throw in a recent separation from your husband, a painful experience that Chabal *had* gone through. She certainly couldn't look down her nose at Jill for having an affair with her boss, as this is exactly how Chabal had come to be divorced and remarried to Langdon.

Chabal and Langdon had now been married almost twenty years, bringing her far more happiness, she knew, than if she'd stayed with her previous husband, not that he was a bad guy. It was just that sometimes in life, people settle for something, not realizing that 'better' is out there, right around the corner. Of course, Chabal couldn't quite grasp how Rick Strong was better than Martin Thomas.

Strong had sexually—no—had been *accused* of sexually harassing a former employee, and for all intents and purposes, this seemed to be a trend in his life, even if married with kids. At least, Chabal thought, when she realized that she was in love with Langdon and not her husband, she'd been forthright and honest, ripping that bandage off as painlessly as possible. Her three children had been the top priority, coming first before Langdon, or John, her ex.

It hadn't been easy, that was for sure. Chabal couldn't even begin to fathom what the additional stress would have been if one of her children had been kidnapped and threatened with execution. For this reason, everything in her wanted to go inside the townhome and pour a tall tequila drink for her and Jill and let the woman cry on her shoulder. Instead, she was parked down the street, needing to pee, following Jill to see if she was somehow involved in the abduction of her own son.

At 10:00, the bedroom light clicked off, indicating that Jill Thomas had gone to bed for the night. Chabal called Langdon to see if this stakeout was meant to last the night through, or if it could be resumed in the morning. He suggested she give it half an hour to make sure it wasn't a ruse and Jill was sneaking out, and then go on home. As they spoke, Langdon said that it looked like Martin was also turning in, and he'd meet her at home in bit. He suggested they might want to be back at their posts by 5:00 in the morning, in case either Martin or Jill were sneaking off to visit their supposedly abducted son before continuing the ploy of grieving parent.

~ ~ ~ ~ ~

Rick Strong looked in his rearview mirror and saw the blue-green truck pull out behind him. What was that color called, he wondered? Jade? No, that was almost the right color, but was actually a piece of jewelry. Turquoise, that's what it was. It stuck out like a flatlander from Mass. at the bar. Thus, Rick knew where he'd seen it, every day, in the dooryard across the street, at that old codger's place. Starling. Jonathan Starling. They'd been neighbors for some years now but had only spoken in passing a couple of times.

He'd also seen the antique truck behind him earlier on his way to work. Was it just coincidence or was the man following him? And for what? Maybe Martin Thomas had hired him to obtain information about his relationship with Jill. Then, Rick remembered their kid had been taken. It was unlikely that the man had hired somebody to follow him around and take pictures of marital infidelities while his little boy was being held captive by some madman.

It must be his wife who'd hired the guy to keep tabs on him. That bitch. Rick could see it now, Valerie striking up a conversation with the crusty old fellow. Starling probably came over to ask for a cup of flour or an egg or something, and next thing you know, they're gabbing away. That woman *did* know how to run her mouth, that was for sure. Didn't know her place, though, no sirree, that she most certainly did not.

Rick busted his ass every day to build a business, a damn fine one, but one that the current governor was trying to destroy. So far, the brew pub had allowed the Strongs to lead a good life in Brunswick. They weren't filthy rich, not yet, but they did okay for themselves. Goddamn food on the table, presents under the tree at Christmas, yes, fucking Christmas, not "the holidays" or some other garbage like that. Cell phones, laptops, and summer camps for the kids, tennis club, expensive clothes, and a cleaning lady once a week for the wife…

Rick had no plans to go see Jill that night, but maybe, he thought, he should change direction and lead the old fool over there so he could report back to Valerie. What the fuck was she going to do about it? She knew which side her bread was buttered on. Not that he really wanted to see Jill, as she mostly just cried now and whined about her missing brat. Rick turned onto Boody Street, the turquoise truck following suit, which could still be coincidence. Rick was only certain he was being followed when he turned left onto Douglas Street. The old fool slowed way down, but then the headlights swung around and followed.

Rick drove the Ford Mustang just below the speed limit, out to the Middle Bay Road and to the back entrance to Brunswick Landing where Jill lived. He revved the engine and opened it up once on the old Naval Air Station, hitting forty as he passed the clubhouse to the golf course, roaring down the road adjacent to the ninth fairway, through some S-curves and out along the airfield. Jonathan Starling and his candy-colored truck disappeared behind him, eating his dust.

He was in no mood to visit Jill and listen to her whine. Or go home and get in a yelling match with his wife about getting somebody to follow him. No, Rick was going to go to the cottage, the one place where he was master of his own castle and didn't have to put up with the pesky annoyances that women brought into his life. Valerie. Raven. Jill. The governor. All women who poked and prodded him as if who they were actually mattered. Didn't they know he was Rick Fucking Strong?

~ ~ ~ ~ ~

Langdon's phone rang. He was just about to drift off to sleep for the night, his arm encompassing Chabal from behind. They'd gotten home roughly at the same time, about forty minutes earlier. He'd checked in with Star, who said that Strong was still at the brew pub, but it looked like it was closing up soon.

It was the ringtone from the Starlight theme song. The one that he'd attached to Jonathan Starling's number. "Hello."

"I lost him."

"What?"

"He must've been on to me."

Langdon cursed silently. The man did drive a turquoise antique truck meticulously restored to a shining gemstone that could probably be seen from outer space. "What happened?"

"He was almost home, veered off path, and then worked his way over to Brunswick Landing. He floored it. The Styleside was no match for the Mustang."

"He didn't go to Jill Thomas's place?"

"No, boss, not unless he parked quite a ways away and walked through the shadows to get there. First place I checked. Then I drove up and down all the streets close by, even those condos across the way and the Rec Center parking lot."

"Okay. Nothing you can do but go home. Let me know if he shows up across the street."

"You want me to stay awake, keeping a lookout?"

"No. If he shows up home, then we already missed what he didn't want us to see. Get some sleep. Call me when you get up in the morning."

"He's up to something, isn't he?" Chabal said, the sleepiness fast disappearing from her voice. "That's why he ditched Star."

Langdon looked at the time. Hesitated. Called Bart.

"What?"

"Could use some help."

"You know how much sleep I've had in the past five days?"

"Star was trailing Strong. He got made. Strong lost him. Not at home. Not at his girlfriend's."

Bart cursed, long and loud, though whether at the situation or at Langdon, it was hard to tell. "I told you he has a rock-solid alibi for the night Eddie was taken. He's not involved."

"Maybe he's got somebody working for him," Langdon said. "The guy has motive and opportunity and is now missing."

"What do you want?"

"Can you put out a BOLO? I mean, like on the down-low."

"You want me to post a 'be on the lookout for a dangerous suspect' on the down-low? What the fuck is this? Inspector Gadget?"

"You got any leads on who took Eddie, then? Anything at all?"

"Nada." Bart sighed. "I'll put the word out. What was Strong driving?"

Langdon gave him the make, model, color, and license plate. There was absolutely no concrete evidence against Strong, but what else did they have?

"Anybody spots him, they'll give me a call, and I'll give you a call. This better not come back to bite me in the ass." Bart hung up.

Chapter 17

Wednesday, October 28th

Jill Thomas woke with a start. Not really from sleep, but from that somewhere in between land of thoughts and dreams, the river Styx whose murky waters separate the living from the dead. In this case, Jill thought, it was quite the opposite, as being awake for her was like death, while sleep temporarily brought solace, however fleeting—until the bad dreams paraded past like sheep jumping a fence to their slaughter.

It was the boatman, Charon, who transported souls across the river to Hades, whose image garnered much of the attention of the art world, Jill knew. But that body of water was named for the Greek goddess of hate, and it was this hate that she felt eating away at her very being. The goddess was the river and the river the goddess, a goddess who loathed death. It was into the river Styx that Thetis, mother of Achilles, dipped her infant son in order to make him immortal, forgetting to dunk the baby's heel by which she held him, and thus allowing Paris to kill him with an arrow years later. What mistake had she, Jill Thomas, made in protecting her son from death?

This, then, was what had startled her from sleep, this overwhelming bitterness and loathing. She hated Martin for hiding in the bottle and erecting a barrier through which she could never pass, finally giving in and leaving him. She knew that it wasn't his fault, that there was a trace of autism in him. This made him brilliant in some ways and unreachable in others. The fact that he had been drunk and passed out the night little Eddie was taken, however, that was unforgivable.

But where had she been? She'd run out on her two men, trying to escape a bland and gray life by falling into the arms of an ass—yes, she full well knew that Rick Strong was the very definition of asshole. But he'd showered her with attention and shown physical desire, the like of which Martin had never done, for Martin had always kept her at arm's length, seemingly keeping the same distance from his own emotions. That inability to find intimacy had grown into a deep chasm and eventually led, after the birth of Eddie, to a physical distancing that prevented them from ever touching, being intimate, or feeling the pleasures of the flesh, even in a nonsexual way.

It was then that the idea came to Jill. It was one of those notions that pass through one's mind lying in bed at 2:00 a.m., here now and then gone in the blink of an eye. She knew that she should get up and at least write it down, so that she wouldn't forget, but this new wrinkle to her life was not going to flit away, oh no.

The cottage. Could Eddie be at the cottage? She'd been there twice. Her mind envisioned the layout. Tried to match up her memories from the video of the masked kidnapper with her baby boy. At 2:30 in the morning, she gave up any pretense of sleep or patience or thought of anything but a driving need to get to the cottage and find out for herself. She pulled on clothes without checking her hair or face in the mirror and eased out the door and into her car.

The late October morning was cold and hard and dark, the sun not due to rise for hours, and even then, a thin, weak sun not strong enough to banish the chill from the Maine morning. The morning was filled with a hard desolation which was unrelenting. Jill felt like this, had felt like this, ever since Eddie had been taken, maybe even before. Her family and friends, her husband and son, were not enough to erase the increasing loneliness that had crawled its way into her heart.

What was wrong with her, she wondered? It was long before her boy had been abducted that this creeping alienation had entered her life. Was it the pandemic? The polarized politics that dominated the news every day had seemingly torn a hole in her soul and filled it with a despair that she was unable to escape. Nothing was right with the world. The one thing that she'd actually felt in quite some time was the abduction of Eddie. For that, she was almost, if not quite, grateful to feel again, even if it was pain and fear that gripped her with an icy claw, and even now, made it hard for her to breathe.

Was it possible that Eddie was at the cottage? This was the single consuming passion driving her forward, propelling her into the night. She parked on the road just past the driveway, and then thought to turn the car around so that it was headed out toward the main road and safety. If she was right, there would be no time to spare in leaving. If she was wrong, it wouldn't matter in the slightest.

She felt her way down the driveway step by step in the starless night, afraid to turn on her flashlight, not wanting to draw attention. There were no cars in front of the cottage. No lights on, but it was the time of night that was the darkest. This was either going to be nothing or an end both terrifying and horrific. Jill did not want it to be true. She did not want to believe it possible.

She knew where the key was, had visited this place before. It was there, hanging on a nail, in the corner of the covered porch. The wooden deck boards complained underneath her feet, warning any inhabitants of an intrusion, announcing her presence with every creak, squeak, and rasp.

The key slid into the lock which clicked open, the noise like a gunshot to her nerves, the door squawking wide. She took a tentative step into the now quiet house, leaving the door open behind her. The door on the right led to the master bedroom. She'd been in there before. Had sex with him in that bed.

There were two more doors on the left. The first one was open. She took her phone out and hit the flashlight app and shone it into the room. There was a bureau, a closet door, a small desk, and a bed. The bed was made and empty. Jill tiptoed down the hallway toward the last door. There was an old-fashioned key, the large brass kind, stuck in the lock. She turned it, expecting it to grate and scrape, but surprisingly, there was not a sound. The door swung open on greased hinges.

She turned on the flashlight. The room was a mirror twin of the last room, except for the boarded-up windows, two of them, and the small boy sleeping in the bed. Jill gasped, then almost sobbed, and went to step forward, but was stopped by an arm that circled her neck and pulled her backward.

~ ~ ~ ~ ~

Langdon's alarm went off. It was still pitch black, and he fumbled for the phone at the bedside table. Only, it wasn't the alarm. It was Bart calling.

"Hello," Langdon said as the sleep fell from him in waves leaving his mind alert, if not his body.

"Got a body out in Phippsburg. Just came over the scanner. The corpse is Jill Thomas, at least according to her license."

"That can't be. Chabal followed her home and watched her lights go out at 10:00," Langdon said. "There must be some mistake."

"Unless there is some other Jill Thomas who just happened to get killed out to Phippsburg, it looks like your client's lights have been permanently turned out."

"Has she been physically identified or just by her ID?"

"Couple officers have been dispatched to notify Martin Thomas. He'll be asked to identify her after the crime scene people are done with her and she's been brought into the morgue up to Augusta."

"Staties out there already?"

"Yep. Kicked everybody else out."

"They can ID her, if they've been working the kidnapping case."

"Couple different fellows than the ones assigned to the command post."

"Haven't you been coordinating the kidnapping case with them?"

"Yeah, missing persons as well as their incident team."

"You going out there? I'm sure they'll let you into the crime scene."

"Yep. I'm on my way," Bart said.

"Can't you identify the body and leave Martin out of it?"

"Kind of want to see what his reaction is."

"Doesn't Rick Strong have a place out to Small Point?" Small Point was past Phippsburg, at the very end of the peninsula.

"Sure does."

"You gonna pick him up?" Langdon walked to the kitchen and hit the button on the coffee pot. It looked to be a coffee day.

"What for?"

Langdon sensed a softening in this stance. The tone was certainly less belligerent. This time, the 'what for' truly seemed to be a question, and not a snarky one, either. "Motive and opportunity, same as with the boy."

"What motive does he have to kill Jill Thomas?"

Langdon wondered that maybe she'd discovered her son being held captive by Rick Strong, is what he thought, but he kept quiet in that regard. "You'll at least bring him in for questioning?"

"When we find him."

"When you find him?"

Bart made some unintelligible noises that could've been a cough, sneeze, burp, but was most likely a clearing of his throat.

"His wife says he didn't come home last night."

"She say where he is?"

"No idea. He's not answering his phone. I'm going to swing by his cottage after I hit the crime scene and see if he might be there."

"Keep me in the loop," Langdon said, but Bart had already hung up.

Chapter 18

"I need to go," Langdon said. "Jill Thomas has just been found dead." He filled Chabal in on the conversation with Bart.

"Where you going? I'm up now. Guess I don't have to go stakeout Jill this morning." Chabal said, shaking her head.

"Wanna go for a ride?" Langdon asked, handing her a cup of coffee. They stood in the kitchen at the granite island.

"Where to?" Chabal took a slug of the coffee.

"Thought we'd go check on Martin Thomas before the police whisk him away. Make sure he's home."

"Make sure he's home?"

"I'd like to eliminate him as a suspect in killing Jill."

"That makes sense."

"A bit later, I thought I might drop you off at the Mall."

"The one down in South Portland? I hate shopping, you know that," Chabal said with a grin.

"I was thinking the Town Mall, right here in Brunswick. I even got you a present yesterday." He held up a Salvador Dalí mask.

"Should I take my own car?"

"I'll bring you back here or drop you there. Don't think I need to watch Mr. Thomas all day. He's going to be busy with the police."

"How about breakfast?"

"If Thomas is there and the police are there, we'll grab some takeout from the diner and come back here to eat."

"Will I have time for a shower?"

"Believe me, the more unkempt you look, the better you'll fit in."

"Unkempt?"

"Think about the worst hangover you ever had," Langdon said. "Couple that with the angriest moment of your life, join those two things together, and *voilà*, you fit the bill perfectly."

"For a homeless person?"

"For the type of women you're going to be hanging out with on the Mall."

"You're terrible," Chabal said. "Just because they're anti-maskers doesn't mean they have poor hygiene."

"Trust me," Langdon said. "They think soap, shampoo, and deodorant all infringe upon their inalienable rights as well."

"Can I at least brush my teeth?"

"Sure. That might be nice, especially if we have time to hop back in the sack. But then you'll need to make your sign."

Twenty minutes later, after feeding dog and taking him for a quick walk down the street, they were in the Jeep on their way to the Thomas home. Dog had been left behind, moping on the couch at being left out. It was just past 5:00 in the morning when they drove past the house, noting the orange Prius in the driveway. Langdon wondered if it was parked at a slightly different angle than the night before, but he couldn't be sure. There was a police cruiser parked behind it and lights on inside.

"Do you remember the description that the girl at Yoga Bear gave you of the car?" Langdon asked. "The one that picked up Ann Morin?"

"She just said it was shiny."

Langdon pointed at the orange Prius. "Like that, you think?"

"Most cars are shiny." Chabal shrugged.

"Talked to a neighbor of Rudolph's the other day. She mentioned she'd seen a bright orange car parked out front of the Morin house a few weeks back. Remembered distinctly that it was that color because she couldn't understand who would buy such a thing."

"That's something to chew on," Chabal said.

They tossed possible scenarios back and forth, hashing their way through two disparate cases that increasingly seemed to be woven together by some very twisted threads indeed.

After an hour, two officers came out with a visibly distraught Martin Thomas. He got in the backseat of the patrol car, not like he was in custody, but rather like a passenger to be transported. Langdon opened the door of the Jeep. "Text me if anybody comes by," he said.

"What? Where are you going?" Chabal asked.

"Thought I'd go inside and poke around a bit."

"How do you plan on getting in?"

"I watched a YouTube video a couple of months back on how to pick a lock. Been practicing at home."

"You're fucking kidding me."

Langdon chuckled. "Yep. Figured that bathroom window is probably still busted. Thought I might wiggle through there."

Chabal eyed his six-foot-four-inch frame, which had added ten pounds in the last few years, and shook her head. "Do you want me to do it?"

"I should be fine."

"Don't keep your phone in your pocket," Chabal said, "in case you get stuck halfway and have to text me to come pull you out."

Having come out to help the search team the day Eddie went missing, Langdon had a decent idea of how to come up behind the house without being seen by the neighbors, none of whom were all that close. It helped that the horizon to the east was starting to show signs of the impending sunrise, giving him a faint light to pick his way through the trees on his approach.

The farmhouse on the far side of the Thomas house had lights on, but the bathroom on this side was well protected by trees. The window had, indeed, not yet been fixed. A piece of cardboard had been taped over the missing glass. Langdon peeled back the cardboard, figuring he could replace it behind him and walk out the back door when he was done, leaving no trace of his visit.

He grabbed the sill and jumped up so that he could get his elbows inside, turning his shoulders sideways to fit through the opening. He'd worn his leather gloves to provide warmth as well as to keep his fingerprints to himself. He'd pulled a skull cap down over his unruly hair and was careful to not rub his face on anything, not wanting to leave any evidence of his presence in case a forensics team returned, which was highly likely now that Jill Thomas had been killed. Having been there a few days earlier investigating the scene at least gave him some plausible deniability if he were to leave behind any trace of physical evidence.

There was nothing out of the ordinary in the bathroom, so Langdon moved to the master bedroom that Martin and Jill had shared, but was now the former's sole domain. The bed was meticulously made, the corners pulled tight, the old military saying that you could bounce a quarter off the bedcover seeming apt. It would appear that the police had not woken Martin this morning, even though they'd arrived around 5:00 in the morning. Not only was he up, but he'd already made the bed. The side table to the bed had a drawer, and in this, Langdon found a bag with a box of condoms. The sales receipt was from two days ago. The box had been opened and several were missing.

It seemed that Martin was having sex with somebody, Langdon mused, or at least had high hopes of doing so. Strange behavior to carry on in the midst of your son being kidnapped, though the comfort of another body might be incredibly helpful in such a situation. Langdon knew this from recent experience, his adult daughter having been abducted by a psychopath. But Langdon had known who had done the taking, and so, could focus his energies to find and recover her, with Chabal by his side. It must be excruciating to just wait, watching the seconds tick by, the impending deadline of the execution of your child growing closer and closer with each passing minute.

In the kitchen was a liquor cabinet filled with half-gallon jugs of various liquors, bottles that the new generation called handles. The coffee pot was on, and three cups were on the counter next to the sink, suggesting that either Martin had a pot already on, or had made one to share with the two police officers when they arrived with the news of the death of his estranged wife. Perhaps one of them had made the coffee as Martin sat and grieved, Langdon speculated, thinking about the man's distraught features as he'd been led to the police cruiser.

Langdon opened the door of a room he'd not been in before. It looked like it was intended to be a bedroom but had been converted into an office. A single bed was pushed against the wall, and a desk looked out through the window toward the farmhouse with the lights on. There was a computer, printer, lamp, and one pen on the desktop. Martin Thomas was an incredibly organized man, Langdon thought, obsessively anal retentive, perhaps had a touch of autism.

In the desk drawer, there were some papers pertaining to the death of Percival and Bernice Thomas. They'd died in June, just days apart, from complications associated with Covid-19. It looked like Martin was inheriting the house out in Oregon, and was splitting a sizable stock portfolio with his sister who lived in Florida. This merely backed up what Langdon had already been told, although the numbers were bigger than he'd expected.

Langdon's phone buzzed in his pocket. Text from Chabal. Get out. Police here.

He carefully set the papers back in the drawer and shut it. Langdon went through the kitchen and slipped out the back just as he heard the front door being opened. He looked at the farmhouse and saw a man watching through a window, though whether or not he saw Langdon, he couldn't tell. Langdon turned his back and slipped into the trees, the sun fully risen now, a tight ball of yellow just above the treetops.

~ ~ ~ ~ ~

Brunswick, Maine, did not, as a rule, have all that many murders. There'd been that incident out at Mere Point last year, but Bart had to go back quite a few years to remember another killing, all the way back to the early 2000s. Hell, they'd only had three assaults all of last year. Not that this case would fall under the jurisdiction of a murder in Brunswick, as the body was found thirty minutes out on a peninsula at Small Point, technically the town of Phippsburg.

Of course, none of that mattered, as all homicides were handled by Major Crime Unit, in this case, the southern division. There had been some jurisdictional issues, but as the murder was potentially tied to the kidnapping, it'd been decided to keep the two cases together. Thus, Bart found himself pulling into the parking lot at the state police facility in Gray just before noon.

Bart arrived at the scene in Phippsburg and positively identified the corpse as Jill Thomas, even if protocol demanded that Martin still be brought in for that purpose. The preliminary analysis was that she had not been killed there, but rather dumped in Cape Small Harbor, where a lobsterman walking his dog before going out on the boat found her body lapping the shore like a piece of driftwood. It seemed that whoever dumped her had not done so in deep enough water. When the Medical Examiner had finished at the scene, Jill Thomas would be brought to Augusta for an autopsy.

Before Bart had a chance to go by and check if he was there, Rick Strong had been rousted from his cottage in Small Point, less than a mile from where the body was found. The forensics people would soon be taking his place apart looking for any connection. In the meantime, Strong had been brought to the Gray facility as a person of interest, with Bart courteously invited to be part of the interrogation.

Bart had given it some thought on the way over, and once inside the building, suggested he be teamed with Detective Morgan for the good old—often highly effective—good-cop / bad-cop interrogation method. Morgan was a ten-year veteran who had proven to be a solid presence in the MCU, but just as important in this instance, she was a very good-looking woman. Bart figured that, given his predilections, Rick might be tempted toward the indiscreet by a pretty lady. Meanwhile, his specialty was bad-cop. His size, over six-foot-five and with a bear-like presence, coupled with a gruff attitude and seemingly permanent dour expression made for a fearsome combination. His receding hairline only added to his intimidating figure, giving him a slightly crazed look that he had practiced in the mirror, rolling his pupils to opposite sides of his eyes, sometimes even scaring himself.

Twenty minutes after arriving, Bart and Detective Morgan were in the interrogation room across a small table from Rick Strong. He'd not yet asked for counsel. The trick was to get him to talk before he did so. There was nothing in the room but the table and three chairs. The window behind Bart and Detective Morgan had been transformed into a mirror by the brightly lit room they were in, though in the dimly lit room on the other side, several state police stood watching.

Strong was disheveled, his normally clean-shaven head now showing gray stubble. His clothes were rumpled, suggesting that perhaps he'd slept in them, and his breath stank of sour booze.

"What am I here for?" Strong asked defiantly.

Bart said nothing.

"You need to tell me what's going on." His voice now had a slight quaver.

Bart said nothing.

"Are you going to talk?" Strong asked in a wheedling tone.

"Do you hate women?" Bart asked.

"What? What the hell are you talking about?"

"What does your wife think about you waving your dick around at anything with boobs?"

Rick snuck a nervous glance at Detective Morgan. "I don't know what you're talking about."

"I understand that there have been several sexual harassment charges against you."

"Is that what this is about? That bitch Burke is a lying…" He trailed off, again casting a flickering peek at Morgan.

"I understand that you have been having an affair with Jill Thomas."

"That's a lie. Who told you that?"

"She did."

Rick slapped the table with his hand. "You brought me here to accuse me of having an affair with Jill Thomas?"

"No. We brought you here because you killed Jill Thomas."

"That's insane… wait… is Jill dead?"

"You tell me."

"I don't fucking know!"

"Why did you strangle her, Rick? Did she find out that you kidnapped her son?"

"What the fuck?"

"That's it, isn't it? She found out that you have Eddie locked away in some hole in the ground and was going to turn you in." Bart glared at the man, rolling his pupils back in their sockets, his face growing red. "You think this whole pandemic is some sort of hoax perpetrated by Bill Gates to add to his fortune. That it's no worse than the flu, that doctors are inflating the numbers to get more federal money, and masks don't do a goddamn thing. That the liberals are all going around waving their arms in mass hysteria, led by some woman governor who's taking away your rights and shutting down your business so that you can't make a living."

"You got that right!"

"And then you had your brilliant idea. You'd kidnap a little boy and make the governor admit she is a lying whore and rescind her restrictions. But she hasn't done that yet, and now you're starting to worry. Will you actually kill the boy, Rick? At midnight on Halloween, will you execute little Eddie?"

"I didn't kidnap Eddie."

"So you say, but then Jill discovered that you did. She followed you or paid you a visit and found her son. She was going to turn you in, so you killed her. You wrapped your hands around her throat and strangled her. Admit it." Bart stood up, knocking his chair over backwards.

"Is Jill really dead?" Rick asked, his voice now trembling.

"Is she?" Bart asked.

"I don't know."

"Why'd you kill her?" Bart slammed his meaty hands down on the table.

"I didn't kill her!"

"Where is the boy?" Bart glared at him, his face inches from Rick's own, his eyes bulging, and then he turned and walked out of the room.

"We just want to make sure the boy is safe," Morgan said. "Maybe you can help us find Eddie?"

~ ~ ~ ~ ~

Langdon sat in his Jeep on Park Row, the short street that ran behind the Town Mall. Out his passenger window he was able to keep a close eye on Chabal, who now stood in a crowd, wearing her Salvador Dalí mask, waving a sign at cars passing on Maine Street that read 'BE PART OF THE HERD.' The number of anti-maskers had swollen, seemingly having doubled overnight, as had the noise they were generating. An equal number of counter protesters had moved closer to the triangle of the Mall occupied by this angry mob, no less vocal.

He felt bad about putting his wife in the middle of all of these fanatics, especially in pandemic times, but Langdon couldn't take the risk he'd be recognized after his confrontation just a few days earlier. Chabal blended in much better. She had a surgical mask on under the plastic art mask and stood to the side of the protesters, but still, he felt awfully guilty.

Bart had supplied them with video footage of the men who'd beaten up 4 by Four at the Brunswick Brew Pub, but it'd be tough to recognize them underneath the Salvador Dalí masks they were most likely wearing, even if they were here.

Langdon figured he could be productive and keep watch on his wife. The first item on his list was to call Richam. "We need to talk," Langdon said when his friend answered.

"It's none of your business," Richam said.

"I'm not in the habit of keeping secrets from my wife," Langdon said.

"What's that mean?"

"I haven't yet told her that I came across you in the apartment of a young and beautiful employee of yours. I haven't done that because she will feel obligated to tell Jewell."

"I just need a few days. Then I'll come clean."

Langdon's phone buzzed with a text from Bart. Strong was alone at his cottage in Small Point this morning. He's in custody now.

Richam's voice broke the silence. "Just two days. That's all I need."

"Tell me what's going on. To be honest, I don't believe you're actually cheating on Jewell. I know you too well. But I need to know."

There was a protracted silence. "Where are you?"

"Sitting in my Jeep on Park Row."

"Why—whatever. I'm at work. I'll be down in a minute."

Langdon called Bart while he waited, but there was no answer. The thought of 4 by Four lying in the hospital crossed his mind. He really needed to pay his friend a visit, but finding the man who had put 4 by Four there seemed of paramount importance right now.

The passenger door opened, and Richam slid into the Jeep.

"I'm glad to know you don't think I'm cheating on my wife," Richam said. "Pretty big of you."

"Jewell told Chabal that she was concerned that you were."

"I love that woman, but there is a bit of crazy in there. You know that."

Langdon laughed. "Yep. But the other day, you seemed pretty cozy with Raven Burke, and then I find you in her apartment?"

"You see me with a woman that is half my age, and you think I'm sleeping with her?"

Langdon held the gaze of Richam. "You don't mind me sharing with Chabal that I saw you at Raven's place?"

"It's a very complicated situation."

"I got time."

Richam sighed. "I think she's my daughter."

Langdon physically felt his jaw drop. "What?"

"I know, right?"

"How?"

"Long story."

Langdon nodded toward the Mall. "I'm keeping an eye on my wife who is hard at it out there 'protesting' the mask mandate and business restrictions imposed by our 'dictator' of a governor. In other words, I've got time."

Richam turned toward the raucous protesters. After a minute, he said, "I guess there's probably a reason for that."

"Tell me about Raven Burke," Langdon said.

"When I first met Jewell, I was sleeping with another woman." Richam kept his eyes turned toward the Mall. "After my third date with Jewell, I was head-over-heels smitten and broke it off with this other woman. Elsie Burke."

"Did you know she was pregnant?"

"No." Richam turned to look at Langdon. "I never saw her again after we broke up. We didn't exactly travel in the same circles. And then a few years later, Jewell and I came to the United States. To Maine."

"How'd you *not* know that this Elsie Burke was pregnant? That she gave birth and had a child?"

Richam shrugged. "She was white. I was Black. Our paths did not cross again after I broke it off."

"Are you sure that Raven is your daughter?"

"That's why I need a couple of days. DNA test comes back Friday."

"Hasn't she been here for some time? Why now?"

"Her mom died a few years back. Before she died, she told her all about me, and where to find me. Seems she'd kept tabs on me. Raven decided to come find me. Did it all legal with a work visa, but when she got here, she was too afraid to approach me. While she was trying to get up the nerve, that whole thing with Strong happened. Then her visa expired, and now she's afraid that ICE is going to deport her. That gave her the courage to confront me with who she is."

"You believe her?"

Richam nodded. "Yes. I believe that the DNA test will confirm that she is my daughter."

"And then you will tell Jewell?"

"I didn't see any reason to tell her if it was not true."

"She does have a crazy side," Langdon said.

"You've been on the wrong side of her temper," Richam said. "Would you be tempted to repeat that particular agony if it was not necessary?"

"Let me know if you need a place to hide out on Friday after you tell her you've fathered a child she never knew about."

Richam laughed. "You'll keep my secret until then?"

"You bet. Can you go visit 4 by Four this morning?"

"Why not you?"

"I have to keep an eye on my wife. I'd ask you to do that, but if that crowd realizes there's a Black man watching them, they might change out their Dalí masks for their pointy hats and string you up like a piñata."

Richam looked back out the window at the mob. "They might just do that," he said. "What has the world come to when this happens in Brunswick?" He opened the door. "I will go by and visit with 4 by Four. Hours start at 10:30?"

"You got it," Langdon said. "And Richam?"

Richam had stepped out and was about to shut the door but paused. "What?"

"Congratulations on having a girl. Maybe Friday we'll have a baby shower."

Chapter 19

Chabal took a deep breath and tried to retain her sanity. She'd never seen—heard, felt—such anger as it rippled through the crowd of anti-maskers. She'd never taken the time to ponder the why, only going so far as to think how childish it was to throw a hissy-fit because you were required to wear a face mask for the health of all. Whether or not it worked shouldn't matter, Chabal thought, as it just wasn't that difficult of a thing to do. Of course, she could better understand the restrictions on businesses affecting people's financial security, if not wholly agree with them. But the outraged enmity of the concentrated mass of people on the Town Mall was chilling.

Of course, she'd seen a person lose their shit before, and seen many a fight that involved the same unbridled animosity that seethed and surged around her. She had, after all, grown up with four brothers. Heck, at one point when not quite a teen, she'd climbed onto the dinner table and stepped across to plunge a fork into one of those brothers, an act that she couldn't explain then or now. But for there to be over one hundred protesters harnessing that pulsating hatred into one acrimonious belch was overwhelming.

Her mission was to see if she could find any of the men present at the beating of Jimmy 4 by Four, ideally the man who did the deed itself. All signs currently seemed to point at Rick Strong as the kidnapper and puppet master, but this appeared only to be possible if, a reasonable assumption, others were involved, given Strong's alibi. Also, they'd kept tabs on him as of late, and he hadn't led them to Eddie. Even if the man in the QAnon shirt was not part of the kidnapping, he still needed to pay for putting her friend in the hospital. But it sure as heck wasn't easy to fake this act. Chabal made sure not to stand too close to the street, for fear of being spotted by somebody she knew, or find herself on the side facing the mob who'd shown up to protest the protesters.

These counter protesters seemed a little more controlled, perhaps not as angry, but just as loud. This hatred between the two groups seemed symbolic of what was tearing the country apart, Chabal thought. Right here in Brunswick, Maine, population 24,000, was playing out a microcosm of the entire nation's unhappy angst, and here, as across the country, neither side seemed to have the slightest understanding of the other nor seemed willing to even try. It was that old saying that to understand somebody else, you needed to put yourself in their shoes. Chabal had literally done this, swallowed up by a crowd of people caught up in an outrage she couldn't comprehend, even if now, at least, she appreciated that it was real and not contrived.

Four hours into her protest, she decided it would be okay to get a bite to eat. Danny's hot dog stand was on the border of the Mall between the two warring factions, a no-man's land where anti-maskers and maskers both were accepted. She found herself in line behind a man wearing a Dalí mask, there always being a line at this Brunswick institution, even when the mall wasn't filled with opposing armies. Chabal kept her own mask on, feeling the eyes of the woman behind her boring into her back, Sally something-or-other, who she vaguely knew.

"This is the best part of this shithole town," the masked man in front said to Chabal.

"What's that?" she asked.

"This hot dog stand. The chili dog is off-the-charts good."

Chabal nodded. "You're not from here?"

"Fuck no."

"Where you from?"

The man waved his arm to encompass most everything. "Out there. How about you?"

"I came down from The County," Chabal said the first thing that popped into her mind.

"The County?"

"Aroostook County. Up by Canada. Everybody in Maine just calls it The County."

"You just come down for the protest?" The man stepped to the front of the line and ordered two chili dogs.

"Damn straight," Chabal said in her deepest voice. The guys in the stand knew her well. She ordered a dog with bacon and catsup.

"I'll get the little lady's as well," the man said. "You want chips or a drink?"

"I'll take a water, thanks. You don't have to do that."

"Always happy to buy lunch for a good patriot, especially one with such a nice body." The man's voice reflected what she knew was a leer behind the mask, almost as if buying her a hot dog gave him that right.

"Why, thank you," she said as sweetly as she could.

They stepped around behind the stand and surprisingly, there was an empty bench. Chabal realized it was because it was located in no-man's land.

"How about we sit and eat?" The man sat down, and she followed suit. "Name's Earl. Earl Franklin."

Chabal took his proffered hand, and he held on too long. "Annabelle," she said.

Earl pushed his mask up on top of his head and took a bite of his chili dog. Chabal had to stop herself from bolting. It was the man who'd put 4 by Four in the hospital. The person she was looking for, and now that she'd found him, what the hell was she going to do? She hadn't expected to be sitting on a bench sharing lunch with him.

"You gonna eat?" Earl asked, his second bite finishing his chili dog, all but the bit oozing down his beard.

Chabal pulled her phone out and looked at the screen. "My friend just texted me," she said. "Hold on." She hurriedly texted Langdon. Behind Danny's. On bench. With Q.

Earl grabbed her phone and looked at the screen. "What're you doing?"

"I told you. My sister is trying to find me. We came down from The County together."

"What's 'with Q' mean?"

"I just..." Chabal had no lie ready to her lips. She snatched her phone back. "Give me that."

Earl looked up and saw Langdon coming across no-man's land. "You bitch," he said and punched her in the cheek, his second chili dog flying to the ground as he turned to flee.

A police officer happened to step around the corner and witnessed the blow. He caught Earl by the arm as his partner stepped up next to him. "Hold on, fellow, what's going on here?"

Earl tried to jerk his arm free and the other officer took out his taser. "Hey, calm down."

"This man is wanted for assault. At the brew pub the other night," Chabal said, rubbing her jaw. It wasn't the first time she'd been punched, and it wasn't the hardest. "And he just hit me."

"Help!" Earl yelled. "I'm being attacked by the cabal of Satan-worshippers."

"Take it easy, buddy, we just need to ask you a couple of questions."

A crowd of unfriendly faces had circled around them. "They're agents of the pedophiles!" Earl yelled. "We've got them right here, don't let them get away!" He grabbed the officer holding him by the elbow.

"Settle down, everybody," the officer with the taser said.

Chabal saw Langdon trying to fight through the crowd.

"Bring the storm!" Earl screamed. "Bring the storm!"

The mob contracted as if gulping down the two officers in one massive bite. Chabal saw Earl slipping through the crowd. She fought to follow him but was knocked to the ground. She fought her way to her knees and saw one of the officers on the ground being pummeled by countless punches and kicks. She tried to get to him but was unable to gain any headway. There was a roaring in Chabal's ears as if the keening of some terrible beast, and then a gunshot rang out, everything paused, and the momentum was broken.

"Back away from them!" a young police officer yelled in a high-pitched voice.

The beast who was the mob eyed him, measuring the danger. Sirens split the air, and the air went out of that mob as it dissolved into individuals weighing the wisdom of continuing the assault, before dissolving into retreating individuals slipping away as suddenly as they had come together, leaving the two police officers on the ground. Langdon was on the ground next to Chabal asking her if she was alright as the sun broke through the clouds.

~ ~ ~ ~ ~

"Earl Franklin is notorious," Bart said. He was seated in Langdon's kitchen.

"Mr. Earl Franklin is going to get an ass-kicking," Chabal said. She had an ice pack on her swollen cheek and fire in her eyes.

"A rising star in the QAnon ranks," Bart said. "He's been gathering quite a following, preaching that the day of reckoning is coming soon, and the president's secret agents are going to bust the cabal of pedophiles wide open and return him to power for four more years."

"Where's he from?" Langdon asked.

"Originally, Alabama. For the past couple of years, he's been all over the place. After the George Floyd incident, his popularity soared," Bart said.

"Why's that?" Chabal asked.

"He became the anti-crusader against the Black Lives Matter movement. A poster child, of sorts. Minneapolis, Portland, Seattle, D.C.—somehow he's been in attendance at all of them."

"Sounds like a real charmer," Langdon said.

"He was sure sweet-talking me," Chabal said with a grin. "Said I had a nice body. Pretty much figured buying me a hot dog was going to get him laid."

"Laid *out*," Langdon growled.

"Not that you were much help when I needed you," Chabal said, needling him.

"What the hell was the plan, anyway?" Bart asked.

"Chabal was going to try and get a lead on the guy who did a number on 4 by Four," Langdon said. "Also, anything about the kidnapper. Could be the two things are even connected."

"Why'd you sit your ass in the Jeep and send your diminutive wife into the fray?" Bart asked.

"She blends in better than I do," Langdon said. "Plus, she has a nice body and attracts creeps."

"Helluva plan."

"It worked," Chabal said. "Because of my smoking-hot body."

"Yeah, worked real well," Bart said. "Got you punched in the face, and two of my brothers in blue almost torn apart. A few tweaks to that plan, and you could've burned down the entire town."

"Didn't exactly expect the protesters to go berserk like that," Langdon said. "Brunswick is a powder keg these days. You're right about burning the town down. It ain't exactly the way life is supposed to be, not currently, anyway."

"You get the whereabouts of Earl?" Chabal asked.

"He was staying out to the Greenlander Motel," Bart said. "Paid up through November first, but was gone by the time we showed. In the wind."

"Do you think if we can catch the kidnapper, all this is going to go away?" Chabal asked. "I mean, is that the focal point of the whole angst, or will that just cause an eruption?"

"You think Earl is in on the kidnapping?" Bart asked.

Langdon shrugged. "Hard to tell. What'd Strong have to say?"

Bart shook his head. "Nothing. Said that he was pissed off at his wife because she had the neighbor across the way following him, so he went out to their cottage at Small Point without telling her. Had a few drinks and went to bed. Funny thing is, the guy who lives across the street is Jonathan Starling. You know anything about that?"

Langdon grimaced. "Yep. I asked Star to keep an eye on him."

"Strong was quite proud of how he caught onto a bright turquoise antique truck following him and then lost him," Bart said. "Putz."

"You gonna charge Strong with the murder?"

Bart, again, shook his head. "Doubt it. Not unless forensics turns up something, or he has a change of heart and confesses. The fact that he was having an affair with a woman who turned up dead less than a mile from where he was sleeping, alone, is pretty damn suspicious, but just circumstantial. Probably hold him for another day at most, and then we'll have to turn him loose. He was waiting for his lawyer when I left Gray."

"What now?" Chabal asked.

"I'll see if we can make any connection between Strong and Franklin," Bart said. "In the meantime, we'll keep digging."

"I might go over and pay Mrs. Strong a visit," Langdon said. "See if she has a change of heart about her alibi for her husband. It's one thing to protect a man you love and think is innocent, quite another to lie for a creep who is having an affair on you and might be a killer. If she changes her story claiming she was with Rick the night of the kidnapping, I imagine that might be enough to bring charges and keep him locked up. Pose it as the safety of her and her kids sort of thing."

"Go ahead and take first crack," Bart said. "If you come up empty, I'll send a couple officers over to rattle her tree as well."

~ ~ ~ ~ ~

"You're the man who attacked Rick," Valerie Strong said when she opened the door.

"Sorry, ma'am. I lost my temper when I discovered he was sleeping with the mother of that kidnapped boy. Name is Langdon."

He paused, looking at the floor, searching for words. "The parents originally hired me to find their boy. Which I haven't..."

She nodded in acknowledgment of those fully-loaded statements. "How can I help you?"

"I was wondering if we might talk."

Valerie seemed to contemplate what that might entail. Her black hair fell in waves over her shoulders, and her face was carefully made up in a desperate attempt to retain her youth and a beauty that impending middle age seemed to be eroding. "Come in," she said, opening the door wide.

"Are your children home?" Langdon walked past her and directly into the kitchen.

"They're upstairs playing video games."

"Do they know their father... has been called in by the police?"

"I told them that he had to answer some questions to help them find who murdered that woman out to Small Point. Said it was just because we live nearby."

"But you know different?"

"What are you asking me, Mr. Langdon?"

"You know that he was having an affair with her." Langdon figured it was long past time for obfuscation. In three days, the abductor of Eddie Thomas was going to execute the boy, and earlier this morning, that boy's mother had been found dead.

"Yes."

"Which makes him the most likely person to have killed her."

"Do you think that my husband is a praying mantis, Mr. Langdon?"

"What?"

"Do you believe that he would fuck this woman and then kill her?"

What Langdon thought was that this usage of the f-word was not normal for Valerie Strong. "I believe that it is the *female* who bites the head off of the male and eats him for the protein," is what he said. "Statistics do show that there isn't much separation between sex and murder."

"Sit down, Mr. Langdon." Valerie pulled out a chair for him, moved around the table, and perched herself on a stool at the island. "Do you believe that Rick killed that woman? Is he under arrest?"

Langdon realized that she wasn't certain whether Rick had been taken in for questioning or had been arrested. "How long have you known that Rick has been sleeping with Jill Thomas?"

"How long has he? You seem to be the one informed here."

"According to her, they've been together about eight months now."

Valerie grunted in what may have been anguish. "Why?"

"Your husband is not a very nice man, Mrs. Strong. I got involved because I'm investigating him for a separate sexual harassment claim."

"Has he been arrested?"

"My understanding is that he has been taken into custody as a person of interest," Langdon said. "Unless they have some concrete information, they will have to let him go within forty-eight hours."

"Why are you here, Mr. Langdon, exactly?"

"The night that Eddie Thomas went missing," Langdon said, "you told the police that you, Rick, and the boys were at your cottage in Small Point all night. Is that true?"

"I think so."

"What do you mean?"

"We fought, okay? He slept in the guest bedroom." Valerie shrugged. "He was there when I got up around 9:00. I can't imagine that he slipped out, kidnapped a boy, and then came home and put his pajamas on."

"Can you believe that your husband would do something like this?"

"Why?"

Langdon looked around the kitchen. It was a modest home for a successful business owner, the appliances dated, the table worn, the walls in need of painting. "He seems quite angry with the governor and the governmental restrictions due to the pandemic."

"Rick might have his failings, Mr. Langdon, but he'd never hurt a child."

"How about a woman?"

Valerie sniffled and looked away.

"Has Rick ever hit you, Mrs. Strong?"

"No," Valerie said with such little conviction that, to Langdon, it sounded an awful lot like yes.

"Where was your husband last night?"

"The police asked me that. Like, a hundred times."

"I am trying to help you."

"No, you're not trying to help me," Valerie said, anger surging forth in her voice. "You are trying to get me to turn against my husband."

"Unless the police find proof that your husband is the killer, Mrs. Strong, you can expect that they will be bringing you in for questioning. Do you have somebody who your boys can stay with?"

"What?" Her eyes went from angry to fearful. "Why would they bring *me* in?"

"You are one corner of a sex triangle," Langdon said in a calm voice, even if his words were inflammatory. "Nine times out of ten, when one of the corners of that triangle is killed, it is one of the other corners who is the murderer."

"Corners?" Tears were now streaming down Valerie's face.

"Did you kill Jill Thomas?"

"No!" Her voice rose to a shriek. "I think you should leave now."

"If you didn't kill her, then most likely, Rick did. Do you want him coming home to you and the boys, or can you give me something that will keep him in jail?"

"Rick wouldn't kill a woman."

"Not even the governor?"

Valerie stood up. "Please leave, Mr. Langdon."

Langdon rose to his feet. "I just want to save the life of a four-year-old boy, Mrs. Strong. Some monster is holding Eddie Thomas hostage and has threatened to execute him in three days' time. I just want to find out one thing. Where is the boy?"

Chapter 20

Chabal sat in the parking lot of the Yoga Bear Studio waiting for Jewell to arrive. With all that was going on, she'd forgotten to ask Langdon about seeing Richam getting into his Jeep earlier. Perhaps it was the getting punched in the face by some whacko who believed there was a pedophilic sex trafficking ring being run by Congress, or maybe it was the near riot that followed. Whatever the case, the meeting of her husband and Richam had slipped her mind.

She texted Langdon. What did you and Richam talk about this morning?

While waiting for his reply, Chabal shook her head in bewilderment at all that was going on. Rumor had it the governor was considering calling out the National Guard to Brunswick to keep the peace. The attack on two police officers had rocked this sleepy town to its very core. The incredibly controversial election just around the corner and the ongoing pandemic had created a deep sense of angst across the entire country. But add in a kidnapping, a death threat if demands were not met, and now the murder of the boy's mother? Chabal shook her head in consternation. What was this world coming to?

Her ruminations were interrupted by a reply from Langdon. You at the yoga place?

Chabal thought, *That wasn't really a reply to my question, now was it?* Yes. Richam?

It's complicated.

It always is.

Can we talk about it later?

Jewell pulled into the parking lot. Okay. But you better be ready to dish.

Chabal got out of her car as her phone buzzed. K.

"Hey, girl," Jewell said. Her face was lined and tired-looking. "Hope you haven't been waiting long."

"Nope. Just got here. You doing okay?"

"Yeah, got a lot on my mind. A yoga session should be good for me. Bring me some inner peace, or some shit like that, right?"

"Don't know about that. Almost killed us last time, if you remember rightly."

"Maybe a kick in the ass is what I need."

Chabal wondered what Langdon was holding back on her. "Let's get our yoga on, then," she said.

They paid their fifteen bucks day-use to the gruff Dianne, who again railed against Chabal for not having her driver's license to fill out her paperwork correctly. *Obviously, a lot of felons tried to hide out in yoga studios*, Chabal thought. After paying to be verbally abused, the young whippersnapper, Karen, twisted them into pretzel positions and demanded they stay that way until they cried for mercy.

"You okay?" Karen asked the supine Chabal after most of the class had filtered away.

Chabal was lying in the savasana pose that the class had ended in. "Why is this called savasana?" she asked without opening her eyes.

"It means 'corpse pose'."

"Gotcha," Chabal said. "Do you drink alcoholic beverages, Miss Karen?"

"I prefer a vegetable smoothie," Karen said. "But I will have the occasional tequila shot."

Chabal opened her eyes. *Wow*, she thought. "Can I buy you a tequila shot at Goldilocks?"

~ ~

Jewell was down with the plan. They met and parked in the adjacent lot whose signage said quite distinctly that parking was for the bank or UPS Store only, but both were closed, so they chanced it. Karen was all of twenty-five years old but looked younger and thus had her license carefully scrutinized. She was quite chatty, and Chabal and Jewell knew all about her by the time they tipped back the second tequila shot.

They were sitting at a high-top across from the bar. There were only seven other people in the cavernous space. Jewell had ordered some mozzarella sticks, wisely reasoning that if they were going to be drinking tequila, they should not be doing so on empty stomachs. And it was Jewell who ordered the second shot, seemingly embracing the idea.

"I ran into our old friend, Ann Morin, the other day," Chabal said to Karen. "She said to tell you hi."

"Really? What's she up to? I mean, like, where's she been?"

Chabal leaned closer, conspiratorially, and whispered, "I think she's having an affair."

Karen giggled. "I thought so. Right? Didn't I tell you I saw her get in a car with some dude and kiss him?"

"Orange car?" Chabal asked.

"Might've been," Karen said. "I mostly remember how shiny the car was and how naughty the kiss was."

"Can't blame her, now, can you?" Chabal said. "Have you seen her husband?"

Karen puffed out her cheeks, this being an effort on her thin face. "Rudolph?" She burst out giggling, and Chabal and Jewell followed suit.

Jewell waved to the waitress and held up three fingers. "Did you know that she was a mail-order bride?"

"Yeah," Karen said. "She mentioned that."

Jewell nodded. "Russian, some small village in the middle of Yakutsk or something."

"I guess that explains why she married Rudolph," Karen said. "It was worth it to come to America. Especially after her last boyfriend."

"What about her last boyfriend?" Chabal asked. "Dish, girl."

Karen leaned forward. "He was a gangster. Some kind of hit man from Odessa in the Ukraine."

"No way," Chabal said.

Karen nodded sagely. "No lie. Then something bad happened, and she had to escape him. She never told me what that bad thing was, but I'm thinking it was pretty terrible."

"So that's why she became a mail-order bride," Chabal said. "To get away from her ex and start a new life in America."

"What is it about coming to America that makes certain people want to cheat on their spouses?" Jewell asked. "Is it true that this place is Satan's playground?"

"Stop joking around," Chabal said. She tapped the table, drawing Karen's eyes to her. "Jewell has a strange sense of humor, sometimes."

"What makes a man think he can buy a woman?" Karen asked, her eyes hot. "I'm glad that Ann left him, to get away. Sometimes us girls have to use what we have to get what we want, am I right?"

Chabal had gathered that Karen had grown up a privileged white girl in Brunswick, gone away to college, and had married a lawyer. Her only occupation seemed to be teaching five yoga classes a week. She was not sure what trials and tribulations the young woman had faced but didn't want to pass judgment. Every woman had a story of inappropriate behavior by a man of one sort or another. Such behavior knew no economic or social limitations but was an equal opportunity offender.

"Damn straight," Chabal said. She wondered again what Langdon hadn't told her about Richam and why.

The tequila arrived, and Jewell held up her shot glass. "May their pricks wither and fall off," she said.

Karen slammed hers back without hesitation and Chabal followed suit, albeit more slowly, and only drank half the burning liquid. "I hope Ann found somebody to treat her right," she said.

"Like a princess," Jewell said.

Karen looked left and right. "She did. She said they're in love, and they're going to run away together and start a new life."

"I didn't think you'd seen her in months?" Chabal asked.

Karen giggled. "I saw her two weeks ago. She told me not to tell anybody. But now that you just saw her, I guess it's okay."

"So? Who is the mystery man she won't tell me about?" Chabal said.

"Don't know." Karen shook her head. "All she'd say is that he's wonderful and that they're going to be together soon, for all time, not just a stolen hour or two, here and there."

"And they went away somewhere?" Jewell asked.

"I don't know if they've gone yet or not. She said they couldn't leave right away, but then they'd be going to the West Coast. I've always wanted to go to California. Hollywood. Malibu. Wait, didn't you say you just saw her?" Karen turned to look at Chabal. Karen's eyes were slightly glazed, whether from the exotic thoughts or the tequila, it was difficult to say. "I should get going," she said, wariness creeping into the glaze. "My husband will be wondering where I am."

"Are you okay to drive?" Chabal asked.

"Absolutely. I've got a wooden leg." Karen laughed loudly at her own joke.

"Let me get you a cab," Chabal said, pulling out her phone. Brunswick was still old-fashioned in that way. A few of the checkered-yellow vehicles were usually parked just across the way at the 7-Eleven.

Karen shook her head. "I'm fine," she said and walked out the door.

"Looks like her tequila shots are on us," Jewell said. "Millennials." The two women looked at each other and laughed.

~ ~ ~ ~ ~

It was seven o'clock before Langdon got a chance to visit with Martin Thomas. The man's eyes were red, and his face showed the strain of the day. It was a difficult thing to identify your wife in a morgue, even if you had been separated for some time. Mercifully, she hadn't been in the water for long when the man walking his dog found her.

Langdon thought it prudent to not mention that he'd just been in the house earlier that day. He also thought it wise not to bring up the fact that, if the police couldn't get anything on Rick Strong to stick, they'd be over, probably by tomorrow, to search for any evidence that Martin Thomas may have been involved in the death of his wife.

"Why?" Martin asked. They sat in the kitchen, across a table from each other.

"Why what?"

"Why me? My parents die of Covid, my son is kidnapped and threatened with death, and now my wife has been murdered."

Langdon shook his head. "It can be a cruel world. Did you speak with Jill recently?"

"We had three briefings with the police yesterday. Three times for them to tell us they had nothing. Knew nothing. No leads. Nothing."

"Did she let on anything to you?"

"Like what?"

Langdon sighed. "I don't know. Any suspicions on who took your son?"

"You think the person who took Eddie is the one who killed Jill?"

"Be quite a coincidence if it wasn't." Langdon did *not* believe in coincidences.

"Jill was the love of my life," Martin said.

"What'd you tell the police? Any bit helps."

"They think the same as you. That the kidnapper is also the killer."

"Serves to reason," Langdon said.

"It's that frickin' Rick Strong, isn't it?" Martin stood up and grabbed a handle of gin and a tumbler. He filled a bowl with ice and set it on the table, then poured the glass half full, added two ice cubes, and just a splash of tonic. "How about you?"

Langdon eyed the drink. "Got any brown liquor?"

Martin pulled a bottle of Jim Beam from a cupboard that Langdon knew was there from his search earlier that day. "Help yourself." He sat back down and took a good haul from the drink.

Langdon poured himself a double and added a couple of cubes from the bowl. "Why do you think it's Rick Strong?" he asked, sitting down.

"Well, for starters, he doesn't believe that Covid is real."

"How do you know that?"

"Before Jill moved out, before I knew they were... sleeping together, she used to quote him all the time. 'Rick says that it's no more than the flu, Rick says it's a conspiracy by Bill Gates, Rick says frickin' this and frickin' that.'"

"Rick Strong is definitely a prime suspect, but so are you," Langdon said.

"Me?"

"In cases like this, it is often the estranged spouse who is the murderer."

"I loved her. Even after she left me for that Neanderthal, I still loved her." Martin finished his gin and tonic and rose to make another. "I would never kill her."

"Was Jill acting strangely in any way yesterday?" Langdon asked.

"Plus," Martin said as if he hadn't heard the question, "the restrictions imposed on his business have got to be killing the man. Isn't it obvious that Strong is the one who kidnapped my son and killed my wife?"

"Without proof, there is nothing anybody can do."

"What if I were to pay you to take care of the situation?"

Langdon thought he knew where this was going but chose to

ignore it. "You *are* paying me to rectify the situation, Martin. I will find whoever is behind this."

"How much would it cost to make Rick frickin' Strong disappear?"

"It has been a very long day for you. I will chalk this up to lack of sleep, grief, worry, and too many movies," Langdon said. "But do not bring it up ever again."

Martin put his head down on the table. "I'm sorry. I don't mean it. I'm just venting."

Langdon had meant to broach the subject of Martin having an affair with Ann Morin but decided the time was not right. And besides, what evidence did he have? That an orange car had been spotted in connection with Ann on two separate occasions? No, best to file that one away for now. "Help me by giving me something to use. Some way I can get proof," Langdon said.

"I followed her to his cottage out to Small Point once, you know," Martin said. "Early on, I used to watch her, you know, like some sick addiction to pain. Usually, he came to her place at Brunswick Landing, but this one time, I followed her out to Small Point. She parked a couple of blocks away and snuck down the street and into his place. I sat down the road staring at his frickin' Ford Mustang and imagined what they were doing in there. That's where she was found, wasn't it? Out that way somewhere?"

Langdon's phone buzzed. Text from Chabal. Can you pick me and Jewell up at Goldilocks?

Sure. 20 min.

"I believe so," Langdon said. "In the harbor, there."

"Was Rick at his cottage?" Martin asked.

"I don't know," Langdon lied. "I got to go, Martin. You going to be okay?"

Martin held up his empty tumbler. "As long as the refills are free," he said, already a bit of a slur to his words.

Chapter 21

Thursday, October 29th

The next morning, Langdon and Chabal were in the living room, recliners back, watching the morning news and drinking coffee. Dog lay between them. Between the impending election, the virus, and the kidnapping, the news was actually quite eventful. And then it went up a notch.

"We have breaking news on the kidnapping of Eddie Thomas," the news anchor said, her voice unusually strained. They looked at each other, then back at the television. "Another video has been sent that we will play in just a moment. I warn that the material is of a disturbing nature, and you might not want to watch or have young children watch. We at News Station WMJX are playing this at the request of the state police. We do not know why this request has been made but have complied for the safety of Eddie Thomas."

The camera cut to a video of a dimly lit room. As before, a man sat on a wooden chair underneath a dangling light bulb in an otherwise dark space. He wore the signature Dalí mask and a red sweatshirt hoodie pulled over his head, zipped up to just below his neck. He had on khakis, and black gloves on his hands, making the only visible part of him his hazel eyes. Eddie Thomas sat next to him, a small smile playing at the corners of his mouth.

The man began speaking in the mechanically-altered voice. "It is not me who is the clown, but this monstrously cynical and so unconsciously naive society, which plays the game of seriousness in order to better hide its madness. There is only one difference between a madman and me. The madman thinks he is sane. I know I am mad. In sixty-three hours, the boy sitting next to me will cease to exist. There is no need for the muckamuck who plays at being governor to wait until that last fateful moment. If she were to make a public statement today saying that mandatory masking and all business restrictions due to the false virus will be suspended permanently, why then, Eddie Thomas will walk free. Within the hour of that statement. Of course, if the governor proves herself to be the two-faced politician that she is and rescinds this order, I will abduct and execute a child every day until she realizes the error of her ways. Surrealism is destructive, but it destroys only what it considers to be shackles limiting our vision. A true artist is not one who is inspired but one who inspires others."

The screen went black and then flashed back to the newscaster.

"Holy cow," Chabal said.

"Did he look like the guy who punched you?" Langdon asked.

"Guy had hazel eyes, alright," Chabal said. "Same size." She shrugged. "Could be."

"Rick Strong is in jail."

"Who's to say when the video was recorded?"

"The guy said sixty-three hours," Langdon said. "Suppose he could've arranged for it to be dropped off this morning and played at 9:00."

"Or somebody did this to exonerate Strong because he is in jail."

"I'm thinking your friend from the Mall."

"Kind of blows holes in the Martin Thomas theory," Chabal said. "If this was a plot to kill his estranged wife and send her lover to jail, he most likely wouldn't have sent this video."

"It certainly complicates things," Langdon said.

"As if my head didn't hurt enough already."

"You were pretty lit up last night."

"Ugh. You're telling me." Chabal rested the side of her coffee cup against her forehead.

"Everything okay?"

"Besides getting beaten up by some dink who thinks the president is the answer to Satan-worshipping pedophiles who have infiltrated our political and social system disguised as liberal snowflakes?"

"I guess that deserves throwing a few back." Langdon chuckled. "You said you were doing tequila shots?"

"Karen's idea."

"Karen?"

"The instructor from Yoga Bear."

"You mentioned something about that, but I couldn't make heads nor tails of what you were talking about."

Chabal groaned. "She spoke recently with Ann Morin, who said she was going to run off to the West Coast with her new man."

"She still around?" Langdon asked.

"Think so, but no idea where."

"The West Coast is a pretty broad area."

"All she knew. I might've slipped up, too many tequila shots, and she skedaddled before I could get any more."

"Martin grew up in Oregon. In fact, just inherited a house there," Langdon said.

"That's on the West Coast."

"Yes. Yes it is."

Chabal took a sip of coffee and sighed. "The plot thickens. Get anything else from Martin last night?"

"One interesting tidbit. Said he followed Jill out to Rick Strong's cottage once, sort of torturing himself with their being together. Said Jill parked her car a couple blocks away and walked to Rick's place, presumably so that no nosy neighbors would report back to the wife."

"That might explain why her car wasn't at his cottage. I'm betting he's had a chance to get rid of it by now."

"Not if he was in lock-up all night," Langdon said. "I called Bart on my way to pick you up and told him. He called back after you passed out and said they found it—right where Martin said it would be."

"Convenient," Chabal said.

"Why's that?"

"Don't you think that if Rick Strong murdered Jill Thomas that he'd get rid of the car? Instead, you get a lead on the car from her husband who she left because she was cheating on him with the man who is currently in jail for killing her?"

"Thought had crossed my mind," Langdon said. "But I'm betting dollars to donuts that this murder is related to the kidnapping, and what motive would Martin Thomas have to abduct his own son?"

Before Chabal could answer, Langdon's phone rang. "Hey, Bart," he said.

"You see the latest video?"

"Yep. Kinda wondering why the news is playing them. Seems like you might want to downplay the whole thing. Take away the kidnapper's power."

"The note that came with the video said to play it at 9:00 this morning or expect a finger at 10:00."

"He's one sick son of a bitch," Langdon said. "Can I get a copy of the video?"

"Sure thing."

"Do you know when the video was made?"

"Tech guys are tearing it apart, but so far, nothing you can't see with the naked eye."

"Strong could've made it before you arrested him. How'd that go down, anyway?"

"We're turning him loose."

"Who? Strong?"

"No, the fucking Stay-Puft Marshmallow Man."

"He was sleeping… was *screwing* Jill, she's found dead close to his cottage, and her car is parked around the corner, and you're letting him go?"

"Listen, we gotta charge him with a crime or cut him loose, but right now, we don't have enough to make anything stick. Just got off the phone with Jackson Brooks at MCU. They're flushing him out the door as we speak."

Chapter 22

"They're letting Strong go?" Chabal asked.

Langdon nodded. "Not enough to hold him."

"We still figure he had help?"

"Maybe we're looking at this in the wrong way. Maybe we should be trying to figure out where Eddie is being held instead of who has him."

"Easier to figure out where he is if you start with who has him."

"The police have been through Strong's house and his cottage with a fine-tooth comb and come up with zilch."

"I take it when the police showed up at Martin's house while you were tossing the place that they searched it," Chabal said. "Maybe it's not either one of them?"

"Earl Franklin," Langdon said.

"Guy breezes into town with his QAnon conspiracy theories and anti-masking rhetoric, and Eddie Thomas gets abducted and is being held hostage in an attempt to get the governor to ease restrictions. What a feather in his cap it would be if he can get the governor to bow to his demands."

"That's exactly why it's not gonna happen. That old mantra that the U.S. doesn't negotiate ransoms. As soon as they do, every Tom, Dick, and Harry will be demanding payment for something or other."

Chabal sat up excitedly. "And he probably knows that."

"Why bother, then?"

"The eyes of the world are on Brunswick, Maine, right now. He's already won. What a theatrical masterpiece, organized by him."

Langdon slowly nodded. "Further proof that those supposedly at war against the insidious cabal of pedophiles don't care about the welfare of children."

"You think he might just let Eddie go? He'll have made his point."

"Not if Eddie's seen his face—and he's had the kid for a few days now. What are the odds? He can't chance it. As of now, he's walking away scot-free."

They sat quietly on that thought and sipped their coffee. "You're supposed to bring me up to speed on what is going on with Richam," Chabal said after a bit. "Something about 'complicated.'"

"You could say that." Langdon smiled wryly. "He's not having an affair on Jewell. Raven Burke just might be his daughter."

"His daughter? You sure this isn't a soap opera we're living in?" Chabal took another sip of coffee and snickered. "You know, like *Days of Our Lives*, or some shit like that?"

"If it was a soap opera, he'd have been sleeping with her when he discovered she was his daughter," Langdon said.

"Gross." Chabal made a face. "But true."

"He was having sex with Raven's mother when he first started dating Jewell back in the D.R.," Langdon said. "Once he realized that he was serious about Jewell, he broke it off with the other woman, but it seems the seed may've been planted."

Chabal snickered again. "And she came looking for her daddy?"

"Her mom came clean before she died, and Raven decided to come see for herself. She was hesitant to approach Richam about it, and then the whole sexual harassment thing with Strong happened. She lost her job, work visa out the window, and she was afraid that ICE was going to deport her. Facing all that, she got up the gumption to approach Richam."

"Is he the father for sure?"

"They get the paternity test back tomorrow, but he seems to think that, yeah, she's his."

"And he hasn't told Jewell what's going on?"

"He thought it best not to risk her wrath until he was sure."

Chabal made a face. "Fair enough. I suppose you want me to keep my mouth shut until tomorrow, then?"

"If possible."

Langdon's phone buzzed. Rudolph Morin calling. "Langdon," he answered.

"You find who took my wife?"

"Not yet, Mr. Morin. We do have reason to believe that she was in contact with a man, but we do not yet have his name."

"Contact with a man?"

"You said your wife was going to Yoga Bear for the past year or more?"

"Three times a week. Sometimes more. Costing me a goddamn arm and a leg, it was."

Langdon smiled, thinking about Rudolph paying his wife to go sleep with somebody else. "According to Yoga Bear, she hasn't been there in the past six months."

"You said that. I say bullshit. Was why I had to eat a frozen dinner three times a week. Think I'd know if she was here or not."

"It sounds like she might've been seeing a man instead."

"A man?"

"I think your wife is having an affair on you, Mr. Morin."

"With who?"

"That I don't know. Not yet. Do you want me to continue my investigation?"

"I didn't think they were hers," Rudolph said.

"What's that?"

"I got home a few months back and there was a pack of Chiclets on the table. I asked her about them and she said that she'd bought them, even though I never, ever saw her chew gum. I thought I'd do something nice for her, you know, surprise her, but no stores even carry Chiclets anymore. Somebody told me you had to order them from Amazon. Ha. Order goddamn gum from Amazon."

"Do you want me to continue searching for your wife, Mr. Morin?"

"Paid you, didn't I?" The phone went dead.

"How'd that go?" Chabal asked as Langdon set his phone down on the armrest of the sofa.

"Seemed to want to brag that he tried to buy his wife Chiclets as a surprise."

"And that didn't make her stay with him? What a shocker."

"Never got them. He couldn't find them at any local stores and couldn't see buying gum from Amazon."

"You tell him about Prime?"

"Slipped my mind." Langdon's phone buzzed. Email. From Bart. He got up and went over to the computer on the desk in the corner of the living room. "Bart sent us the video from this morning."

Langdon brought up the email and clicked on the attachment, bringing up the video. He hit play, and Salvador Dalí again entered their morning. After it was done playing, Langdon repeated the opening line. "*It is not me who is the clown, but this monstrously cynical and so unconsciously naive society, which plays the game of seriousness in order better to hide its madness.*" He swiveled in his chair to look at Chabal who still sat on the sofa. "An odd choice of words to use, don't you think, to say that the government is duping people with Covid."

"Odd choice indeed," Chabal said, looking at her phone. "Probably because they're not his words, but the words of the real Salvador Dalí."

"What do you mean?"

"That's a famous quote from the surrealist master himself," she said. "What's the next line?"

Langdon played the video, pausing it after the next line. "*The madman thinks he is sane. I know I am mad.* What the hell does that even mean?"

"Another quote," Chabal said, looking at her phone. "But you got me on what it means. Didn't Socrates say that he was smarter than just about everybody because he knew he was ignorant, and they didn't? Seems to be about the same thing."

Langdon nodded. "He knows he is mad so that makes him saner than most." He hit play, letting the next sentence play aloud. *In sixty-three hours, the boy sitting next to me will cease to exist. There is no need for the muckamuck who plays at being governor to wait until that last fateful moment.* "That's not a Dalí quote, is it?"

"No," Chabal said, scrolling through her phone. "This is the real message, and the other part is garnish."

"Sounds about right," Langdon said. "The muckamuck who plays at being governor?" He typed the word into the computer. "Muckamuck means food. Or plenty of food." He read through Wiktionary. "'A muckamuck is somebody of high importance.' It originated from Chinook Jargon, whatever that is."

He again hit play, listening to the next section. *If she were to make a public statement today saying that mandatory masking and all business restrictions due to the false virus will be suspended permanently, why then, Eddie Thomas will walk free. Within the hour of that statement. Of course, if the governor proves herself to be the two-faced politician that she is and rescinds this order, I will abduct and execute a child every day until she realizes the error of her ways.*

"He's certainly a callous asshole," Chabal said.

"Two-faced politician. Is that a reference to the secret cabal of political pedophiles?"

"Sounds like it. Even though he's the one threatening to execute children, he's trying to place the blame on the governor."

"I don't think the QAnon people care much about rationality," Langdon said. He again hit play. *Surrealism is destructive, but it destroys only what it considers to be shackles limiting our vision. A true artist is not one who is inspired but one who inspires others.*

"Another Dalí quote," Chabal said.

"That might be the entire crux of the thing, right there," Langdon said. "He is not inspired, but rather, trying to inspire others."

"To do what?"

"Tear down the government."

~ ~ ~ ~ ~

An hour later, Langdon found himself at the diner. When he'd asked Chabal if she wanted to go out for breakfast, she groaned and said something about getting herself together first, and that was likely to take some time. When Langdon sat down next to Danny T. at the counter, the man also groaned.

"No," Danny T. said.

"Good morning to you, too. No, what?"

"No to whatever you want me to do."

"Thought I'd buy you breakfast."

"I already ate."

"You don't want more?"

Danny T. flicked his tongue nervously over his lips. "I might have another bite or two."

Another bite or two turned out to be the Lumberjack Special of pancakes, French toast, eggs, bacon, sausage and English muffins. "This the guy who beat 4 by Four down the other night?" Langdon asked, sliding his phone with the picture of Earl Franklin on the screen over toward Danny T. but not so close that he might mistakenly eat it.

"That's him, sure enough," Danny T. said nervously.

Langdon took the phone back. "I'm sending you this picture and one of Rick Strong. Thought maybe you could ask around about them."

"Ask around?"

"First of all, I'd love to find the man in photo number one. His name is Earl Franklin. He's one of those traveling QAnon fanatics spreading lies and hatred across our country."

"They're the guys who think the president is some mysterious source named Q and is gonna bust a child sex ring wide open, ain't they?"

"You got it."

"Selling kids for sex ain't right."

Langdon stared at his uneducated friend with a troubled look. "It's not true, Danny T. You know that, right? It's a conspiracy theory that has been totally debunked."

"Like the man on the grassy knoll. You know, the Russian who really shot Kennedy?"

"Even more far-fetched than that," Langdon said.

"Something about Hillary Clinton I never much liked."

Luckily, the food arrived, making it hard for Danny T. to continue talking.

"You find Earl Franklin for me, and I'll pick up your diner tab for a month," Langdon said. "And 4 by Four will owe you one."

Danny T. choked on his food. "A month?" he finally managed to ask.

Langdon chuckled. "Yep. And ask around and see if anybody has ever seen him with Rick Strong."

"This about the kid who got taken?"

"It might be."

"You think it was Hillary Clinton?"

"*What?*"

Danny T. swallowed what may have been an entire pancake. "You know, who took that boy."

Chapter 23

"What is he doing here?" Rick asked. He'd been dropped off at the cottage by the police only to find his wife and Earl Franklin there. "Where are the boys?"

"The police seem to be looking for me about that little mix up at your bar the other night," Earl said.

"The boys are at home. They can take care of themselves," Valerie said. "Earl showed up needing a place to stay, so I brought him out here."

"You're a fucking moron," Rick said. "The police think I killed that woman, and you think it's a good idea for *him* to hide out *here*?"

"Don't talk to my sister like that," Earl said, coming to his feet.

"You need a place to hide out, and you're going to get in my goddamn face?" Rick's face turned a deep red.

"Is it true? Were you screwing that woman?" Valerie asked, also standing up. The three of them were in the small kitchen of the cottage.

"None of your goddamn business," Rick said. "Sit your ass down."

"None of my business? None of my business? I'm your wife, aren't I?"

"Has your pecker been wandering as of late, Rick?" Earl stepped closer so that his nose was just inches away from Rick's. "I told you that you best treat my sister like a queen, or I'd bitch slap some sense into you."

"Did you kill her?" Valerie asked.

"No, I didn't fucking kill her," Rick said. "Did *you* kill her?"

"What? No, I didn't kill her. Why would I..."

"You were dipping in the honey jar, weren't you, Rick?" Earl said. "You told me that that boy's mother worked for you. But it was a little bit more than that, wasn't it?"

"Let's all sit down and take a deep breath," Rick said. "I'd say I'm not the only one the police are looking for."

"What's that supposed to mean?" Valerie asked.

"They spent a good hour asking me questions about you, Val," Rick said. "Once they realize I didn't kill Jill Thomas, well then, you're the next one on their list. Yes, I was sleeping with her. The police know that. Now you know that, but I think you already knew, didn't you?"

"You know I'd never hurt another person," Valerie said. "Not like that. Not just because she was screwing my husband. God, she can have you, for all I care."

"The police don't know that. They're going to come after you hard, and you better be ready," Rick said. "Now, can we please sit down?"

Earl grudgingly stepped backward two steps and slid into a chair. Rick followed him over and sat across from him. Valerie stood seething in the middle of the kitchen, finally exhaled, and joined them.

"The police are after you for beating up that guy down to the brew pub?" Rick asked. "How'd they get onto you?"

"Turned over your cameras, didn't ya?" Earl took a sip of the Pabst Blue Ribbon he'd been drinking when Rick arrived. "Must've matched my face with that face recognition software shit they got nowadays."

"How do you know they know you?"

Earl squirmed a bit in his chair. "I might've told 'em."

"You told the police who you are?" Rick asked, his voice struggling with control.

"Not exactly," Earl said. "I told a little lady, and I figured she told them."

"Why is it you figure she told the police?"

"Cause I punched her in the face, I reckon."

"Why'd you punch her, Earl?" Rick asked, his voice rising slightly.

"Well, I didn't know it at the time, but turns out she's the wife of that fellow you had trouble with. Chabal Langdon. I was out protesting and grabbed a chili dog from that stand there, and we started talking. Then I seen on her phone how she'd texted something about Q, and next thing I know, that fellow is coming across the grass toward me."

"And that's when you punched her?"

"Yeah, I gave that bitch a good one and lit on out of there, only this cop, he come around the corner of the stand and grabbed my arm, but I managed to get away."

Rick turned his head to look at his wife. "Val, did you get that neighbor of ours from across the street to follow me?"

"Follow you? No. Who're you talking about?"

"That old geezer with the green truck."

"Jonathan? No, I haven't spoken with him in months."

"He was sure enough following me Tuesday night. You sure you didn't put him up to it?"

"I swear on my mother's life I didn't." Valerie crossed herself.

"I suppose I'll have to ask him myself why he was following me," Rick said. "Were you home with the boys all Tuesday night? You didn't go out anywhere?"

"Why?"

"Can the boys verify that you were home all night?"

"Yes."

"Not after they fell asleep, they can't," Earl said.

"The police come by and search the house yesterday?" Rick asked.

"Yes."

"They're probably going to come by again and ask you some questions. Maybe search the place a little more intensely. Just answer their questions. Let them look around. You got nothing to hide."

"Where're you going to be?"

"I got some things to take care of. Starting with that Langdon and his wife, what'd you say her name was?"

"Chabal," Earl said.

"Earl, he's going to come along and help me out. You go home now. I don't want the police showing up and having the boys home alone answering their questions. Get now."

"You coming home later?"

"I said get."

Valerie started to retort, thought better of it, got up and left.

"Whatcha thinking?" Earl asked.

"I figure you might stay at that other place. Police don't know about it. You can lay low there until things blow over. First, you got to help me fix something."

"You fix that guy Langdon," Earl said. "I'll take care of his woman. Show her what a real man is."

~ ~ ~ ~ ~

"Rick Strong been home today?" Langdon asked Star over a cup of coffee.

"Don't think so," Star said. "The missus went out with some other fellow about an hour back."

"Another man?"

"Yeah. Didn't get a good look at him. Had a hoodie pulled up over his head. Almost like he was trying to hide his face."

"The guy driving a car?"

Star shook his head. "Don't think so. They took Val's car, and there aren't any other cars parked around that I haven't seen before."

"Like, maybe he spent the night?"

"Could be," Star said. "Didn't keep watch yesterday with Rick in jail and all. Figured I'd give myself a day off."

"Ready to go back to work?"

"What do you want me to do?"

"You know the asshat that clocked 4 by Four?"

"He might get out later today," Star said.

"4 by Four?"

"Yeah, I just got back from the hospital. Told him he could stay here for a couple of days until he gets his feet back under him."

"That's good of you." Langdon suddenly felt very guilty. "I haven't even gotten a chance to get in and visit him."

"Yeah, he mentioned that."

"Been pretty busy."

"Yeah."

"A woman was murdered. Her boy kidnapped. Kidnapper's threatening to execute him."

Star smiled. "I'm not judging you. Those days are long past."

"You picking him up?"

"He has to get the final okay, but yeah, if he does, I plan on getting him."

"Maybe we can have a get-together. I could pick up some takeout. Get the gang together." Langdon thought of Chabal with her bruised cheekbone, Bart who hadn't slept in a week, Jewell thinking her husband was having an affair, and Richam with a newfound daughter.

"If that makes you feel better. What about the asshat who hit him?"

"You mind walking around town showing this around?" Langdon asked. He pulled out his phone and opened the camera. "See if they've seen this man?"

Star took the phone and held it close. He grabbed a pair of readers from the table and put them on. "Is that the fellow who kicked in 4 by Four's ribs?"

"Yep. Footage provided by Rick Strong, nonetheless."

Star handed the phone back. "Can't be certain because of the hoodie he had on, but he looks a lot like the fellow Val Strong just left with about an hour ago."

~ ~ ~ ~ ~

"What are you doing here?" Ann Morin said with a surprised look on her face. "I thought we weren't going to see each other until Sunday?"

Martin Thomas stepped through the door and pulled it shut. "Thought I'd swing by at nap time for a brief respite." He kissed her on the mouth and stepped inside, pulling the door shut behind him.

Ann grabbed his hand and pulled him behind her to the master bedroom. He closed and locked the door behind them, and they fumbled with each other's clothes. They tumbled into the bed, she still wearing her blouse and bra, he with his socks on, and rocked their way to a quick climax, or at least he did.

"Can you stay for dinner?" Ann asked as they lay on their backs breathing hard.

"No. I'm supposed to be at the police station at 4:00. They have some questions they want to ask me."

"That's okay," she said. "In two more days, we'll be together forever."

"I didn't want to tell you this on the phone, but I can't go with you."

"What do you mean?"

"Too much going on. I'll follow you out, and we'll be together as I promised. I just can't go right now. But you have the key and the address. In a week or so, I'll follow you out."

"You promise?" A hard glint came into Ann's eyes. "I don't intend on losing you. Losing us."

"I promise. Just until things settle down."

"I'll do anything to protect us. Whatever you want."

Martin turned on his side and kissed her. "I have to unwind this whole kidnapping mess. Who knows? Maybe the people who took my son will let him go a few days after the stroke of midnight on Halloween. I can't very well go taking off until I make sure of things."

"I'll wait and we'll go together," Ann said.

Martin shook his head. "Stick to the plan. Alaska Airlines, 5:05 p.m. out of Logan."

He stood up and began getting dressed.

Chapter 24

Friday, October 30th

Langdon and dog went into the bookstore early to do some work in the office. It probably could've been done from home, but sometimes it was good to get away. Dog was always up for any sort of adventure.

The get-together to welcome 4 by Four the night before had been put off. They'd decided to keep him for another night at the hospital. Star was planning on picking him up this morning when he got the thumbs up to leave.

Langdon had just about forty-two hours to find Eddie Thomas. Would Salvador Dalí actually execute a four-year-old boy, he wondered? Or was it just for show? The governor had made no comment in regard to the threat, actually, a whole series of "no comments" to the questions hurled at her by the media. As of now, the current phase of reopening businesses hadn't changed though, with a second wave of Covid enveloping Maine, a state that, until now, had stayed relatively virus-free, much stricter mask regulations were being promised, as well as another likely shut down of certain businesses.

Rick Strong. Earl Franklin. Martin Thomas. It was most likely one of these three men who had taken Eddie and killed Jill. Maybe a combination of them. If it wasn't any of them, Langdon thought, then he stood little chance of finding Eddie. Star had made large photos of Earl Franklin and done the downtown Brunswick loop of establishments with no luck whatsoever. Langdon had not heard back from Danny T. He wondered if the man was actually looking, or had just agreed to do so to get Langdon off his back.

Then, there was Ann Morin, Langdon thought, who was talking about going to the West Coast, possibly California. Or maybe it was Portland, Oregon, whatever that beach town was where Martin Thomas had just inherited a house. Was Martin the man that Ann was having an affair with, and were they planning on going west together? Certainly not without his son, but maybe once this thing was done and over, he'd be happy to leave Brunswick in his rearview mirror.

Langdon unlocked the door to the bookshop, letting dog run through, and locking it behind. He looked at the time on his phone, just after 6:00 in the morning, and wondered what time Richam and Raven would get the results of the blood test back. If his friend was right, and Raven Burke was his daughter, Langdon didn't envy Richam the conversation that would follow with Jewell.

The office door was open and there was a light on. Langdon thought that it might be that time when he should start carrying the Glock. Dog brushed past him, rushing his way through the door. Langdon went to call him back, thought better of it, and followed him. Star was sleeping on the couch, his face being energetically licked by dog.

"What are you doing here?" Langdon asked.

Star sat up, rubbing dog's head. His hair was mussed atop his head and his eyes were blurry. "Internet was down at home. Figured I'd come in here last night and use the computer to do some research. Thought I'd close my eyes for just a minute."

"What kind of research?"

"The two guys you got me looking for. Strong and Franklin."

"Find anything?" Langdon sat down behind his desk.

"That I did. Was going to call you and realized it was 3:00 in the morning." Dog had climbed up and was attempting to sit in Star's lap to better allow for his head to be rubbed.

"Yeah? What'd you find?"

"Found out that Earl Franklin's sister is Valerie Franklin."

"Valerie Franklin?"

"Actually, that used to be her name. Then she got married to a guy by the name of Strong. Rick Strong."

"Valerie Strong is the sister of Earl Franklin," Langdon said slowly. "How about that?"

~ ~ ~ ~ ~

Richam thought it best to have Raven present when he broke the news to Jewell. Raven hadn't liked this particular plan very much but had agreed. Not that it was that big of a deal, Richam argued to himself. So what if he had a daughter from a relationship that occurred before he'd met Jewell? Well, not technically before, but he'd indeed broken it off when he realized that he was serious about Jewell. He'd told Langdon that it had been after the first few dates, but the truth was that it had been more like six months.

Jewell had run down to Portland to meet a client in her office. She worked for Christian Helpers for Entering Refugees and Immigrants Services and Hospitality, or simply, CHERISH. Little did she know that her husband was about to put her to work helping an immigrant who was actually her stepdaughter gain citizenship. Jewell was mostly doing her work from home in these trying times, but immigrant services couldn't be done solely via the computer monitor, and she occasionally had to confer with her clients, officials, doctors, or landlords face-to-face to make things happen.

Currently, Richam and Raven were sitting in the living room of his house awaiting her return. He was holding the printout from the results of the paternity test. He looked at the paper, reading, *Richam Denevieux is **not** excluded as the biological father of the tested child.*

His eyes skimmed down. *There is a 99.9% chance that this man is the biological father of the child.* That was pretty definitive. He was the father. He'd had almost two weeks to wrap his head around this possibility, the lab being incredibly slow, most of their resources turned toward the virus and not such things as paternity.

He had printed the results from his confidential portal after Jewell left. Then he'd called Raven, greeting her as his daughter, and convincing her to come over. They hugged, tears had been shed, and now they sat nervously waiting for Jewell's arrival. Richam had done the math around Raven's birthday and shared with her that she was conceived approximately four months after he'd started dating Jewell.

The silence was such that they both heard the car coming down the long driveway to the ranch that Richam and Jewell had lived in for the past twenty-seven years. Richam had started as a waiter at the Wretched Lobster, worked his way up to being the bartender, the host, and finally the owner about ten years back. They'd raised two wonderful kids, the oldest, Will, almost the same age as Raven.

The door opened, and Jewell swept into the house. Richam loved the energy that his wife possessed, except when he was in the doghouse, for then that formidable vitality could be focused and directed at him like an alien ray gun. And it most certainly burned. Richam tried very hard to not be the target of his wife's ire.

Jewell had natural black, curly hair that she let grow out, picked it to stand up, and then hair sprayed to hold into place. This added approximately seven inches to her height of five-foot nine-inches. Her eyes were dark brown and they flared like hot coals when she came into the room and saw Raven and Richam sitting there.

"You're Raven Burke," Jewell said.

Raven nodded.

"Baby, let me—"

"Shut it," Jewell said holding up her hand. "Are you fucking my husband?"

Raven smiled, a tight glimmer of teeth, but her eyes holding Jewell's. "That woul' be a sin," she said.

"Yes, very much so. He is a married man, and you're half his age. And if you are, I'm going to kick your ass before I get started on him."

"That, too—"

"How old are you, anyway?" Jewell stood over Raven staring down at the girl.

"Jewell, let me talk," Richam said. "She's my daughter."

Jewell had swung around as if to light into Richam, but froze as the words worked their way into her head. "Daughter?"

Richam nodded. "I got the paternity test back this morning. Ninety-nine percent certain."

"You mean you're not having an affair?"

"No, baby, I love you. I'd never cheat on you." Richam stood up but knew it was not quite time yet to enter his wife's space. "Sorry, I just wanted to be sure before I shared it with you."

Jewell turned back to Raven. "You're his daughter?"

"Ya," Raven said. "He's my father."

"You're from the D.R.?"

"Ya. I came here about a year ago."

Jewell looked back at Richam. "How long have you known?"

"I told him two week' ago, Mrs. Denevieux," Raven said.

"We went in to get the cheek swabs for the paternity test immediately," Richam said. "What should have taken, at most, two days stretched until this morning because of Covid. I just kept thinking I'd have a definitive answer one way or another, and the days kept sliding by."

"I am just happy that you are not having an affair." The tenseness in Jewell's shoulders relaxed a notch, as far as it ever did.

"I'd never do that. You should know better," Richam said.

"Does that mean you're my stepdaughter?" Jewell looked back to Raven.

"I suppose so," Raven said with a broadening smile.

"Who was your mother?"

"You didn't know her. She lived in Santo Domingo," Richam said. "I knew her from when I worked in the city."

"How old are you?" Jewell asked, not acknowledging her husband.

"I am thirty-one, Mrs. Denevieux."

"When is your birthday?"

"In January. The nineteenth."

Jewell's shoulders and eyes escalated in intensity as if a trigger had been pulled. "You're seven months older than Will. My son."

~ ~ ~ ~ ~

Star left to go home and shower and get ready to pick up 4 by Four, leaving Langdon to order books and pay some bills. He thought he should wait until 8:00 to call Bart, in case his friend had finally gotten a chance to get some rest. There was another request for that Kevin St. Jarre fellow, author of *Aliens, Drywall, and a Unicycle*, and Langdon decided to stock the title even though it wasn't a mystery. Had to go with what the people wanted, he thought, wishing at the same time that politicians felt the same way.

At 8:00 on the dot, he called Bart.

"What?" the surly cop answered.

"And a fine morning to you, you big, lovable teddy bear," Langdon said.

"And what is so fine about it?"

"The sun must've come up, and another day has begun."

"Don't know if you've been outside, but if the sun is up, you can't tell. The clouds are black as night, and icy rain fills the air."

"Aren't you the poetic one," Langdon said, needling the man. He was perhaps the only person that knew the gruff bachelor liked to dabble in writing poetry in his free time. "I'm in my office at the bookshop. Got here before the sun was due to rise. As a matter of fact, there was still a Star out when I got here." Langdon chuckled at his own joke.

"You call me for a reason?"

"The Star I'm talking about is Jonathan, and he spent the night here surfing the 'net, and he uncovered something that it looks like it might have slipped past our boys in blue."

"You got something you want to tell me?"

"Earl Franklin is the brother of Valerie Strong, wife of Rick."

This caused a pause of silence. "Son of a gun."

"Not really cause to bring him in again, one would think," Langdon said. "But most certainly an interesting tidbit. You have any information on what Earl might be driving? I couldn't find anything."

"He lost his license and doesn't drive. Took a bus here. Arrived in Brunswick two days before Eddie Thomas was abducted. He was staying out to the Greenlander Motel until the day of his scuffle. Then he disappeared. No credit card purchases. Phone has been turned off. Probably using a burner. He's ceased to exist."

"You think he's hiding out at Strong's house? Or maybe his cottage?"

"He wasn't there the morning that Jill Thomas was found dead. We searched both places."

"Probably worth another look," Langdon said. "You bring him in on assault charges, maybe he'll crack, decide to turn on Rick, and tell us where the boy is."

"You don't know they took Eddie Thomas," Bart said. "Man, you gotta get off that particular horse."

"I'd sure like to get the chance to ask them if they did," Langdon said.

Bart agreed to send officers to double-check the Strong residences and keep Langdon in the loop before hanging up the phone.

Langdon watched the videos sent in by the kidnapper again, and then again. It was on the third pass of the most recent video that he paused it and replayed a part in the middle. *In sixty-three hours, the boy sitting next to me will cease to exist. There is no need for the muckamuck who plays at being governor to wait until that last fateful moment.* Something was tickling Langdon's brain. He'd heard somebody say muckamuck in conversation recently. Who had it been? He typed it into the computer, noting again that it was a person who thought they were all that and a bag of chips, and that it was derived from Chinook Jargon, whatever that was. He hit the link to find out what that was at the same time his phone buzzed.

"Hey, Danny T., you find out anything?"

"Well, I been asking around like you wanted, about Strong and Franklin, but nothing much came up yesterday. Few guys knew Strong owns the brew pub, one even mentioned that he didn't much believe in masking, but otherwise, nothing much really."

"Star found out that Earl Franklin is Rick Strong's brother-in-law," Langdon said.

"Huh, that might explain what I came across this morning."

"What'd you come across this morning?"

"You betting on your Vikings this weekend? Thought you might want to give me a touchdown and I'll take the Pack."

Langdon sighed. This was how Danny T. worked. If he had information, he took his payment in favorable sporting event odds. Luckily, the bet was usually just five bucks, never more than twenty. "You got the Packers and seven points," Langdon said. "What do you got?"

"For a ten spot," Danny T. said.

"You got it. Now spill what you found."

"I came into the diner this morning to get breakfast, you know—hey, you're still paying my tab for a month if I help you track down those guys, right?"

"Yes, Danny T.," Langdon said through gritted teeth. "You went into Rosie's this morning," he prompted.

"Fantastic," Danny T. said. "I showed Rosie the picture of Strong, and she knew him, you know, them both owning restaurants in town. Said he'd been in earlier, asking around. Then I showed him the picture of Earl Franklin, and she didn't know him, not at all, but said that he'd been with Strong this morning."

"Asking around?"

"Rosie said they was asking about you and Chabal. Said they had something for you. Rosie, she said she'd heard about you busting Strong's nose and thought this was a bit suspicious, is what she said."

"What were they asking about?"

"They was looking for where you lived. Rosie told them to get lost and not be stirring up trouble in her diner. You know Rosie, she can be pretty damn scary if you get on her bad side and—"

"They wanted my address?"

"Yeah, that's what I been saying. They offered up fifty bucks for anybody that could tell them where you lived, and Rosie kicked them out, told them to get lost, like I said."

Langdon knew it wasn't hard to find an address. Being a PI and gaining a few enemies along the way, he took precautions, but knew that anybody with any internet savvy could probably find where he lived. He realized he'd missed the last thing Danny T. had just said. "What's that?"

"Rosie said that Ray followed them out to the parking lot and spoke with them. They might've given him money, she said, and she wasn't going to be letting ole Ray back into the diner ever again, not unless he had some—"

Langdon hung up the phone and went to the door, calling Chabal as he went. He was out the back of the building and to his Jeep as the call went to voice mail.

Chapter 25

Langdon floored the Jeep out of the parking lot, past the fire station, and onto Maine Street barely looking for oncoming traffic. Dog could sense the anxiety, and whereas he'd typically think this was some big game derived for his pleasure, now sat in the passenger seat with his ears pinned low and a guttural whine coming from his throat.

Even with the bad weather, the protesters had swollen to a larger number yet again today, both for and against masking, many of them spilling onto the street. Cops faced off against them, trying to keep them on the Mall, and Langdon noticed pushing and shoving here and there. With all the police resources required to keep the protesters in line, what was being done to find Eddie Thomas, he wondered? The state police were technically in charge of the kidnapping case, but they certainly relied on the local police to do a lot of the footwork and to make connections.

Langdon passed the church at the top of Maine Street. This turned his thoughts to the pastor from a church down in southern Maine who'd presided over a super-spreader wedding event earlier in the summer. What was wrong with people, he wondered, when they couldn't recognize the truth of things? The Bowdoin campus was quiet and forlorn-looking. Only freshman had been permitted to return in-person this fall, and there were heavy restrictions on any sort of social gathering.

These thoughts buzzed around the central driving fear within his brain. Chabal was home alone, unsuspecting, and Earl Franklin and Rick Strong were coming to pay a visit—no, more likely, were already there. Langdon had no doubt that Ray from the diner would sell him out for fifty bucks. The man would sell out his own mother for half that. He tried to call Chabal again, to no avail, but he was almost home now.

The Langdon house was at the back of the Meadowbrook development, its backyard the vast, mostly forested plot known as the Brunswick Town Commons. Langdon turned onto his street and saw a bright red Ford Mustang in his driveway. Chabal's car would be in the garage if she was home, and he assumed she was, as he likely would have known of any plans she had to leave the house that day. For the second time this morning, Langdon wished he'd started carrying the Glock. Nothing to be done about that now, because it was in a locked box in his bedroom closet.

He parked beside the Mustang and raced across the front yard and through the front door. Chabal sat on the couch facing him. Next to her was Earl. He had a knife in his hand, what may've been a Bowie, with a seven-inch blade and a clip point. The tip of the steel was pressed lightly into Chabal's neck just under her chin, causing her to tilt her face up toward the ceiling. Rick sat in Langdon's reading recliner, his feet up on the footstool, and a pistol held casually in his lap.

"Let her go or…" Langdon said. He could hear the lameness to the empty words.

"Welcome home," Rick said. He was grinning broadly. "I hear that you've been looking for me. Here I am."

Dog growled low in his throat, and Langdon motioned for him to stay put. "What do you want?"

"I want answers, asshole."

"Answers to what?"

"Why did you come into my brew pub and attack me the other day?"

"Can you have your brother-in-law ease up on the knife-to-neck thing?"

Rick laughed. "So, you have finally made that connection. It's about time." He looked at Earl and gave a short nod, and the blade came away from her neck, but only just, leaving a small, red dot behind.

"A woman hired me to investigate you for sexual harassment of your employees. When I heard that you were carrying on an affair with Jill Thomas, I assumed that you'd done the same to her, and she'd succumbed to your pressure." Langdon shrugged, taking another step into the living room. "Sorry. I might've gotten a bit carried away."

"And who hired you to investigate me?" Rick asked. "Ah, don't bother. I'm betting it was that cock-tease, Raven Burke."

"How about we put the weapons away and talk this through," Langdon said.

"You also seem to think that I kidnapped Eddie Thomas and killed his mother." Rick pointed the pistol at Langdon. "I don't particularly care what you think, but I would like to know what your fat buddy thinks."

"Fat buddy?"

"Don't play coy with me. Sergeant Jeremiah Bartholomew. Why is he after me?"

"What do you mean?"

"I just spent twenty-four hours at the state police lockup in Gray. Your fat friend came in and played bad cop and then turned me over to some broad with huge knockers. I'm thinking he thought I'd confess to every sin I'd committed with those bazookas waving at me. Why does he have me down as the number one suspect?"

"Come on, Rick. Don't play dumb. You're smarter than that." Langdon edged another half-step closer. "Your business is being destroyed by Covid restrictions. You're an avowed anti-masker. You were having an affair with the mother of the kidnap victim. The kidnapper is threatening to kill the boy unless government restrictions are loosened. Then Jill Thomas turns up dead less than a mile from your cottage where you spent the night alone."

"Somebody is setting me up. I didn't kidnap that boy, and I'm no murderer."

"Okay, so put away the gun and tell your QAnon bro to put his blade back in his pants."

"Where do you get off running around spreading rumors about me?" Rick asked. "Come into my place of business and headbutt me? What makes you so special?"

"Yep, I'm a real muckamuck, aren't I?" Langdon said.

"What?" Rick had a quizzical look on his face.

The confusion appeared to be genuine as far as Langdon could tell. "Whatever. How about we put down the weapons and…"

"Not on your life," Earl said. "This bitch and I have something to work out between us."

"Get your hands off of me," Chabal said.

Earl reached over and cupped her breast in his hand and then squeezed so that she flinched in pain. Chabal swept her arm outward, knocking the blade away from her neck. Langdon took one step forward and kicked Earl under the chin, snapping his head back and sending the Bowie clattering to the floor.

Rick leapt from the recliner with the pistol extended in front of him. "Don't move!"

Dog shot across the floor and flew through the air, his teeth sinking into the man's bicep, causing him to shout in pain.

One part of Langdon's mind wondered where dog had learned that particular stunt, as another quickly calculated his own next move.

Earl grabbed Chabal by the hair as she attempted to stand up and brought her face smashing down into his rising knee. Chabal slumped to the floor. Earl's eyes were glazed from the kick, his mouth twisted in primal ferocity. Langdon tried to remove that feature from his face by smashing a punch into his teeth.

Rick had slung dog into the wall and now stepped forward, the gun still in hand, and crashed it in a sweeping blow to Langdon's ear. Langdon stumbled forward, falling onto Earl on the couch, as dog again came charging across the room and bowling into Rick, who grabbed the canine by the collar and hurled him across the room. Earl had his arm around Langdon's neck, pinning him down on the couch as Rick brought the pistol once again to bear on Langdon. Chabal rolled her small but sturdy frame against the man's legs, and he lurched to the side, the pistol firing into the wall.

Langdon bit Earl's arm, sinking his teeth into the meaty flesh, and was rewarded with a howl of pain and Earl releasing his hold. He jabbed a short punch into Earl's neck and flung himself sideways into Rick who was trying to regain his balance and turn the weapon back toward Langdon. Their two bodies collided, sending them both spilling to the floor, the gun finally coming free and sliding across the hardwood.

Rick grabbed Langdon's face and tried to find his eyes with his thumbs, so Langdon grabbed Rick's penis with his right hand and twisted, making him scream in a high-pitched falsetto. It'd be some time before Rick Strong used that particular appendage again, Langdon thought with satisfaction.

Earl was crawling across the floor, the pistol just feet from his grasp. Langdon judged that the man would get there and aim and fire before he could, and so, grabbed Chabal's arm and pulled her through the archway into the kitchen with a whistle for dog to follow. The three of them limped their way to the first-floor master bedroom, slamming and locking the door, as Earl screamed for them to come back and take their medicine.

Langdon hustled around the bed to the closet. The key to the lockbox was hanging on the wall. He pulled it free and opened the metal box, pulling the Glock out, slipping a clip in, and racking the slide as he came back around the bed. He pulled open the door and stepped into the hall, gun in two hands, as he heard the squealing of tires. He took the few steps back to the front door and saw the Mustang disappearing down the street.

Langdon went back to the bedroom where Chabal and dog were huddled on the floor. "Are you hurt badly?"

Chabal shook her head to the negative. Dog was licking the blood from her face. "Might've broken my nose," she said. "You okay?"

"Yep. But getting fairly angry."

Chapter 26

Chabal's nose was most likely broken but after a quick internet search, they decided it wasn't worth going to the hospital. It wasn't like it was crooked. Langdon had fared the best out of the three of them with only a ringing in his ear and a scratched face. Dog had a pretty bad limp, but they decided to hold off on visiting the vet for a day or two to see if it got better on its own.

Langdon called Bart, who came over with Jackson Brooks of the Maine State Police and took their statement, after which an arrest warrant was issued for Rick Strong along with new felony charges against Earl Franklin. After the police left, the three of them licked their wounds, sitting in silence in the living room, each lost in their own thoughts. Langdon assumed that dog's thoughts had to do with eating or chasing rabbits.

Star called to let them know that he was picking up 4 by Four from the hospital and wondered if the group would be getting together. Langdon told him about the visit from Rick and Earl, and asked if they might come to his house at 5:00. Star said that as long as 4 by Four was up to it, that would be no problem. Langdon texted the plan to Richam, Danny T., and Bart. Nobody replied.

Nonetheless, at four o'clock, Langdon called Goldilocks Tavern and ordered three large pizzas. As he prepared to go, Chabal insisted that she go with him. They both left the house armed, leaving dog behind, who for the first time in his life, seemed to be okay with that. Langdon first swung by Moonshiners, the liquor store, to pick up a handle of Glenlivet, a box of wine, and a case of beer. The pizza smelled delicious, making Langdon realize he hadn't eaten all day.

It was unlike Danny T. to pass up free food, so Langdon called him. A bit of arm twisting ensued, and the man agreed to come over, the Langdons swinging by his apartment to pick him up. The man did not have a car, and cab fare would stretch his slim wallet.

"What happened to the two of you?"

"Do you know where Ray lives?" Langdon asked.

"Ray?"

Langdon told Danny T. about the visit from Rick and Earl. "I believe that tomorrow I'd like to go thank Ray for his part in this. See if he knows anything more about those two right-wing nuts."

"You know," Danny T. said, "I'm not really even all that hungry. Can you just drop me back home?"

"I'm not involving you in any of that," Langdon said. "This is just to celebrate 4 by Four getting out of the hospital. Pizza smells good, doesn't it?"

As they passed the First Parish Church, Star's turquoise truck pulled out in front of them from Boody Street, and they followed it back to the Langdons' house.

"You look like hell," Langdon said to 4 by Four once they were seated around the dining table.

Langdon and 4 by Four had beers in hand, and Chabal had poured a glass of wine. Star, the recovering alcoholic, had a ginger ale, and Danny T., a Dr. Pepper. The three pizzas were opened up in the middle of the table, and each of them grabbed a slice of pie.

"Ha," 4 by Four said. "That's the pot calling the kettle black." His right eye was several different colors, there were stitches in his left cheek, and he was hunched forward from cracked ribs. Quite a contrast for the usually dapper lawyer. "Star says you ran into the same guy as attacked me."

Langdon gave a tight grin. "I'm not sure how Earl walked out of here. Gave him a good solid kick to the chin. It was Strong who gave me the cauliflower ear. Hit me with a pistol and then tried to scratch my eyes out."

"Appreciate you kicking him in the face," 4 by Four said.

"You supposed to be drinking?" Star asked. The question could've been directed at any of the three of them with drinks in hand. Nobody deigned to reply.

"Your friend Earl Franklin is a whackadoodle," Langdon said to 4 by Four and filled him in on Franklin's leadership role in QAnon.

"What about all the drops?" Danny T. asked when Langdon was done.

"Drops?" Chabal said.

"You know, all the posts from Q, the secret insider fighting the evil pedophiles," Danny T. said.

"It's all made-up bullshit, Danny T.," Langdon said. "Did Hillary Clinton get arrested? I believe that was a staple of the QAnon conspiracy theory, wasn't it? That Hillary is behind this cabal of cannibals and child rapists?"

"McCain didn't resign from the Senate, Pope Francis wasn't arrested, and Zuckerberg didn't leave Facebook and flee the country," Star said. "Why would anybody believe any of that malarkey?"

"All I know is that it's bad to molest children and drink their blood," Danny T. said. "You'll see. On election day, the people will stand up and speak, and the storm will come and then we'll have the great awakening."

"When did you buy into all this stuff?" Langdon asked.

"I've been following the breadcrumbs on 8kun," Danny T. said proudly. "I'm a baker, now."

"You know 8kun is linked with neo-Nazis, white supremacy, and is hosted out of an internet provider in Russia, don't you?" Star asked.

There was a knock at the door and Richam, Jewell, and Raven came in without waiting for an answer. Richam pulled out chairs for both Jewell and Raven before sitting himself. "Are we interrupting something?" he asked, looking around.

"Not at all," Langdon said with a sidelong look at Danny T. "Just talking politics, which perhaps is best left off the table right now. Grab a slice, beer in the fridge, scotch on the counter next to the boxed wine."

Richam fetched a glass of wine for Jewell, raised his eyes when Raven asked for a scotch, neat, but did as he was told, and grabbed a beer. "I thought 4 by Four was the one who got beat up," he said, sitting back down and eyeballing Langdon and Chabal.

So, Langdon shared the story again. "That's been our day," he finished up. "What about yours?"

Richam took a slug of beer. "I think you all know Raven Burke," he said. "What you probably don't know is that she is my daughter."

4 by Four choked on his beer, which, judging by his face, was not a good thing to do with cracked ribs. Star nodded as if it all made perfect sense, and Danny T. reached for another piece of pizza, as if this was no big surprise.

"Her mother recently passed, and Raven decided to come look me up. I didn't even know she existed until a few weeks back," Richam said. "I knew her mother back in the D.R.," he added.

Langdon was watching Jewell. She seemed to be biting back any comments of her own, which for Jewell, meant that she was handling it remarkably well. He raised his beer. "Welcome to the family."

"It was Rick who di' that to your ear?" Raven said. "I am sorry that I got you involve' with him."

"Him harassing you seems to be only the tip of the iceberg when it comes to the wrongdoings of one Rick Strong," Langdon said. "We think that he might be the one who kidnapped that boy, Eddie Thomas, and also killed the mother, Jill."

"I saw on the news that her body was foun'," Raven said. "I di' not realize she was murdered."

"She was strangled," Langdon said. "And I—we—think that Rick was the one who did it, but we don't have proof as of yet."

"An' this other man?"

"Rick's brother-in-law and fervent QAnon supporter." Langdon looked over at Danny T. as he said this, as did Chabal, Star, and 4 by Four. "We believe they are in this together. What we don't know is where the boy would be if it is them. Earl is from out-of-state, and the police have carefully searched Rick's home and cottage."

"Rick has another place. One where he took women that his wife di' not know about," Raven said.

"Why didn't you tell me this before?" Langdon asked. "That would've been good to know about, a crib, especially as we're investigating him for sexual harassment of employees." Silently, he wondered why Jill Thomas had not told him of this place either.

Raven gave a small shrug. "When I tol' another lady who work' at the brew pub what Rick was doing to me, she say for me to not go to his apartment. That's all she woul' say. I thought that was where he live'."

"This woman, she definitely said 'apartment'?" Langdon asked.

Raven nodded. "Ya."

The door opened, and Bart came through the door. "Ouch," he said, looking at Chabal's face, which had turned several new colors since he'd last seen her. "You look worse than 4 by Four, and didn't even go to a doctor, much less a hospital."

"I just did it to meet some nurses," 4 by Four said. "Even got a phone number from one young lady who said to call when I felt up to it."

"Speaking of young ladies, who are you?" Bart asked, looking at Raven.

"That's Richam's daughter," Danny T. said.

"Wasn't asking you," Bart said. He'd never liked Danny T. very much. "But, no, it's not. I've known Tangerine Denevieux since she was two years old, and this fine young woman, while looking a bit like her, is most definitely not her."

"She is Richam's daughter with some white woman back in the D.R.," Jewell said.

"Meet Raven Burke," Langdon said.

"Isn't she the one who hired you to investigate Strong in the first place?" Bart asked. It was difficult to flummox this gruff policeman, but flummoxed he certainly appeared to be.

"Yes, she is. Raven, meet Bart. His bark is much worse than his bite."

"Nice to meet you," Raven said.

Bart eyed her like she'd insulted him. "How old are you?" he asked.

"Seven months older than Will," Jewell said pointedly.

Bart went and got a beer, the sounds of opening the fridge and beer loud in the muted room.

"Raven was just telling us that she heard rumors that Strong may have a crib where he likes to take women," Langdon said to Bart.

"Or kidnap victims," Chabal said.

"First I've heard about it," Bart said. "Jill Thomas said that Strong came to her place. Matter of fact, that was why she moved out, because Martin started staying home due to Covid, and they had no place to meet. Strong corroborated that."

"Maybe he never took her there," Chabal said.

"Why not?" Bart asked.

"Could be one of those pleasure rooms like in that *50 Shades* movie," Danny T. said. "Stuff she wasn't into."

"Or he has another woman shacked up there," Richam said.

"How many women does one man need?" Jewell asked.

"Are you seriously telling me there's only two slices of pizza left?" Bart asked.

Langdon wasn't sure about the deftness of this change of topic but welcomed it. "Didn't know Danny T. was gonna have five pieces."

"If you check his pockets, you might find another couple of slices," Star said.

"What do Brunswick and Maine's finest have in the way of updates?" Langdon asked.

Bart swooped the last two pieces onto a plate, rolling one up like a taco and shoving half of it into his mouth. "Not much," he said, chomping away. "Forensics found a hair from Jill Thomas at Strong's cottage, but he readily admitted she'd been there before. Body was wiped totally clean."

"The body was wiped clean?" Chabal asked.

Bart looked down at the table. "Looks like whoever killed her stripped her naked and cleaned her with Clorox," Bart said.

"Maybe she was already naked," Star said.

Bart shook his head. "No signs of recent sex, consensual or non."

"Maybe things were getting hot and heavy, and then he killed her?" Langdon asked.

"Suppose it could be," Bart said. "Not the way it usually goes down."

"Don't some people get off on being strangled during sex?" Danny T. asked.

"There was no sign of sex," Bart repeated, eyeballing Danny T.'s pockets.

"Any leads on Strong or Franklin?"

"Got some intel on Franklin. He's one messed-up individual, but nothing hinting he's a murderer or kidnapper. Strong is clean as a whistle, unless you count cheating on his wife as a crime." Bart cast a nervous look at Jewell. "Of course, he'll burn in hell for those indiscretions, but we can't lock him up for it."

Richam cleared his throat but said nary a word.

"I think home invasion, assault, and threatening with a deadly weapon warrants putting somebody behind bars," Langdon said. "You catch him, and we'll find that boy, and then we can work on putting together a case against the prick."

Bart nodded. Langdon decided to join Raven in a glass of brown liquor. The group relaxed into simple conversation and let the troubles of the world fade for the next couple of hours.

~ ~ ~ ~ ~

"Can I help you, ma'am?" the officer at the desk asked. He might've been staring at her chest, and his mouth might've been open.

"Um, I was wondering if I could talk to somebody in charge?" Annika Morin was in a low-cut green dress and heels.

"Sure thing, ma'am. My name's Lieutenant Walton. What can I do for you?"

"I, uh, was just over to the courthouse filing a restraining order against my husband for domestic abuse. They said the judge wouldn't get a chance to look at the papers until Monday at the earliest."

"Generally takes a few days, at least. And that's only for a temporary restraining order, ma'am. Final one might take three weeks." The lieutenant moved his eyes up to her face and once again became lost, this time in her plush lips.

"Thing is, officer, thing is, that I was needing to go back and get something from the house."

"You're not staying there?"

"Not for almost two weeks." Annika emitted a tiny sob. "He hits me."

Lieutenant Walton stood up to his full five-foot-seven inches and hiked up his pants. "That bastard," he said.

"I am scared of him."

"You want an escort to pick up a few of your things, is that it?"

Annika nodded faintly. "*Da*. Yes. Please."

"Please, have a seat." Lieutenant Walton pulled out a chair for her, and once she sat, took a seat across from her at the computer. "What is your name?"

"Ann. Ann Morin."

He clicked her name into the keyboard. "Ann Morin from Washington Ave. out to Bailey Island?"

She sniffed. "That's me."

"We got a missing person report on you. Filed by Rudolph Morin."

Annika reached across and put her hand on his, leaning forward, desperation in her eyes. "I'm not missing. I am right here."

"Yes. Yes you are." He nodded appreciatively. "Do you have some identification?"

She handed him her driver's license. "He wants to lock me up and keep me a prisoner."

Lieutenant Walton pecked into the keyboard. "I have updated the missing person report and will happily escort you out to your house to get what you want. If your husband so much as looks cross-eyed at you, I will bust him on assault charges."

She leaned forward and grasped his arm. "Thank you so much."

Annika knew that Martin would be furious if he knew she was here, but she had to make certain that her name wasn't on some watch list before she traveled. She guessed that Rudolph would have told the police she was missing. Plus, she needed to get James' blanket. She couldn't leave without that.

Chapter 27

Saturday, October 31st

Langdon arrived at the police station at 8:45 a.m., fifteen minutes before the scheduled briefing with Martin Thomas. Bart met him in the front lobby to escort him back to the conference room.

"You were looking for that lobsterman's wife, weren't you?" Bart asked. "The one who reported her missing?"

"Ann Morin?" Langdon asked.

"That's the one," Bart said. "You need look no more."

"What do you mean?"

"She came in yesterday and talked to a lieutenant. Wasn't even aware she'd been reported as a missing person. Said she left her husband because he was abusive and said she'd started the process of getting a restraining order."

"That sounds like one case solved," Langdon said. "I believe I might owe Rudolph some of his retainer back."

"Rudolph, that's his name." Bart guffawed. "Walton, he's the one who took her out there, he said that his nose fit the name perfectly."

"Took her out there?"

"Yeah, she wanted to pick up some things, and Lieutenant Walton went out to make sure Rudolph, ha, ha…" Bart shook his head. "To make sure that Rudolph didn't get rough with her. Sweet as honey, the lieu said. And, hot as apple pie, whatever that means."

"Hmm. Interesting," Langdon said. He thought about sharing with

Bart his suspicions that Martin Thomas might be having an affair with Ann Morin, but decided to take a run at it himself first. "Where'd she give as an address?"

"Couldn't tell you," Bart said. "Is it important?"

"Maybe." Langdon shrugged. "Maybe not."

"You're not going to tell Rudolph where she's at, are you?"

"You know better than that. Thought I might swing by and talk to her, clear a few things up."

"I'll find out and let you know."

They'd been talking and walking and now entered the conference room. Martin Thomas was already sitting there with Jackson Brooks, head of the Major Crime Unit for the state police. Langdon knew the man well, as a sexual fling between his wife of the time, Amanda, and Brooks had been one of the reasons for his divorce. Then, he'd been angry with Brooks, but that separation had led Langdon to Chabal, and over the years, he'd actually come to forge a friendship with the man. This friendship with both Jackson Brooks and with Bart was the only reason he was being allowed into the room.

The outlook was bleak. The governor had refused to consider the kidnapper's demands, as was protocol. The governor had gone on all of the news stations with Martin Thomas the day before and would again later today, pleading with the kidnapper to let the boy go. Brooks and Bart both tried to convince Martin that there was a very good chance that the kidnapper would let the boy go, but the words sounded hollow in the room.

It was unlikely, over the past eight days, that the boy had not seen his abductor's face. Perhaps the man had kept the Dalí mask on whenever interacting with the boy. If that was the case, there was no need to follow through on any threat to execute Eddie. And even if Eddie had seen his kidnapper's face, there was a big difference between kidnapping a young boy and killing him. If the man was as unhappy as his words suggested, though, he might kill Eddie just to cast the governor in a bad light.

After a half hour, Langdon asked if he might have a private word with his client, and Brooks and Bart left him alone with Martin.

"Sergeant Bartholomew says that you have a theory that Rick Strong and his brother-in-law, Earl Franklin, are the kidnappers," Martin said.

"A theory, but no proof," Langdon said.

"Jill was found out near his summer cottage at Small Point, and he just happened to be there? And his wife did not know where he was that night? The man has been sleeping with my wife for the past eight months. A man who has knowledge of my house, my son, and has a motive for taking him hostage. It sounds like more than a theory to me."

"He has a strong alibi for the night Eddie was taken," Langdon said.

"But Franklin does not. I suppose if I were to kidnap somebody, I'd have somebody else do it, all the while establishing a strong alibi for myself."

"Yet, you have no alibi for where you were the night Eddie was taken," Langdon said.

"What's that supposed to mean?" Martin's eyes were red-rimmed to begin with but now flashed with anger. "Are you suggesting I kidnapped my own son?"

"Did you?" Langdon asked.

"Fuck you."

"Your story was that you were home with Eddie, passed out. Alone." Langdon shrugged. "It'd sure help to have an alibi."

"Why would I kidnap my own boy and threaten to kill him if the governor doesn't lift the Covid restrictions? Why in God's name would I do that?" Martin stood up and walked to the door.

"Do you know Ann Morin?" Langdon asked his back.

Martin froze and turned slowly around. "Who?"

"Ann or Annika Morin."

"Name doesn't ring a bell," he said.

"That's funny," Langdon said. This was make or break time. "The instructor over at Yoga Bear, Karen I think her name is, said that you were having an affair with Ann."

"Karen? Who the hell is that?"

"Seems they were pretty good friends, Karen and Ann." Langdon continued the lie. "Karen said that Ann left Rudolph for you. Told me your name and described you to a T. She said the two of you were planning on running off together."

Martin came back and sat down. "I don't know what you're talking about." But his tone was weaker, and his body language deflated.

"I think you do. Tell me."

Martin sighed. "Okay. I've been seeing Ann. So what?"

"Was she with you the night that Eddie was taken?"

"No."

Langdon considered lying and saying Karen had said they were together that night, but that was a stretch. "Not at any time? Can she vouch for you? Did you call her in the morning to let her know that Eddie had been taken?"

Martin shook his head. "We didn't see each other when Eddie was with me."

Langdon seemed to remember Jill saying the same thing about Rick before admitting that to be untrue. "Why have you kept this secret?"

"She's been hiding out from her husband," Martin said. "He's a mean cuss. Beat her a couple times a week. Raped her. Threatened her. If I brought her name up, he would've found her. She was scared of him. So, I agreed to keep her name out of it. Figured, what did it matter?"

"We're trying to save the life of your son, and you're withholding important information?" Langdon asked. "That sounds like a big deal to me."

"I'm sorry if you think that. I was just trying to protect Ann."

"Karen said the two of you were going to leave Maine. Run off to Oregon. Something about inheriting your parent's house in some beach community."

"Yeah, once this was all over. Hopefully, we'll be able to take Eddie with us. Leave this place behind. Too many bad memories. Rudolph. The kidnapping. Then Jill getting killed." Martin started to cry. "God, I just hope that Eddie comes back okay."

"Were you leaving any time soon?"

"No. Not for a while. Why?"

"When was the last time you spoke with Ann?"

"Been a couple of days," Martin said.

"Did you know that she is filing a restraining order against Rudolph?"

"We talked about that ,but figured what was the sense. Just lay low until we can blow town. Why?"

"She came in here yesterday. Talked to somebody about it at the town hall. Then, she got a police escort out to her old house in Harpswell to pick up personal belongings."

Martin shook his head. "I don't know anything about that. Like I said, I've been pretty preoccupied. Seems like maybe she changed her mind. Probably didn't want to bother me."

"Where's she been living?"

Martin measured Langdon. "You won't tell Rudolph?"

"I'm not a big fan of domestic abuse," Langdon said. "Especially when it's a man beating a woman who he feels he purchased online from Russia."

Martin appeared to be contemplating. "She's renting a room at the Pleasant Motel. One of their efficiencies."

Langdon knew the place. It was located on Pleasant Street, though it didn't seem a place that was all that pleasant, even if cheap. "You got her phone number?"

Martin gave him the number.

"You want to give her a call right now, and see if the three of us can sit down together?"

"I got to be back here at noon. But sure, let's give it a try. Can we keep the police out of it?"

"I don't see why they need be involved," Langdon lied.

Martin hit the number, listened for a bit, then left a message saying to call him back.

"You'll call me when you hear back from her?" Langdon said.

"Absolutely. Whatever helps find Eddie safe and sound."

There was a knock at the door, and Bart poked his head back in. "I got a few things to go over with Martin if you two are all done."

"Yeah, we're all done for now. I got some things to take care of," Langdon said. "Call me when you hear back," he said to Martin.

"That address you asked about?" Bart whispered as quietly as his deep voice allowed as Langdon stepped through the door. "Room 19 out to the Pleasant Motel."

~ ~ ~ ~ ~

Langdon could take a right out of the police station back to his office, or go left down the street to the motel. He figured it couldn't hurt to go see if Ann Morin was indeed there. Langdon had bad memories of the place as, years ago, back when it had been called something different, he'd been responsible for the death of a friend there. It was a U-shaped building with parking in the middle. Room 19 was in the back right corner. There was no answer and no sign of life.

The woman in the office did not seem to care much about protecting the privacy of her guests and readily told Langdon that the room was occupied by Ann Morin. She'd checked in last Sunday and paid for a week in advance. The manager, or so the tag on her blouse said, had never personally seen the woman. For fifty bucks, she quickly agreed to let Langdon into the room. The bed was made. There were no clothes or toiletries in the room. It looked as if it had never been used.

Langdon texted Bart. Something odd about Ann Morin. She does have a room rented at Pleasant Motel but never stayed in it. I have reason to believe she might be connected to kidnapping. Can you see what you can find out? Langdon knew that if he told Bart about her affair with Martin that the gruff cop would immediately confront the man about it, and that would do little but make Martin clam up.

He put the phone on speaker and lay it in his lap, calling Rudolph Morin as he drove back to the office. The man answered on the fourth ring but didn't say a word. The loud sound of an engine could be heard in the background. "Mr. Morin, we need to talk."

"You know where Ann is at?"

"I don't think she wants to be found," Langdon said.

"I know she doesn't want to be found," Rudolph said. "She goddamn came out with a cop and stole a bunch of her stuff. That ain't legal, I tell you. I'm gonna sue the goddamn police department for every red cent they got."

"We agreed when you hired me that if she was safe and sound and didn't want to be found that I wouldn't tell you her whereabouts."

"I don't goddamn care what we agreed. If you ain't gonna tell me where she's at, ain't much use talking to you."

"I wanted to return some of your retainer," Langdon said hurriedly before the man could hang up. "I believe I owe you about a thousand dollars."

"You should owe me the entire goddamn thing if you ain't gonna tell me where she's at."

"Can you come to my office and pick up your money, Mr. Morin?" Langdon didn't want to make the run out to Bailey Island. What was normally a beautiful drive would seem grim on this particular day, and he was fairly strained for time if he was going to chase down a kidnapper and save a boy's life.

"I'm coming into the wharf now," Rudolph said. "Give me time to unload my haul and I'll be there. 'Bout noon."

"High noon," Langdon said, and hung up as he pulled into the parking lot behind The Coffee Dog Bookstore and his office.

Chapter 28

"What's up, babe?" Langdon asked Chabal as he entered the office. He felt guilty locking the door behind him, but soon enough, they'd open back up, and he was sure his regular patrons would understand. He could always blame it on Covid.

Chabal looked up from her laptop screen. "Not too much. Valerie Strong has agreed to see me and Star at noontime. She seems to have a fondness for him. What'd Bart and Martin have to say?"

Langdon relayed the events of his morning so far. "Martin is definitely in a relationship with Ann Morin. She may have been at the Pleasant Motel, but she's gone now. Something a little odd about that whole thing."

"Odder than the fact that he's having an affair with a married Russian mail-order bride while the possible execution of his son looms at midnight tonight?" Chabal asked. "I can see why he might just keep his mouth shut about her."

"I suppose. I just sense there's more to the story."

"Hear anything from Raven?" Chabal asked.

"She texted Greg asking if they could talk. Nothing yet."

"He's the waiter at the brew pub?"

"That's the one. Talked to him a bit. Seems like a good sort. He might shed some light on this mysterious apartment of Strong's."

Chabal looked at her phone. "I need to go. Star and I are going to prepare our strategy for our meeting with Valerie. I'll see if she knows anything about the place."

"You're going to miss seeing Rudolph Morin," Langdon said with a smile.

"That's too bad. He's such a lovely man. He's coming here?"

"I thought it'd give me a chance to dig something more out of him about Ann. He didn't seem very happy that she came by to pick up some of her things with a man in blue. Downright upset when I refused to share her address at the motel, even if it looks like Ann is gone from that particular place."

"Are you going to tell me how you got him to come by?" Chabal asked.

"I offered him half his money back."

"Generous of you. Especially seeing as she paid him a visit on her own and you have no idea where she is now. Getting paid for achieving zilch is kind of nice, isn't it?"

Langdon chuckled. "At least we gave it a go. Plenty of people out there getting paid for not even trying, unless you count scrolling through Facebook and Twitter."

"Don't forget Instagram. Plenty to keep people busy."

"Leave the office door open, will you? Wouldn't want to miss Rudolph showing up." Langdon had a direct view of the front door of the bookshop from his desk.

"Gotcha, boss. See you back in a bit?"

"I'm going to try and talk with Jill Thomas's parents up in Bowdoinham. I'll let you know."

Chabal left with a wave of the hand. Langdon figured he might as well make the call now. He wasn't thrilled to be bothering the grieving mother and father of a recently murdered woman, but it was for the sake of their grandson *and* to find who killed Jill. Langdon spoke with Hugh, the father, who agreed to meet with Langdon at 2:00.

Why was Ann Morin's motel room empty? Langdon wondered, tipping back in his chair and closing his eyes. The room was paid for until tomorrow. It was possible that she'd left a day early—but why? It made no sense. If she was going to be staying with Martin, why didn't he just say so? It could be that she had just gone to another motel or hotel, afraid that Rudolph would find her after visiting him the day before. Martin and Ann were planning on moving to Oregon when this whole thing was in their rearview, but until then, where was she hiding?

And where was Eddie Thomas? It could be that he was at this mystery place of Rick Strong's. That made the most sense. If there was even such a place. This was based on Raven Burke's memories from almost a year ago as a passing statement from another waitress. If there ever had been such a place, why hadn't Rick taken Jill there? It was likely that he no longer had it. Possibly, with the downturn of the economy with the pandemic, Rick had to let his hump place go.

A banging on the glass door of the bookshop jolted Langdon back to the present. Rudolph Morin had stopped banging long enough to press his bulbous nose against the glass to peer inside. Langdon hopped up to let him in before the man returned to trying to shatter the glass.

"Come on in," Langdon said opening the door. "Sorry, the bookshop is closed down for a few days. Hope you don't mind if I lock us in?"

"Just give me my money, and I'll be on my way," Rudolph growled.

"Sorry, but there are a few things you have to sign."

"Like what?"

"A paper saying you received a thousand dollars back, for one," Langdon said. "Also, a statement saying that our business together has been concluded."

"That so I can't sue you for being useless at your job?"

"Your choice." Langdon started to close the door.

"Wait," Rudolph bellowed, blocking the door with a forearm that looked like a concrete block. "What about my money?"

"If you want the money, you have to sign the papers."

"Okay, okay. Let me in, would you?"

Langdon let the man pass through the door and locked it behind them. "Straight back to the office," he said and followed the lobsterman back into the office. "Have a seat."

"Just give me the papers and a pen and the money, and I'm gone."

Langdon sat down behind his desk and reached into a drawer. He pulled out a receipt book and wrote on it that one Goff Langdon had returned a thousand dollars to one Rudolph Morin. He made an X and placed it in front of the man while he pulled out the papers for the conclusion of the contract.

"You know, she wasn't always so unhappy," Rudolph said. "I think there was a time she actually loved me. Then James died."

Langdon paused. "James?" He decided to play it as if he had no knowledge.

"Our little boy."

"You had a child together?"

Rudolph exhaled a large breath. "That we did. Goddamn SIDS got him. Things were never the same after that."

"When was that?"

"Almost four years ago. He was just five months old. Put him in his crib and found him dead." Rudolph's voice cracked. "It was me that put him down to sleep. She blamed me for it. I didn't do anything different. Lay him on his back. Found him on his stomach. Never even saw him roll that way before. He'd flip from his stomach to his back, but not the other way. No sir."

"I'm sorry to hear that."

"I kept thinking she'd get past it, you know? And it'd be like before, but she just kept getting more distant. Then she was gone."

The man was suddenly a human being, Langdon thought, just like turning a switch. The death of a baby has spun many a happy parent into a spiral of grief. Maybe Rudolph had been one such.

"I just think if James was still with us, you know, everything would be fine," Rudolph interrupted Langdon's thoughts. "What can you do?"

"I'm sorry, Mr. Morin. For everything."

"Yeah, well, give me that goddamn paper to sign."

Langdon slid the paper across the desk, and Rudolph signed it. Langdon wrote him a check, and walked him to the door, neither one of them saying another word.

~ ~ ~ ~ ~

Chabal turned onto Maine Street and drove past the Town Mall. There had to be close to a thousand people spilling over into the street. The National Guard had arrived and was trying to contain the gathering, which was more of a mob than a crowd, verging on a riot instead of a protest. Signs jutted up into the sky. Dalí masks covered the faces of the people on the closer side by the memorial, while Covid masks hid the features of the throngs on the gazebo side. Camo was the reigning uniform of the Dalí crowd, and black clothing and umbrellas the attire of the VAIN group. Chants, slogans, and insults were being bandied back and forth. It was just one spark short of a wildfire.

Star let Chabal in with a big smile. She thought back to the first time she'd met him over twenty years ago. He'd still been drinking then, but soon after had quit imbibing, and hadn't touched a drop since. Star attributed his recovery to working in the bookshop; Langdon and Chabal who had welcomed him; the community of Brunswick who embraced him.

"We have just twelve hours to save that boy," Chabal said.

The smile waned. "That fellow won't really kill him," Star said, the words filled with more hope than conviction.

"We can't allow it to happen," Chabal said. "If the boy knows who the kidnapper is…"

"Rick Strong coming to your house and attacking the two of you certainly makes him look guilty."

"Him and his brother-in-law, Earl."

"So, how do we get Val to talk?"

Chabal shook her head. "I don't know. Maybe by sharing what we know about her husband sexually harassing employees, carrying on an affair with Jill Thomas, and keeping a secret place to take his women."

"I'll play good cop," Star said. "She likes me."

"Where's 4 by Four? I thought he was staying with you."

"Wanted to go home this morning. Had to track his car down, as Strong had it towed from his parking lot. Drove himself home." Star looked at a clock on the wall. "Almost time to head across the street."

"Why noontime?"

"The boys were going out somewhere."

"No sign of Rick or Earl?"

Star stepped to the window, opening the curtain further, and nodded down the street to where a Ford Crown Victoria was parked. "State police keeping an eye on the place. Been there all night and morning." At that moment, the Strong boys wheeled bikes out of the garage and rode down the street. "Looks like we're on."

Star led the way to the front door and tapped the doorbell. Valerie Strong opened the door. She looked like she hadn't slept, her hair was disheveled, and her makeup was smeared under her eyes. "Hi, Jonathan," she said.

"Hello, Val. This is Chabal."

"You're that man's wife, aren't you?" Val said.

Chabal figured she could say the same to her, but refrained. "Goff Langdon is my husband."

"I'm so sorry about everything that is going on," Star said.

"Come on in," Val said, opening the door wide. She led them to the living room where they sat down. She did not offer anything to drink.

"Is there anything I can do for you?" Star asked.

"What happened to your face?" Valerie asked looking at Chabal.

"Your brother smashed it into his knee. After he stuck a knife in my neck and groped me."

Valerie shook her head. "Earl was never any good. Don't know why I've stuck with him all these years."

"He was with your husband at the time," Chabal said. "I think they planned on killing us, but not before they had their fun with me."

"They are two peas in a pod, those two." Valerie shook her head wearily. "Earl, he's just like his daddy. My daddy. And Rick's no different. Looks like I made the bad old mistake of marrying my father."

"You're the victim here, just as much as me," Chabal said. So much for the good cop / bad cop routine. "Langdon was hired to investigate Rick for sexually harassing an employee. Then he discovered that the man was having an ongoing affair with Jill Thomas. Might be time to leave the man."

"He didn't kidnap that boy," Valerie said. "He might be a morally repugnant man, but he wouldn't take a child."

"How about kill a person?" Chabal asked. "Like me the other day."

Valerie shook her head from side to side. "I don't know. Maybe. If Earl egged him on. He's hit me before. Just once. He was very angry. Like he wanted to kill me. It scared me."

"Was Rick truly with you the night that Edward Thomas was taken?" Star asked.

"Yes."

"No chance he snuck away?"

"No. I don't think so. He slept in the guest room, but I didn't sleep much that night. I would've known."

Chabal believed her. "How about Earl?"

"He was staying at some motel out to Cook's Corner. Can't say for sure, but don't think he would've been involved. That QAnon mumble-jumble he's always spouting is about a cabal in the government that mistreats children. Can't see how killing a little boy would be something he's involved in. Don't make sense."

"We heard that your husband might have an apartment in town," Star said. "Do you know anything about that?"

"An apartment? No." She shook her head. "We got this house and the cottage out to Small Point. Why would he need an apartment?"

"We heard it was to take women to," Chabal said.

"Fuck," Val said. "You think you know somebody, and then one day, everything you thought to be true is false." She sighed, stifling a sob. "I don't know anything about an apartment. He certainly didn't take me to it."

"He's probably making monthly payments," Star said.

"Rick handles all of our finances," Valerie said. "Would never share any details with me. Now I know why."

"Does Rick have a desk? A computer?"

"The police took the computer. Searched his desk." Valerie stood up and gestured for them to follow. She led them to a small room that looked to be a former bedroom converted to a home office.

"Do you mind if we look through his papers and effects?" Chabal asked.

"Knock yourself out. Doubt you'll find anything. The police have been through everything."

An hour later, Chabal had to admit that she was right. If there had been anything to find, it was gone now. She'd have to get Bart to check on what the police had.

~ ~ ~ ~ ~

Danny T. was nursing his way through an afternoon cup of coffee at Rosie's Diner when he heard somebody say Langdon's name behind him. He spun the stool slightly so that he could peek a glance. Rudolph Morin was talking intently to a thin man. Danny T. knew Rudolph well, having once worked a fishing boat out of Mackerel Cove where the man moored his boat. That was before Danny T. had cut the line to an expensive fishing net to save his friend's arm. The boy was safe, but the net went to the bottom of the Atlantic Ocean, after which Danny T. was blackballed from that particular career by the angry boat owner, who happened to be a cousin of Rudolph Morin. It didn't matter that the friend's arm was attached to the son of the boat captain.

"Langdon wouldn't tell me where she was. Thinks I want to hurt her. I just want her back, is all," Rudolph said.

The thin man, who had his back to Danny T., replied, "She doesn't answer her phone?"

"Think she got rid of it. Maybe got a new one, or one of them burner ones. She seems to be under the impression that I'm some danger to her. Ain't no such thing."

"What do you want from me?"

"Find her. Get a message to her, is all."

"I might know where she is staying," the thin man said. "I'll deliver your message tomorrow."

Rudolph suddenly looked up at Danny T. There was no recognition in his eyes, but there was suspicion. He whispered something to the other man and stood up, throwing money down on the tabletop. The thin man took a last drink of coffee and followed Rudolph out the door.

Chapter 29

Greg had finally replied to Raven's text message. He agreed to meet her at the Wretched Lobster for a drink. She'd suspected that he'd had a thing for her, back when she worked with him at the brew pub, back before her life fell apart. Now, she was rebuilding it better than ever before. She had a place of her own. A job. And a father. Jewell was a bit testy about it, but had accepted her, and Raven was sure that her surliness would dissipate over time. Richam had been having sex with Jewell and Raven's mother at the same time, but that had been over thirty years ago. A lot of water had passed under that particular bridge since then.

She was at a high-top table in the bar waiting for Greg to arrive. At the next table, even if socially distanced, were Richam and Jewell. It was his place, after all. She couldn't very well tell him he couldn't be there, but it was kind of nice to have an overly protective father, something she'd never known.

Greg came down the stairs, spotted her, walked over, and sat down. "Long time, no see," he said.

"Hello," she said.

The waitress appeared and Greg ordered a beer, "How've you been?" he asked.

"Up and down." Raven smiled. She'd always like him, but perhaps just as a friend. "How've you been?"

"Same as everybody else during this pandemic," Greg said. "How about you? You just up and disappeared."

"I ran into some problem. Rick fire' me because I wouldn't have sex with him, and I try to bring sexual harassment charge against him."

"He's a snake," Greg said. "I should've quit when you told me what he was doing to you. I'm sorry. Truth be told, I didn't quite believe it, didn't want to believe it."

"Not your problem," Raven said.

"Could've told me you got fired. Maybe I could've helped you out."

"Things got a little crazy. I lost my place. Couldn't get a job. I wasn't thinking straight."

"I just thought you were ghosting me," Greg said.

Raven smiled. "That why you took almost an entire day to reply to my text?"

"Maybe," Greg said sheepishly. "Why'd you contact me now?"

"Things are going better. I'm getting my life back on track. I actually work here now."

"That's great. They hiring? Think I'm going to shitcan that job. Tell Rick Strong what I think of him. Boomers, you know?"

"Don't do it on my account," Raven said.

"He's sleazeball *numero uno*," Greg said. "Ever since you told me what he'd been saying to you, I been paying more attention. Don't know how I ever got the job, you know, not having…" He trailed off, his face coloring.

"He has to hire the occasional male for appearance's sake," Raven said. "I can ask my employer. He might be able to help you out." She stole a glance at Richam sitting at the next table.

"Thanks, that'd be great. What happened to the sexual harassment charges?"

"My phone got turn' off and I got kick' out of my place. When the human right commission couldn't reach me?" Raven shrugged. "They threw it out."

"That sucks."

"I've hire' a detective to try and prove he is a ba' man. So he won't hurt no more women."

"That's why you contacted me," Greg said, realization dawning on his face. "You want information."

"Ya, and also I know you're a goo' man."

"What do you want to know?"

"I hear rumor of an apartment that Rick has to take women to," Raven said. "Do you know it?"

"You remember Sarah Brown? She started working at the pub right before you left." Greg looked nervously over his shoulder.

Raven nodded, even though she did not remember the person. "Ya."

"Back when restaurants were being closed down, Rick told her he was going to let her go. Said he had a place she could stay, if she needed it. No monetary charge, if you know what I mean."

Raven tried to keep the excitement from her face. This had been almost too easy. "Does she know where this apartment is?"

Greg nodded. "She not only knows where it is. She lives in it."

Raven's mouth gaped open. "How can she do that?"

"I threatened to punch out Rick because of it. Especially after what you'd said to me. Told her I couldn't believe it, that it was despicable. You know what she said? She just laughed and said it was just sex. He only comes over about once a week, lasts ten minutes, and she has a place to live, with all her expenses paid. She begged me to not say anything."

"Do you know where?"

Greg smiled. "I've been there. It's not far from here, actually."

"When was the last time you were there?"

"Couple weeks ago, why?"

~ ~ ~ ~ ~

Hugh and Jane Lunt lived in a modest cape in a small neighborhood in Bowdoinham. They were approximately sixty years of age. He was a robust man of medium height and wore a sports coat even on a Saturday. Jane was a slight figure, unlike her daughter had been, with a tired smile and worry lines creasing her face.

Langdon sat at their kitchen table with a cup of coffee. Across from him was a framed quote saying, 'Victory in Jesus'. A black Lab sat on the floor with alert eyes, even if its body was growing older. The house was very neat, or what he'd seen of it so far, which was not much.

"Again, I am sorry for your loss," Langdon said.

"The Lord has a plan for all of us," Jane said.

"Jill hired you to find Eddie?" Hugh asked.

"Yes. If it's not too much, I'd like to ask you a few questions."

"You think the person who took Eddie is the same one as killed our Jill?" Hugh asked.

"It is certainly quite possible."

"Why?"

Langdon opened his palms up in front of him. "I don't know. Maybe she figured out who took Eddie and confronted them. Or tried to get him back."

"Is this man really going to kill Eddie?" Jane asked.

"I hope not. How often did you talk with your daughter?" Langdon asked.

"I went down to Brunswick to watch Eddie three days a week," Jane said. "Until the pandemic came along, that is. Martin's been working from home and…" She choked up, pulling a Kleenex from a pocket and blowing her nose.

"You'd go to the house? Were there ever any visitors?"

"No. Sometimes we'd go out to White's Beach. Or Popham Beach."

"Just you and Eddie? Would Jill go with you? Martin?"

"Martin was usually at work."

"How is your relationship with Martin?"

"He loved Eddie and Jill, that was quite clear." Jane blew her nose.

"He could be a bit aloof," Hugh said.

"Aloof?" Langdon asked.

"Not in a bad way," Hugh said hurriedly. "Just far away at times. Like he was somewhere else."

Langdon had noticed that very trait in Martin Thomas. There was something detached about the man. "Who were their friends?"

"Jill would set up play dates for Eddie," Jane said. "I think she became friendly with the mothers. I don't know their names. I think one was Susan."

"There was that friend from UMO," Hugh said. "What was his name? The one who has the place in Harpswell that Martin and Jill would watch in the winter?"

"Oh, yes. The artist," Jane said. "Rowan Coffin."

"What do you mean, they'd watch his place?" Langdon asked.

"He goes south somewhere for the winter," Hugh said. "To warmer climates."

"Is he around now?"

"I wouldn't know," Hugh said. "Why?"

"Do you know his address?"

Hugh shook his head. "No."

Langdon looked at Jane who also shook her head to the negative.

"I think they remained friends with a few other people from UMO, but nobody local," Hugh said.

"Jill kept up with a couple friends from high school," Jane said. "Hanna Libby. And, oh, yes, Faith Williams. I think they talked just about every week."

Langdon had them write down a list of names, asked a few more questions, and then left them to their sorrow. He wondered why they weren't with Martin as the deadline for Eddie loomed. It must be a terrible thing to have a grandson kidnapped and a daughter killed, all in one week. He was impressed that they were holding up so well. The list of names was sparse, and Langdon figured that the police had followed up on them already, but he thought he should share just to make sure.

He called Bart from the road, and it went straight to voice mail. He left a message that he'd be sending a list of names to make sure they'd been interviewed, but one Rowan Coffin seemed to jump out and that he lived in Harpswell. Langdon asked Bart if he could find an address for him. If Rowan Coffin had gone seeking warmer climates already, perhaps Martin Thomas had access to a place that nobody knew about so far.

It was a long shot to believe the man would kidnap, make demands of the governor, and threaten his own son, but maybe that was where Ann Morin had gone. Why would the man keep her whereabouts unknown? If Ann was there, why wouldn't Martin have told Langdon? Langdon could understand that she might want to be hiding out from Rudolph, and that was why Martin didn't bring her into this mess. But now? Ann had gone home and taken her things and begun the filing of a restraining order against the man.

It was a sticky situation, Langdon grudgingly admitted to himself. Martin was having an affair with a married woman, and his son had just been kidnapped, and his estranged wife murdered. He could see why the man might want to keep Ann on the down low. Hide her out in the house of a friend who was a snowbird. Did any of this help answer the one overarching question?

Where was the boy?

His phone buzzed with a call. He grabbed the phone from under the emergency brake of the Jeep, thinking it might be Bart calling him back. It was Danny T. He answered it and hit speaker, laying it in his lap. "Danny T. To what do I owe the honor?"

"I was having a cup of coffee at the diner and heard somebody talking about you," Danny T. said.

"Seems like I'm a hot topic at the diner," Langdon said. "Was it more young ladies wishing I was a single man?"

"Nope."

"You going to make me keep guessing?"

Danny T. sighed. "It was a fellow by the name of Rudolph Morin. He's a lobsterman out to Bailey Island. You know him?"

"Rudolph Morin was talking about me?"

"Said something about you not telling him where somebody was? That make sense?"

Langdon thought that sounded just about right. Rudolph was probably complaining to a buddy. "Yeah, he wanted me to find his wife. Claimed somebody stole her. I had a lead on her, but it went cold. Not that she wanted to be found by him. Gave him half his money back earlier today and told him I wasn't looking anymore."

"Guess he got somebody else," Danny T. said.

"What's that?"

"The guy he was talking to thought he might know where this person was. Rudolph asked him to deliver a message to her. Guy said he'd see about doing that tomorrow."

"Did you know the guy?"

"Nah. A little too well-dressed to be eating at the diner, if you ask me."

"Can you keep your eyes out for him? Ask around and see if you can get a name?"

"Aye, aye, Captain."

Interesting, Langdon thought. Rudolph was proving to be very persistent. If he wanted to tell Ann something, why hadn't he done so the previous day when she came by the house? "Thanks, Danny T., I owe you."

"Pats vs. Bills tomorrow. I got the Pats. Five bucks. You give me fourteen."

"You got it," Langdon said and hung up.

What message was it that Rudolph wanted delivered to Ann, Langdon wondered? It could be just something as simple as he had some personal belonging to return to her. Maybe he'd agreed to sign divorce papers. Or was it a plea of some sort? It seemed that Rudolph truly just wanted Ann to come back to him. If so, what could he possibly send to her that would bring her back? It certainly seemed that Ann Morin was not planning on getting back together with him. Langdon wasn't sure how strong her relationship with

Martin Thomas was, but either way, she was gone from Rudolph.

Rudolph had suggested it was losing their baby boy, James, to SIDS, that had driven a wedge into their relationship. Langdon was not sure how the whole Russian mail-order bride thing worked, but he had his doubts on the sincerity of affection between the participants. It seemed to him more like a mutual agreement, perhaps, where both parties received something they wanted. Even so, when put that way, isn't that what most couples fostered their love on? Sex and security. Like interests at the start are always a good thing, but they can diverge, as well as converge when not there to begin with.

Marriage had always been a business proposition, when looked at cynically, Langdon supposed. Merging of titles, wealth, exchange of dowries, and the desire of powerful men to parade around arm-candy. Maybe Rudolph could really win the heart, or at least the good sense, of Ann, if only given the opportunity. The answer was right there, tickling his senses, of what that might be, when his phone buzzed.

It was Raven Burke. "Hello."

"Langdon. We foun' the apartment."

"Strong's secret place?"

"Ya. Greg says he keeping a girl there now."

"A mistress?"

"Ya. She work' for Rick at the brew pub, and now she work for him in the bedroom."

"Where is it?"

"On Hennessy."

"I'm almost back to Brunswick now. I'll go right over. What number is it?"

"It don't have a number on it. But we're park' down the street now in a blue Honda."

"We?"

"I am with Greg."

"Don't do anything. Stay in the car. I'll be there in five minutes."

Chapter 30

Langdon drove past the blue Honda with Raven and Greg sitting in it, continuing on around the corner, thinking that Rick or Earl might recognize his Jeep on the street. He walked back and climbed into the back of the car.

"Hello again, Greg," Langdon said.

"You still thinking of letting your daughter work at the brew pub?" Greg asked.

Langdon studied his profile trying to discern if the young man was being sarcastic. "She lives in Brooklyn. Be a long commute."

"Ha. Sorry I wasn't more helpful about Raven," Greg said. "I had an idea why she left, you know, when you asked, but I wasn't sure. She just up and disappeared." He gave Raven a pointed look.

"We're going to fix that *mamagüevo*," Raven said. "Excuse my language, but he is a cocksucker."

"Which place is it?" Langdon asked.

Greg pointed down and across the street. "About six places down. Blue duplex. Right side."

The building was a two-story affair with a front porch. There were two front doors. They were painted red. A white railing enclosed the front porch that was common to both sides. The shades were drawn on the right side. As if on cue, the door opened, and Rick Strong appeared. He stepped out, looking both ways, but seemingly, not seeing the three of them in the Honda.

"Call the police and stay in the car," Langdon said.

He was not going to let the man walk away. He'd attacked him. Threatened his wife. And quite possibly had a kidnapped boy inside that apartment, scant hours from potential execution. Langdon stepped out of the car and walked quickly, closing the space. He pulled the Glock from his shoulder holster under his leather jacket. He wasn't going to make the mistake of underestimating the man again. Rick was opening the door of a Chevy Impala, a far cry from his Ford Mustang, but also red in color.

"Hello, Rick," Langdon said as he came up the double wide driveway.

Strong paused, the door open, looking into the car, at the house, and then at Langdon. "What do you want?"

Langdon chuckled. "You're wanted for assault and a host of other charges. The police are on their way. I merely mean to detain you for their arrival."

"I didn't kidnap that boy," Strong said.

"Close the door, Rick."

"It was you who attacked me first."

"You held a gun on me while your brother-in-law fondled, threatened, and hurt my wife, Rick. That is not acceptable."

"Look, can we work this out somehow? What do you want?"

"I want you to close the door and put your hands on the hood of the car," Langdon said. "We'll wait for the police together. Then, we'll see what's inside your secret apartment."

Strong closed the door. "I have a lady friend in there. Do we need to drag her into all of this?"

"Hands on the hood."

"She is not any part of this."

"I'm not going to ask you again."

The anger that had been growing into a living thing since this asshole and Earl had come into his home was now a full-fledged beast Langdon could barely contain. The thought of shooting Strong in the knee was beginning to seem like a fine idea. Perhaps the man saw it in his eyes, because he grudgingly stepped to the front of the car and put his palms flat on the hood.

It was as Langdon stepped up behind him to check for weapons that Earl stepped out onto the porch with a shotgun. "Maybe you best put that pistol down on the ground," he said.

Langdon looked at the armed man over his shoulder. "You pull that trigger, Earl, and you're going to kill Rick here, as well."

Earl shifted his feet. "Step away from him."

"Why would I do that, Earl? So you can murder me? Tell me, was it you who killed Jill?"

"I didn't kill nobody."

"Where's the boy, Earl?"

"I don't know nothin' about no boy. Put your gun down and step into the yard."

Rick turned around and Langdon pressed the Glock to his forehead. "Don't move."

"I said put the gun down!" Earl's voice rose to a shriek.

They heard the wail of a police siren. Langdon judged it was leaving the police station, coming down Stanwood, and would be there in less than a minute. "What's it going to be, Earl? You going to kill both of us and go to jail for life?"

"Put your gun down!"

Langdon looked at him. He saw the eyes tighten at the corners, and then Earl pulled the trigger, tilting the rifle up as he did so, the blast going overhead. Langdon brought his Glock in a sweeping motion around and Strong shoved him, causing Langdon to stumble, before bringing the pistol to bear on Earl, who dropped the 12 gauge like it had burned his hands.

Strong went to run, stepping around the corner of the car, looking over his shoulder at Langdon, as Raven Burke stepped forward and swung a baseball bat into his face, the impact louder than the shotgun blast had been. Strong crumpled, his nose shattered and spouting blood, unconscious before he hit the ground.

Two police cruisers pulled up with a squeal, more sirens in the background. Bart stepped out of the second car.

"Better call an ambulance," Langdon said. "I believe that Raven has had her recompense, finally, in blood if not in money."

Earl was handcuffed and put in a cruiser. Bart and Langdon went into the duplex where they found Sarah, Greg's friend. But there was no boy. An ambulance arrived, and Strong was whisked away along with two police officers.

"If he knows anything about the boy, he won't be telling us anytime soon," Bart said.

"If he knows anything, then Earl knows it, too," Langdon said. "I'm betting he's ready to talk."

"You want to take a crack at him before we bring him into the station?" Bart asked.

"Thought you'd never ask," Langdon said. They went over to the police cruiser and he climbed in back with Earl.

"What do you want?"

"You're going away for a long time, Earl," Langdon said.

"What for? I didn't do nothin'."

"You held my wife and I hostage and assaulted us. You just tried to murder me with a shotgun. Not sure what—"

"I didn't try to kill you," Earl interrupted. "You know that. It was just a warning shot."

"Tell me where the boy is, Earl, and I'll tell the police that. Help us find the boy and maybe we'll drop the charges for assaulting my wife."

"I don't know where no damn boy is."

"Why'd you come to Maine, Earl?"

"To protest the bullshit restrictions on people's goddamn rights is why."

"You came to kidnap a boy and hold an entire state hostage, is more like it."

"I want to talk to a lawyer."

"You got here two days before that boy was taken, Earl, and you and Rick planned it out. He's going to let you go down for this, you know. Because you're the one that went in the house and took him. His word against yours. He's a local businessman, and you're a well-known rabble-rouser. Give me something, Earl, so I can help you."

Earl turned his face away and stared across the street.

"Last chance, Earl."

After a minute, Langdon got out of the car. Bart was standing there waiting. "You get anything?"

Langdon shook his head. "No."

"You think him and Strong took the boy?"

"I don't know. I'm beginning to think I may have gotten turned around on this one."

"We'll take him in and grill him at the station," Bart said. "I got that address you asked about."

Langdon pulled the paper out of his pocket with the other names on it. "I got these names from Jill's parents. The Lunts. You probably checked them out already."

"Who was this Rowan Coffin? First we heard about him."

"Hugh and Jane said that Martin and Jill would watch his place in the winter. He's a snowbird. Worth asking Martin about, anyway. Maybe send a couple officers over."

"What are you going to do?"

"Reindeer games."

~ ~ ~ ~ ~

Rudolph Morin lived in a bungalow on Bailey Island, overlooking the Giant Stairs, a natural rock formation that led into the Atlantic Ocean. The house was essentially built backward, the front door and porch facing the sea rather than the road. It had a low-pitched roof, was well-kept, and had neighbors close on either side. Langdon wasn't sure if he should walk around to the backward-facing front or go in through a door he saw on the side of the home. He chose going to the front.

Shadows from the homes and trees crept out into the ocean as the sun descended in the west. Langdon had parked next to Rudolph's truck, so he figured he was home. The man made him wait a good two minutes before opening the door. "What do you want this time of night?"

It was just after 5:00, not really night at all, but Langdon knew many lobstermen were on the water long before first light, especially if they were going out deep like Rudolph did in the colder months. "Thought maybe I could ask you a few questions?"

"I thought me and you was done?"

"Can I come in?"

"What for?"

"About Ann."

Rudolph stepped aside. The interior of the house was an open design, the kitchen, living, and dining rooms all sharing one space. There were three doors leading to other rooms, two of them open. The house was up on a platform and had no basement. There were exposed rafters overhead, and everything was quite neat and tidy.

"I heard tell that you were trying to get a message to Ann," Langdon said, sitting down in a well-worn armchair.

"What business is it of yours?"

"What do you want of her?"

"What any man wants of his wife, I suppose." Rudolph sat down facing Langdon. "Did you decide to help me find her?"

"I need to know what message you're trying to get to her."

"It's personal. None of your damn business."

Langdon settled back in his chair, studying the man. He certainly didn't seem like a kidnapper, but then again, who did? He was most definitely not the man in the video. But the description of the man that Danny T. saw in the diner could most certainly be the man behind the Dalí mask. One thing Langdon knew for sure was you could usually learn more by listening than by talking.

Rudolph cleared his throat. "You really here to help me?"

"Depends."

"Told her I loved her. Said I'd let her go out more. Even take her to dinner and such. Let her buy more clothes and shoes and shit like that." The man's voice was shaky.

"Did you tell her you wouldn't hit her anymore, as well?" Langdon asked.

"Who the hell said anything about hitting her?" Rudolph blustered.

Langdon sat quietly.

After almost a minute the bravado again seeped from the lobsterman's body. "It was only the twice. I didn't mean to. You know how women can be. She just kept at it until I lost my temper."

"You tell her in the message that that would never happen again?" Langdon asked.

"Yeah, I tol' her alright."

"Who was the man who was delivering the message?"

"Sawyer. Sawyer Delisle."

"How does Sawyer Delisle know where to find Ann?"

"What in thunderation are you going on about? What's it matter?"

Langdon sighed. Said nothing.

"He's the husband of Ann's yoga instructor."

"Karen?" That actually seemed very plausible, Langdon thought. "Did your message say that you'd figured out a way to replace your boy?" he said.

"Replace my boy? James?"

"Did you take Eddie Thomas from his home?" Langdon asked.

"Eddie Thomas? You mean that young'un that went missing? Hold on now, what the hell're you suggesting here?" Rudolph struggled to his feet. "You saying I took that boy to hold over the government?" His face was blood red, and he looked like he might wrest Langdon from his seat.

"I'm asking if you took him to replace your own son?" Langdon stood to face the man. "So as to get your wife back. The plan was never to turn the boy back over, was it? What were you going to do?"

"Get out of my house, goddammit."

"Answer the question."

"No. No I didn't. I wouldn't steal no little boy. Never."

Langdon believed him.

~ ~ ~ ~ ~

"They're sticking to their story," Bart said. "They claim they have nothing to do with Eddie Thomas. They don't like the Covid restrictions, but they'd never take a young boy and threaten to kill him." They were sitting in the command post at the police station. They were the only two there, the others all out chasing down leads in a last desperate attempt to find the kidnapped boy.

"What'd they say about coming to my house?" Langdon asked.

"Strong said they just wanted to rattle your cage a little. You did go into his place of business and headbutt him."

"Because he was carrying on an affair with the mother of little Eddie," Langdon said. "Who, by the way, is now dead."

"Said he had nothing to do with that. Thought his wife was having him followed, got angry, and went out to the cottage and drank himself to sleep. Woke up with the police pounding on the door."

"What about her car parked on the next street over?"

"Claims to know nothing about that."

They were at a table that seated twelve. The four corners of the room had cubicle desks with computers on them. A dry-erase board with names, places, numbers, and more filled one wall. Pictures of the PD staff down through the years adorned the opposite wall.

"What'd the officers say who picked him up?" Langdon asked.

"Said he was pretty dazed and confused."

"Hungover? Or in shock from having killed somebody?"

"Definitely reeked of alcohol."

"Suppose if you murdered somebody, it might prompt you to tip a few back."

"Could be."

Langdon looked at the clock. It was almost 8:00. "I went to have a conversation with Rudolph Morin. It turns out his wife is having an affair with Martin Thomas."

"Am I the only one in this town not getting laid?" Bart asked.

"Also turns out that Rudolph and Ann's marriage went downhill after their infant son died."

"Died?"

"SIDS. Under a year old. Be about the same age as Eddie Thomas, if he was still alive."

"Huh," Bart leaned his bulk forward over the table. "You thinkin' that Rudolph might've gone and gotten himself a replacement to win the heart of his wife back?"

"Thought had crossed my mind."

"He the same size as Dalí?"

"Not at all. But Danny T. saw him talking with a guy who could be. Was trying to get a message to Ann."

"You know who this guy is?"

"Husband of Ann's Yoga instructor. Guy by the name of Sawyer Delisle."

"I'll have a couple guys go have a chat with him," Bart said.

"Right enough," Langdon said.

Bart's phone buzzed, and he answered it. After a few grunted questions, he hung up, turning back to Langdon. "Nobody home at that artist's house. Rowan Coffin. No lights on. No cars in the drive. Locked up tight as a clam's ass at high tide."

Chapter 31

It was just about 11 o'clock, one hour before the witching hour, the time when All Hallows' Eve changed over to All Hallows' Day. It was a time to honor saints and martyrs, a holiday that somehow had taken on spooky connotations over the years, probably because of this celebration of the dead.

Langdon was in the command center with Bart, Martin Thomas, Jackson Brooks, and one officer he didn't know. The others were out hunting for Rudolph Morin or providing logistical support to the National Guard troops, who were busy containing the protesters and counter protesters on the Mall. The governor had been strangely quiet, avoiding ordering a curfew on the streets of Brunswick, seemingly intent on not allowing the kidnapper to claim even the least accomplishment.

Bart had sent a patrol car out to bring Rudolph in after Langdon had shared the information about the young infant boy dead from SIDS and his obsession with finding his wife and bringing her home again. Rudolph had not been home. A BOLO had been put out on him but, so far, no luck. Sawyer and Karen Delisle had proven to be of no help. Under duress, they gave the address at the Pleasant Motel for Ann. It was there that he had planned to deliver the message on the following day. The message pretty much just contained what Rudolph had told Langdon, that he loved her, and would let her do more stuff if she'd just come back. Nothing about a replacement son.

Bart had just emerged from the interrogation room where he'd been taking another crack at Rick Strong and Earl Franklin, to no avail. The police had been holding off sending them down to Portland while they saw how the midnight deadline played out. Rick had seemingly opened up and spilled his guts, allowing that he hated the mask mandate, business restrictions, thought the pandemic was a hoax, was a philanderer, was often inappropriate with his female staff, had a kept mistress in an apartment, carried on an affair with Jill Thomas, had attacked Langdon and Chabal in their home—but had *not* kidnapped Eddie nor killed Jill.

A television flickered in the corner, waiting for the final impassioned plea from Martin that had been filmed earlier and played every hour on the hour since six o'clock.

"They won't really kill him, will they?" Martin asked. "I mean, what good would that do?"

"I can't imagine they want to add murder to the list of crimes against them," Jackson Brooks said. As the head of MCU for the state police in Maine, Brooks had been in many terrible situations, but the strain of this particular case showed clearly on his face.

"They'll let him go, you'll see," Bart said. "It was all just a publicity stunt to draw attention to the mask mandate and business restrictions."

"Why wouldn't the governor just pretend to ease up until Eddie was set free?" Martin asked in a small voice. "Then she could re-impose anything she wanted. Once my boy was let go."

"There was the threat that Salvador Dalí would abduct and kill a child every day if that happened," Langdon said.

"You give people like this an inch and they think they can keep taking," Brooks said.

"We're not talking a business negotiation here," Martin said. "We're talking about a human life. A little boy. *My* little boy." His eyes flashed angrily.

Langdon had his concerns about Eddie being let go. Whoever had taken him had most likely killed Jill Thomas, and it was also likely that the boy could ID his kidnapper or where he'd been held or something that would lead authorities to the abductor and murderer. There was a theory out there, he knew, that it was always easier to kill the second time around. There was no death penalty in Maine, but those charges should be sufficient to keep the kidnapper behind bars for quite some time. Whoever *he* was, he couldn't gamble on letting the boy go.

"And it's not a political decision," Martin continued. "These people who run the government don't get to decide whether or not my little boy lives or dies. They don't. It's not their choice. The only person who gets to sit in judgment of Eddie's life is God. And God would not let him die."

"We can only hope for the best," Langdon said.

"This person is going to kill Eddie. I just know it," Martin said, desperation tinging his words. "I can tell that he is a cultus man. Evil at the core."

Bart turned the volume up on the television as a news anchor came onto the screen with the now familiar banner below, WHERE IS THE BOY?

"We are just one hour away from the threatened execution of a four-year-old boy," the woman said, her face somber and lacking the usual dramatic urgency to her voice. "The governor has made it clear that she will not negotiate with the kidnapper. We go next to Alyssa Ward who is outside the Brunswick Police Department right now. Alyssa, do you have any updates for us?"

The camera changed to show the outside of the police department where Langdon and the others sat. A small crowd had gathered, but most of those still up at this hour were down on the Mall. There had been talk of marching on the police station, but the National Guard had dissuaded the crowd by their overwhelming presence. A young woman with dark hair was bundled in a parka and mittens, a scarf around her neck, but no hat on her head. She was standing next to the spokesman for the Maine State Police.

"Can you tell us if you have any leads on the kidnapper?" the newswoman asked. The night sky was overcast, only a dim light filtering through from the waxing moon.

Langdon knew there were no leads. The spokesperson for the police would now proceed to say a lot of nothing, the message behind the words being that the police had met a dead-end. He'd mention that they had two suspects in custody and were searching for a person of interest. Langdon didn't believe Rudolph was a kidnapper and a murderer. He was a lobsterman who'd been hurt by the Covid restrictions, true, but he seemed genuine in his assertion that he'd never endanger a boy, or take the child of another, knowing the pain that that loss could inflict.

Strong's house and cottage were being gone over again with a fine-tooth comb, the evidence teams hoping to find a clue, the slightest indication of where Eddie might be, anything that would lead them to his whereabouts. Langdon didn't much like the man, nor his brother-in-law, Earl. As a matter of fact, he detested both men, one for the arrogance, the other for the ignorance, and both for the entitlement that they felt. At the same time, he had his doubts that either of them would kill a small boy.

What if the plan was to release Eddie, something they weren't able to do from jail? If they admitted to knowing his whereabouts, they were confessing their guilt. But if they were held captive, what would happen to *their* captive? Working on the theory that they were indeed the abductors, was there a third party involved, or was Eddie Thomas trembling in some dank basement or closet with no food and water? Langdon shivered. Rick and Earl couldn't admit their knowledge, not without admitting their guilt, and any confession would lead to quite a bit of jail time.

The television crackled, drawing Langdon's attention back, this time to a video he'd already seen several times that day. Martin Thomas stood next to the governor at a podium. The Maine state flag hung behind them, the blue material with a moose, a pine tree, a seaman, and a farmer representing the traditional values of Maine. Below the north star was the state motto, *Dirigo*, 'I lead.'

"My role as governor dictates that I do what is best for the people of Maine. Yesterday we saw the single highest increase in cases, hospitalizations, and positivity rates from the Covid-19 virus. If we do not contain this outbreak, we will have opened a Pandora's Box that will not be easily closed. As a result, we will be returning to lower indoor gathering limits, postponing bar and tasting room re-opening's for now, and will be removing several states from quarantine exempt status. Maine people realize that this is a team effort of social and personal responsibility. We don't drive on the wrong side of the road. We wear seat belts. We wear masks to prevent the transmission of the virus. Above all, we, the people of Maine, will not be held hostage by a sole malcontent, nor by radical influencers from out of state, but will stand firm, shoulder to shoulder, and reject domestic terrorism. At the same time, we beg of the person responsible for abducting Eddie Thomas to let the boy go. I believe that his father, Martin Thomas, would like to say more on that matter."

The governor stepped to the side and back a step and Martin Thomas approached the center of the podium. He cleared his throat, staring down at his hands, before raising his red-rimmed eyes to stare straight into the camera.

"I don't know who you are and I don't care. Just let my boy go. He has done you no harm. It is not Eddie who brought the pandemic to the world, to the U.S., to Maine, to Brunswick. He is an innocent child, for God's sake."

Martin gulped in a huge breath of air and then exhaled with a slight slurping sound. He took out a handkerchief and blew his nose.

"Eddie has a birthday coming up in early December. He will be five years old. Next fall, the virus willing, he will be starting kindergarten. He likes Star Wars action figures, and has a knack for painting that surpasses both me and his mother."

Martin blew his nose again. His normally perfectly-immaculate presentation had broken down, his hair ruffled along with his jacket, bow tie askew, and stubble on his chin.

"Eddie has recently lost his mother. Let him come home so that we can recover together. I beg of you. Let my son go."

The news anchor came back on the screen, and Bart turned it off. "We are doing everything we can," he said quietly.

"I know," Martin said. If anything, his disarray from the earlier recording had grown worse. "What is the next step?"

"Try to find Rudolph Morin to see if he has any involvement," Bart said.

"Then what?"

"We wait and hope for the best, Mr. Thomas."

Martin gave an almost imperceptible nod of his head. "I am going home in case the kidnapper drops Eddie off there. I will have my cell phone with me. Call me if you have any updates. Anything at all. Please find my son."

The local cop, state cop, and PI watched as Martin Thomas shuffled his way out of the command post. Langdon stood up suddenly and followed him through the door and down the hallway. He waited until Martin stepped out into the parking lot before laying his hand on the man's shoulder.

"It's going to be okay," Langdon said.

Martin looked around wearily. "How do you know?"

"Can I do anything?"

"Find my son."

"Would it help if I came and sat with you?"

"No. I am not very good company right now." Martin turned and started walking to his bright orange Prius.

"Do you have somebody to be with you?" Langdon asked. "Ann?"

Martin paused and turned. "Ann and I are on a hiatus until this has been put behind me. I am fine by myself."

Chapter 32

Sunday, November 1st

Langdon and Chabal were nursing at least their fourth cup of coffee of a very long night when the phone buzzed just after 5:00 a.m. It was Bart, beckoning them to the station, his voice, normally gruff, subdued. They drove past the Mall, empty now at this time of the morning, picket signs and trash scattered about, the only remnants of the crowds that had surged there the night before.

The command post, desolate the night before, was now crowded with police officers, politicians, National Guard, representatives of the governor, and various others.

As they entered the room, Jackson Brooks walked up to the television monitor bringing a hush to the command post that was quieter than the night before when there had been only the four of them there. Faces were somber. Langdon sensed that most knew what was about to be said or shown. The prognosis did not look good.

"This arrived this morning," Jackson Brooks said. "The media has agreed to hold off on airing this while we research the authenticity." He hit play.

The television hummed to life. A light illuminated a small space that was swaying to-and-fro, making Langdon's head churn, lack of sleep, coffee, and lack of food perhaps contributing to this. There was the figure of a man standing over a bundle lying at his feet.

The man turned and showcased the familiar Salvador Dalí mask. Langdon realized that they were on a boat, and that the bobbing of the screen was the waves rocking the vessel.

"I have been quite clear in what the repercussions would be should the governor ignore my demands," Dalí said. "The virus is a hoax, perpetuated by the government, the muckamucks who hold us, the people of the United States, hostage every day. They attempt to take away our rights. Close our businesses. Make us wear masks. Just so as to flout the power they have, like the olden plantation owner snapping his whip. Enough is enough. We will no longer be held captive to a hostile authority. Surrealism is destructive, but it destroys only what it considers to be shackles limiting our vision. Thus, I suggest, that people rise up and throw off the bonds that hold us prisoner. It is time to rise against a tyranny that has subjugated us for too long. If the price for this spark to freedom is the life of an innocent, so be it."

Dalí turned his back and lifted up what looked to be a figure wrapped in a black trash bag with duct tape covering most of the surface. "You had your chance to save this life," Dalí said, looking directly into the camera. He then dropped the figure over the side of the boat. He picked up a flashlight and video camera and shone it onto the angry waves to show it bobbing, and then followed the rope back to the deck where it was attached to a concrete block.

Langdon's eyes followed the arc of the flashlight as Dalí picked up the anchor meant to send Eddie Thomas to Davy Jones' locker, and that is when he saw it. On the wall, in the cabin, was the decorative antique steering wheel that he'd seen before. Then the flashlight changed course, pinning the concrete block balanced on the side of the boat.

"Let the revolution begin." Dalí pushed the concrete anchor over the side and again shone the light to show the bagged figure sucked underneath the water. The flashlight went out and then the video went black.

Jackson Brooks looked out over the muted room. "We need to find this bastard. Anybody have any ideas?"

"It can't be Strong and Franklin," a blue uniform said. "They been in lock-up."

"Unless they had an accomplice," Bart said. "Or the video was made at another time to be delivered today. There was no time stamp on it. The techs are reviewing the original as we speak."

Langdon cleared his throat. "I know that boat."

"What?" Brooks burst out.

"There is a decorative antique steering wheel in the cabin. I've seen it before. The boat is Rudolph Morin's."

Brooks rewound to the spot where the wheel was visible and froze it. "Are you sure?" he asked.

"Absolutely," Langdon said.

"Son of a bitch," Bart said. "Dalton, where do we stand with Rudolph?"

"He never came home last night, sir. We got two officers outside his house out to Bailey Island, and a BOLO out on him, but so far, nothing."

"Find out if his boat is at its mooring. Get a car out there right now. Call in the sheriff to see if he has anybody closer. Hell, get the Coast Guard over there, give them something to do," Bart said. "Go, now."

"He moors at Mackerel Cove. His boat is the *Annika*," Langdon said.

Bart swung his head around. "Named after his wife?"

"I assume."

"Okay, people," Bart said. "This is the situation. Rudolph and Annika Morin lost a baby to SIDS about four years ago. She recently left him for another man. He has been trying to get her back. The thought is that he may have kidnapped the boy to replace their own, all in an attempt to get her to come back to him."

"But why kill the boy?" Brooks asked.

"Maybe she wanted no part of him, especially with a kidnapped kid. Hell, the guy is ugly as hell. He makes me look like Rock

Hudson," Bart said. "Eddie has seen his face, so he dumps him in the Atlantic and tries to put it off on the anti-maskers."

"He's pretty much an anti-masker, anti-government-interference kind of guy," Langdon said, but something was tickling his mind.

"Or maybe he faked it?" Brooks said. "Everybody thinks the kid is dead, and him and Annika ride off into the sunset together?"

"Max, add Annika Morin to that BOLO. Check toll booths, bus stations, train depots, airports, you know the drill. Let's find Rudolph and Annika. Maybe we'll get lucky, and Eddie will be with them."

The room suddenly buzzed with energy, breaking the gloom and doom the video had produced. Purpose and hope had been provided, at the very least something to do. Langdon was watching the video play through for the third time when Bart came back into the room.

"We got him," he said. "Rudolph Morin just showed up at home and is in custody. He's being brought in as we speak."

~ ~ ~ ~ ~

Langdon and Bart sat across the table from Rudolph. It was not the dimly-lit interrogation room of movies and televisions but a spare room that housed no one-way mirror, actually had no windows at all, and had several framed pictures on the walls. The seats were padded and the floor was carpeted. It was now 8:00 a.m.

The *Annika*, Rudolph's lobstering boat, had been secured in its mooring at Mackerel Cove. Forensics was on its way, but there would be no immediate information. If the boy were to be found, it'd be crucial for Rudolph to tell them, that is, if he hadn't really dumped him over the side to dispose of evidence that could send him to prison for life.

Rudolph's normally puffy cheeks had added an outer layer of swollen redness to match his eyes and nose. "What in hell is going on?" he asked.

"You tell us," Bart said.

Rudolph looked at Langdon. "Is this because I fired you?"

"We're trying to find Eddie Thomas," Bart said.

"What in the good goddamn does that have to do with me?" A light flickered in his eyes and he swung his eyes back at Langdon. "You told him that I took that boy to get Annika back, didn't you?"

Langdon didn't say anything.

"Did you take the boy?" Bart asked.

"I told him already," Rudolph said. "I didn't take no goddamn boy. Wouldn't do no such thing. Not now. Not ever."

"Where were you last night?" Bart asked.

"What goddamn business is it of yours where I was?"

"We received a new video of that kidnapped boy, Eddie Thomas. Just about five years old. The abductor dumped him over the side of a boat into the ocean. Killed him. Murdered him," Bart said.

Rudolph looked at Bart and back at Langdon. "I didn't kill no boy."

"Where were you last night?" Bart asked.

"I was out."

"Out where?"

"Drinking."

Bart looked patiently at him. "Drinking where, Rudolph?"

"Down to the Tin-Top."

"The Tin-Top?" Bart raised his eyebrows. "Is that a bar? Don't think I know it."

Rudolph looked sullenly at him. "Guy over the bridge on Orr's Island has a place a few fellows get together at."

"Like a speakeasy?" Langdon asked. Bart shot him a look that told him to shut up.

Rudolph scowled. "Don't know what no speakeasy is. Just a place for guys to hang out."

"What's the guy's name who owns the place?"

"What do you need to know that for?"

Bart stood up and leaned over the table. "You are here on suspicion of murder. We need to verify your whereabouts."

"Leo. Leo Hall. He can vouch for me."

"What time you leave?" Bart asked.

"Didn't."

"You stayed at this drinking establishment all night?" Langdon asked.

"I told you, it's just a place guys get together. We throw a few bucks in to help pay for the alcohol. Nice little set up behind his house. Sometimes we play cards or cribbage."

"You didn't answer the question," Bart said.

"I was over-the-bay drunk," Rudolph said. "Don't rightly remember, but woke up on Leo's couch this morning, got in my truck, and drove home. Now, here I am."

"You take a boat ride last night?" Bart asked.

"Boat ride? Hell, no. Told you I was buzzed to beat Jesus. Wouldn't go out on no boat in that condition," Rudolph said angrily, and then furrowed his brow. "Why?"

"You said you were 'over the bay'."

"What? Goddammit, man. I was just saying I had too much liquor. I didn't mean I went out on the bay."

Langdon had heard the old-timers use that expression before but thought it was getting less play as of late. "The thing is, Rudolph," he said. "The boat that the boy was dumped overboard from? It was your boat. It was the *Annika*."

"My boat didn't go nowhere last night, much less dump a child into the sea," Rudolph said.

"So you say," Langdon said. "But it was on the video. Plain as day."

"It couldn't be." Rudolph's anger had changed to confusion. "How'd ya know it was the *Annika*?"

"I recognized the antique wheel in the cabin," Langdon said. "The one your ancestor, Raymond was it? Took off his sinking vessel in the War of 1812."

"Lots of people got wheels up in their cabins. Is that all you got?"

"It was pretty distinctive."

There was a knock on the door. An officer motioned to Bart, who stepped out into the hallway with him.

"I didn't take no boy. You got to believe me. Wouldn't never do that," Rudolph said.

"It was your boat, Rudolph. Does anybody else have access to it?"

"No." Rudolph was sullen now. "Nobody going out on my boat but me."

"You see the dilemma, don't you?" Langdon asked. "Do you keep a spare key on it?"

"Sure enough," Rudolph said grudgingly. "But nobody knows it's there. Hangs right behind that old wheel."

Another tickle nuzzled Langdon's consciousness as Bart came back in the room and sat down. He sighed heavily and stared at Rudolph quietly, making the man squirm in his chair.

"Got travel plans today?" Bart asked.

"No. Not going anywhere," Rudolph said.

"Not even to Portland?"

"What? Why would I go down to Portland on a Sunday. No."

"Portland, Oregon, Rudolph."

"What in thunderation are you talking about?"

"It seems your wife has booked plane tickets for two people to Portland for this afternoon out of Boston. 5:05 p.m."

"Don't know where my wife is. Ask him." Rudolph pointed at Langdon. "I hired him to find her, and he couldn't or *wouldn't* do it, and I got no idea where that goddamn woman is. If I did, I'd straighten her out, real quick, I would."

"What do you mean by that?" Bart asked.

"Nothing. Nothing at all."

"The plane tickets are for Annika and James Morin."

"My son?"

"What is your middle name, Rudolph?" Bart asked.

"What's that got to do with anything?"

"Your middle name is James. Same as your boy's was," Bart said.

"Don't know what you're talking about."

There was another knock, and Jackson Brooks came into the room. "Mind if I sit in?"

Langdon stood up. "I was just leaving. Take my seat."

"Where you going?" Bart asked.

"I gotta see about a muckamuck," Langdon said.

"A what?"

"Tell you later. Make sure that Annika and James don't get on that plane."

Chapter 33

"I think the kidnapper might be Martin Thomas," Langdon said to Chabal. He'd grabbed two coffees at the Lenin Stop Coffee Shop and was currently sitting in the office of the Coffee Dog Bookstore with his wife.

"You think Martin killed his own boy?" Chabal asked. They sat at their desk's facing each other in their swivel chairs with coffee cups in hand.

"No. I think he faked both the kidnapping and his son's death."

"What makes you think that?" Chabal smiled. "Not that I'm disagreeing. You know I trust your instincts."

"There's been something bothering me since Thursday. Remember the kidnapping video?"

Chabal nodded. "Sure."

"And how the guy used the word 'muckamuck'?"

"Yeah, we looked it up, didn't we? Meant important people, or people that think they are important, something like that, right?"

Langdon leaned forward. "Something's been tickling what little is left of my brain about muckamuck. I couldn't quite place it. And then last night, Martin called the kidnapper a 'cultus man'. So I looked it up. Cultus can pertain to cults, but the original meaning stems from a bad man. Its origin is Chinook Jargon."

"Chinook Jargon?" Chabal said. "Again? That was where the word muckamuck came from."

"Exactly. As soon as I saw that, it clicked in who I heard use the word before. It was Martin Thomas the first time I sat down with him, Jill, and Bart. It was when they got in the fight about him being drunk and her having an affair with Rick Strong. Martin called Rick a 'high and mighty muckamuck,' or something like that."

"What is Chinook Jargon?"

Langdon looked at his computer screen and read from it. "It is an extinct pidgin composed of elements from Chinook, Nootka, English, French, and other languages, formerly used in the Pacific Northwest of North America."

"The Pacific Northwest," Chabal said slowly. "As in, Portland area."

"Bart just found out that Ann and James Morin have plane tickets from Logan to Portland, Oregon, later today. That, coupled with Martin using the same Pacific Northwest slang reference with the word 'muckamuck,' makes me think that *he* is the real kidnapper."

"Jack called this morning," Chabal said slowly, "while you were down to the station. He couldn't find anything on the videos, but he did point out that the boy and his kidnapper had a fondness for each other. Once when Eddie didn't have a mask on, he smiled up at the guy. I played it back, and it was indeed a very trusting and loving look. And then another time they bowed their heads together, and the kidnapper whispers something to him that seems to settle Eddie down."

"Father and son," Langdon said.

"Why would he kidnap his own son?"

"I don't know." Langdon shrugged. "Let's look at the facts. He was alone with Eddie when the boy disappeared. He's carrying on an affair with Ann Morin, who more than likely knows where Rudolph hides his spare key to his boat, and now it turns out that Ann and James Morin have plane tickets to Portland this afternoon."

"You're thinking that Ann is taking Eddie to Portland, Oregon, as James Morin?"

"Yes, I do."

"Don't they need to provide identification?"

"Not for a child that age," Langdon said. "I'm betting Ann even has a social security card that says James Morin on it."

"You think Eddie Thomas is alive?"

"I do."

"Do you know where he is?"

"I'm betting he's at the cottage of that artist. Rowan Coffin. What a perfect place to hide out. An abandoned house you have the key for."

"Didn't the police go check it out?"

"Yep. Lights out. No cars in the driveway. Nobody home," Langdon said. "But, don't you suppose if you were hiding out, you might put shades up in at least one room, or go in the basement, and perhaps hide your vehicles so nobody knows you're there?"

"Could be," Chabal said and stood. "Suppose we're going for a ride."

The cottage was down a dirt lane off of the Harpswell Neck Road. Langdon was glad they were in the Jeep as it was a bumpy, twisty, path down toward Middle Bay. The mailboxes had all been up on the main road with no marker at the driveway, but GPS seemed to indicate it was off to the left. Langdon went on past, turned around, and came back past the entrance, pulling off to the side as best he could. It was possible they'd need to make a quick exit.

"Got your pistol?" Langdon asked.

He knew she did. He had watched with interest as she'd removed it from her desk and pulled her blouse off before putting on the holster that hung on her left side, the straps over her shoulders and underneath her breasts. He'd been disappointed when she put her shirt back on.

Chabal reached under her blouse and pulled out the SIG P365. It had been a recent gift from Langdon for her birthday. "Sure enough," she said.

"We'll circle the cottage looking for their cars," Langdon said.

"Gotcha, boss," Chabal said in a mocking tone. "I'll follow your lead."

Langdon smiled. It'd taken some getting used to that she was a better shot than he was, but facts were facts. "Don't think we should need the guns, but somebody did kill Jill Thomas, so keep your head down."

"Sure thing, boss." Chabal opened the door and got out. "Can't sit here all day."

Langdon removed his Glock from the console and got out as well. He considered repeating his warning to be careful, but knew he'd be teased for it and decided to lead the way off the road into the woods. It was rough going. Straggly evergreen trees were littered amongst strewn rocks, some the size of a minivan, while their feet stumbled over a mixed scree of pebbles and chunks of stone the size of soccer balls. They were almost upon the cottage before Langdon spotted it.

The windows were dark, but Langdon could see curtains blocking anyone from seeing in, and possibly, light. It seemed serene, almost something out of a fairy tale, but then again, most fairy tales were not actually tranquil behind the scenes. He held up his hand, and they backed carefully away to a vantage point of the driveway. It was, indeed, empty.

It was now 11:00 a.m. Langdon figured that if Ann Morin was indeed taking Eddie Thomas to Logan airport in Boston, they'd need to leave no later than 1:00 for a 5:05 p.m. flight. He began a scuttling walk away from the drive, careful to stay out of sight of the cottage. The forest growth was a mix of Eastern White Pines and other fir trees with the occasional red maple thrown in, giving ample cover.

It was at the back of the house that they found the two cars. They were under a tarp. Langdon picked up a corner and saw Ann's Corolla and Martin's Prius. He looked over his shoulder at Chabal, who mouthed the word, "Jackpot."

Langdon carefully put the tarp back down and motioned Chabal to follow him away from the cottage. After a few steps, he realized that there was another road on this side, from which the cars most likely had come in, rough but passable.

"What's the plan?" Chabal asked.

"Thought I'd text Bart that they are here and then go in and brace them," Langdon replied.

"Why don't we just wait for the police?"

"That's all we need is to have police cars come careening down the road, sirens blasting, warning them to get away."

"You could suggest they come quietly."

"They could be headed to the airport at any moment."

"We can keep watch here and… apprehend them if they try to drive away."

Langdon sighed and looked toward the cottage, now out of sight.

Chabal laughed. "Just giving you a hard time. I know your manhood has been questioned. Martin hires you to find the kidnapper, and he *is* the kidnapper. Didn't think much of your abilities, did he? Let's go brace the motherfucker."

It was Langdon's turn to laugh. First, at her good read of him, and second, at her foul language which, once common, seemed to appear these days only in moments of great tension. Middle age, he supposed. "Right-o," he said.

Chapter 34

They worked their way carefully to the back of the cottage. Langdon felt a bit silly with his Glock out, as it couldn't have been a more serene setting. Middle Bay was the view through the trees, glittering in the sun. A boat motor could be heard coming from that direction. No other houses were visible. The back windows of the cottage were completely covered by heavy curtains.

Langdon made his way down the side of the dwelling, not bothering to crouch below the windows, while Chabal covered him. She then followed him to the front corner. He imagined they worked with the precision of a practiced SWAT team, and then almost laughed aloud at the thought. He certainly hoped that he was not endangering his wife.

"Ready?" he whispered.

Chabal nodded.

He moved to the steps centered in the front of the cottage leading up to a porch that ran the length of the façade. Three steps. He skipped the middle one, Chabal just behind him. As his foot came down on the porch, the front door opened. Martin Thomas stood framed in the entranceway. His mouth made a perfectly round O.

Sitting at a table behind him was Eddie Thomas eating a bowl of cereal. It was the perfect complement to the tranquility of the day. Father and son together. A box of Cheerios on the table next to a half-gallon of milk. *If it wasn't so darn sinister*, Langdon thought, leveling his pistol.

"Hello, Martin," he said. "Do you mind if we come in?"

Martin stood unmoving as if turned to stone. Langdon lowered his Glock to his side and stepped forward, forcing the man into motion, backpedaling into the kitchen.

"What do you want?" Martin asked.

"I was hired to do a job. Figured I'd do it," Langdon said, his eyes sweeping the kitchen.

It looked to have been updated recently, the appliances shining silver and modern, not from the '70s like many summer cottages. There appeared to be no weapons present, although there was a block of knives on the counter.

Martin put his hand on Eddie's shoulder. "Take your cereal into your room," he said. "I need to talk to this man."

"Why do you have a gun?" Eddie asked.

Langdon didn't know what to say, so, said nothing. He put the Glock in his waistband and let his shirt hang over it.

"Off to your room," Martin said.

Eddie dutifully stood up, grabbed his bowl, and went down a short hall and into a room, shutting the door behind him. He seemed to be a very obedient child.

"Where's Ann?" Langdon asked.

"How should I know?" Martin asked. "I told you I haven't seen her in over a week."

"Funny thing about that," Langdon said. "Her car is under the tarp next to yours."

Martin sat down at the table as if his legs had been knocked from under him. "She went for a walk. Get some fresh air. I was just going out to check and see if I could see her."

Langdon nodded at Chabal, and she checked the small living room, and then went down the hallway to the three bedrooms and one bathroom. "Nothing," she said, returning. "Just the boy."

"Keep an eye out for her, would you?" Langdon asked. He sat down across the table from Martin. "Why'd you hire me if you were the one who took Eddie? I mean, what were you thinking?"

"Jill insisted that we hire you. She'd read all about you in that case involving Senator Mercer and thought you were an American Sherlock Holmes."

"Why didn't you get rid of me after she was killed?" Langdon danced around the topic of whether or not Martin was the murderer. He'd get to that.

"Thought it would be bad form. Would make me look guilty."

Langdon nodded. That made sense. "Why'd you kidnap your own son?"

Martin closed his eyes and leaned his head back as if searching for the answer in the dark recesses of his mind. Langdon was about to prompt him again when Martin brought his head down and forward and his eyes snapped open. "She told me she was going to go for full custody."

"Jill?"

Martin nodded. His eyes blazed fiercely with the thought. "She hadn't filed yet, but she told me, threatened me, that she was going to do it. Said I was a drunken control freak with no emotions. That I would burn any sort of empathy, passion, and kindness out of Eddie. My son. She was going to try and prevent me from seeing my own son."

"Most people just hire a good lawyer," Chabal said from the doorway.

"I hit Eddie once," Martin said. "She was going to insist that a therapist talk to him, get him to tell on me. On his own father. No, I wasn't going to let her take him away from me."

"I think I understand the most of it," Langdon said. "You kidnapped Eddie, faked his death, and Ann and Eddie have a 5:05 flight today to Portland. Eddie would be traveling under the name of her dead son, James Morin. From there, they'd go to that beach town where you inherited the house and wait for things to cool down here so you could go join them. You and Ann would then get married, but she'd keep her maiden name, and Eddie would become James Morin, and the three of you would live happily ever after."

"Very good," Martin said. "I may have underestimated you."

"What I don't get," Langdon said, "is why the whole charade about holding the government hostage in an attempt to get them to loosen up their Covid restrictions?"

"I figured I could kill two birds with one stone," Martin said. "There are people out there who truly believe the nonsense that Covid is a hoax. There are people who refuse to wear a mask, for Christ's sake."

"You thought that it would cast a shadow on the anti-maskers," Langdon said slowly. "By showing how radical they were, so radical that they'd kidnap and kill a young boy for their beliefs."

"Not just radical but plain stupid," Martin said "People believe this whole QAnon nonsense. They think that Hillary Clinton is the head of a cabal that molests and eats children. By posing the kidnapper as one of them, I was able to show their true colors. How many people were out on the Mall yesterday? A thousand? More than half of those people were supporting a deranged kidnapper who was threatening the life of a small boy just so they wouldn't have to wear a mask in public."

"That was pretty effective," Langdon said.

"It brought them out of the swamps they live in and cast a spotlight on the ridiculousness of their position."

"Were you hoping the police would target Rick Strong for the kidnapping?"

"The thought crossed my mind. He's one of them, ranting and raving all the time about government interference, but if he gets a pothole on his street, he wants it fixed immediately. He's happy to take a PPP loan, get a stimulus check, send his kids to public school, have the fire department come to his house if needed, but if they tell him to wear a mask, he goes apeshit. You're damn right I was hoping the police went after him."

"His brew pub has been hurt by the business restrictions," Langdon said. "A tad more annoying than having to wear a mask."

"To save lives," Martin said.

"Your parents died from the Covid, didn't they?" Langdon said.

"That's part of it."

"I wasn't particularly close to them, but nobody deserves to die alone like that, not just so people can go out and eat and drink. Come on, man, can't people just wait for the vaccine?"

"Plus, Strong was having an affair with your wife," Langdon said. "Another reason to steer the police toward him."

"That, too." Martin's voice was like sandpaper. "I don't know what she saw in him."

"You loved your wife still, didn't you?"

"She was the one true love of my life," Martin said softly.

"Why'd you kill her, then?"

"What?" Martin slapped his hand down hard on the table. "I didn't kill her. It was Strong that killed her. The police arrested him for it."

"They brought him in for questioning but released him with no charges," Langdon said. "This is what I think happened. Jill remembered this cottage that you look after. Maybe she even recognized something in one of the videos as being familiar, as she and you would sometimes come out here like you were on vacation, back before things went sour. Anyway, something sparked her into coming out here to see if her boy was here, little Eddie, being held captive by his own father. She snuck into the house and found Eddie in bed, but then you woke up and found her. You knew she would turn you in. You knew you'd never see your son again. Not in prison and not after. So, you murdered her. You didn't have much time. Eddie's in his room. Maybe he even saw you hurt his mommy. You had to get rid of the body. You could've just dumped the body in the ocean or buried it in the woods, but no, you thought how convenient it would be to make it look like Rick Strong killed her. You knew about his place at Small Point. Maybe you even followed

Jill there before. So, you dumped her body where it would be found not far from his place. It was just a bonus when it turned out he was there alone that night, although that might've prevented you from planting some evidence there. Did you actually go to the house and realize his Mustang was parked out front?"

"That's not true. None of it," Martin said. "I loved Jill. I would never have harmed her. No matter what she did."

"Kidnapping is bad enough, but murder?" Langdon said. "You'll be old and wrinkled before they let you out of Thomaston, or Warren, or whatever the prison is called now."

"I wasn't even here that night," Martin said. "I was home the whole night. The police woke me up with the news in the morning before the sun came up. It had to be Strong. I'd bet a pound to a penny he's abused women before. She was sleeping with him. I'm thinking they were having a little romp at his place and things got a little too kinky, or maybe she pissed him off and he belted her one. Either way, before he knew it, she was dead. He tried to dispose of the body but effed that up as well. He was probably drunk."

"I don't think he killed her," Langdon said. "And I'm starting to believe that you didn't murder her, either."

"Why don't you put that gun down?" Annika Morin stood in the hallway with a shotgun aimed at Chabal who was keeping watch out the front door. "Before I blow your guts all over the wall."

Chapter 35

"Where'd you come from?" Chabal asked with a perplexed look on her face.

"Not so smart to park on side of road. I recognized stupid bumper stickers on back of Jeep. Started to walk right past it before it clicked. Goff Langdon and his little wifey." Annika stepped forward and raised the shotgun to her shoulder. "Now put the gun gently on the floor and kick it over here."

Chabal did as she was told. Langdon reached his hand to the butt of his Glock as Annika focused on Chabal. She proved to be too cagey for that, swinging the large barrel of the shotgun toward him, almost in lazy contempt. He put both his hands flat on the table.

"There's trap door in bedroom under chair. I came in through there, picking this little baby," Annika waved the shotgun, "up on the way from trunk of my car."

"You did it, didn't you?" Langdon said.

"Martin, get up and move over next to me," Annika said. "And then you sit down in his seat," she said to Chabal with a wave of the shotgun.

"You did what?" Martin asked, looking at Annika and not moving.

"He's talking about framing Rudolph, honey," Annika said. "Sure, that is me. I knew where he kept spare key. Once the police catch on to whose boat it was, they'll go over it with fine-tooth comb, and you know what? They're going to find Eddie's DNA all over it. I'm sure Rudolph was just sitting home watching television by himself like he does every night. No alibi. His boat. Video. DNA. He's going to take fall. Go to prison for murder."

"Not what I was speaking of," Langdon said, "but, in point of fact, he does have an alibi. He went to some place called the Tin-Top and got drunk and slept on the couch there."

Annika looked nonplussed. "He needs to pay for what he did."

"What did he do?"

"He killed my baby." Annika's face was masked in anger. "Stupid fucking *svoloch*."

Langdon assumed that 'svoloch' was a bad thing. "He put him down for the night. In the morning, he was dead. It is horrible, but it happens."

"He killed him with his stupidity. But God brought him back for me."

"Sounds like it was an accident to me," Langdon said. "As a matter of fact, he's pretty torn up by it. There is rarely any fault assigned in a SIDS death."

Chabal had inched forward a step toward Annika, who now turned the shotgun back toward her. "You stay right where you are until I figure out what we're going to do with you. I'd rather not have to clean up blood before flying to Portland."

"You're not going to shoot anybody, Annika," Martin said. "This ends here."

Annika laughed harshly. "I'm not going to jail. *We're* not going to jail. I'm going to take James and fly to Portland and rent a car and drive to Cannon Beach. That is where we'll be, in the mansion overlooking the Pacific Ocean, when you are able to join us."

"You know the boy is actually Eddie, and not James, don't you, Annika?" Langdon asked.

"He is James Morin. He is my son." Her eyes blazed fiercely.

"James Morin is dead," Langdon said.

"The whole point of this was that nobody would get hurt, much less killed," Martin said. "I'm not a murderer."

"If you are too afraid to get your hands dirty, I will do it. Taras taught me to use a weapon. How to kill." Annika's voice had risen to a shrill whine.

"Who is Taras?" Martin asked.

"He is why I am here. He is why I am owed. I will have my fairy-tale ending. I will."

"Did Jill Thomas show up here in the middle of the night?" Langdon asked. "Looking for Eddie. Is that why you killed her?"

"I told you, Rick Strong killed Jill," Martin said.

"No, he didn't," Langdon said. He nodded at Annika. "She killed Jill."

Martin swung around and stood up to face Annika. "Tell me that's not true," he said.

Annika stared at him before letting out a long sigh. "I had no choice. It's like he said. I woke in middle of night to sound in hallway, and I found her in doorway to James's room. I grabbed her around neck and pulled her back out of there, and squeezed and squeezed, and after bit, she was moving no more. I had no choice. She would blow up our plans just like these two. We deserve to be happy. Don't let them come between our love."

"You killed Jill?" Martin stood slumped in the middle of the kitchen. "It wasn't Strong? It was you? Why?"

"I told you, honey, it was for us. She was going to ruin everything. What's it matter, anyway? The whore cheated on you. Left you. Wanted to take your son from you. She deserved to die."

Langdon carefully slid his hand under the table and pulled his Glock from his waistband, laying it on his lap. "How'd you get her car out there and then get back here without a vehicle?" he asked.

Annika laughed harshly. "Guy who owns this place has scooter in shed. I put it in trunk and Jill in backseat. Dumped her in harbor. Brought car to where Martin told me she'd park when she was over there, fucking Rick. Yes, honey, she was fucking Rick. Not only did she cheat on you, but she was also going to send you to prison."

"What now?" Martin asked.

Chabal edged a step closer to Annika. She was now just about five feet from the woman.

"We tie these two up and bring them to Strong's cottage in Small Point," Annika said.

"And then what?"

"We leave them dead inside."

Martin nodded slowly. "That might work," he said.

"Then I come back and get James, and we go down to Logan and fly to Portland. We stick to plan, honey, just like we set up. When things cool down around here, you come out and join us. We'll be happy together. I will make you happy, honey. Please give me chance."

"Okay, baby. We'll do it your way." Martin stepped up to Annika.

Langdon knew it was now or never. Once they were tied up, there was no chance of survival. He pointed the Glock under the table. Annika recognized what he was doing, and she tilted the shotgun and pulled the trigger.

Martin knocked the barrel of the gun upward and the buckshot ripped into the ceiling, showering plaster down on the room like a snowstorm. Langdon held off pulling the trigger, having no clear shot, luckily, as Chabal took two steps and plowed into Annika like a strong safety on a defenseless receiver.

Annika rolled from underneath Chabal and came to one knee, the shotgun still gripped in her hands, the barrel swinging in an arc to point at Chabal on the floor. Langdon couldn't risk a shot for fear of hitting Chabal and came out of his chair, knowing that he was too late, that he couldn't prevent his wife from taking the second blast to the face.

Martin drove a fist into the side of Annika's head, and she toppled to the floor, then kicked her in the jaw and stood over her unmoving body. "I loved her," he said. "My wife. Not you. Never you."

"Daddy?" Eddie stood in the door to his bedroom. He was such a tiny human being. "What's going on?"

Chapter 36

Two weeks later

It was unseasonably warm for mid-November. Langdon, Chabal, and dog were taking a walk at Popham Beach. It was completely dog-friendly this time of the year, especially down by the fort. It was almost 60° with just a tiny breeze coming off the mainland. Dog thought it nice enough to go swimming, in between chasing birds and rolling in the sand.

"It was the Russian all along," Chabal said. "We should've figured. It's always the Russians. At least in the movies."

Langdon chuckled. "If she was better read, Annika may have realized that many fairy tales don't actually have happy endings."

"Are they going to be able to make the murder charge stick?" Chabal asked.

"They should have enough to convict, but she seems to have a fair case for an insanity plea."

"She really came to believe that Eddie Thomas was her son, James, didn't she?" Chabal said.

"I think so. Funny how grief can warp your mind."

"How about Rudolph?"

"He's been visiting Annika as often as they permit. I think the guy really loves her, in his own way."

"Even after she attempted to frame him for murder?" Chabal shook her head. "People sure be crazy."

"Maybe they're both insane," Langdon said. "What makes them so good together."

"Seems that our friend Rick Strong isn't doing so well," Chabal said with a smirk.

"Assault charges, the Maine Human Rights Commission is revisiting Raven's sexual harassment charge, and now I hear that his brew pub is being closed for health violations," Langdon said. "I'd say he's probably had better times."

"Star says that his wife is filing divorce papers, as well."

"Couldn't happen to a nicer guy," Langdon said with a grin.

"Looks like Earl Franklin is going to walk with just a small swat on the backside," Chabal said. "Pig-fucker."

Langdon turned to hide another grin at his wife's language. "Things will catch up to him. He's not smart enough to stay out of trouble."

"What's going to happen to Martin Thomas?"

Langdon picked up a stick and threw it into the waves for dog to chase. "Kidnapping should net him twenty years. Maybe more with the other charges of child endangerment, accessory to murder, if that sticks, and whatnot."

"What's going to happen to Eddie?"

"Hard to say. Maybe Jill's parents will adopt him. Or Martin had a sister down in Florida. Otherwise, he'll go into the system."

"It's always the kids who suffer the most, isn't it?" Chabal said.

"Far too often," Langdon said. "Far too often."

Questions for Discussion

How would you describe the protagonist?

Does Langdon have a compelling voice?

What characters did you identify with? Or like?

What plot twists were unexpected?

What emotions did the antagonist evoke in you?

How do you feel about the romance in the novel?

Do you believe that the events of this book could/do happen?

For additional questions related to this novel, contact the author:

Matt Cost
matthew-cost@comcast.net
www.mattcost.net

About the Author:

Matt Cost aka Matthew Langdon Cost

Over the years, Cost has owned a video store, a mystery bookstore, and a gym. He has also taught history and coached just about every sport imaginable. During those years—since age eight, actually—his true passion has been writing.

I Am Cuba: Fidel Castro and the Cuban Revolution (Encircle Publications, March, 2020) was his first traditionally published novel. *Mainely Power*, the first of the Mainely Mysteries featuring private detective Goff Langdon, was published by Encircle in September, 2020, followed by book two, *Mainely Fear*, in December, 2020, and book three, *Mainely Money*, in March of 2021. Also available is his Clay Wolfe / Port Essex Mystery series: *Wolfe Trap* (June 2021), *Mind Trap* (October 2021), *Mouse Trap* (publishing in April 2022), and *Cosmic Trap* (publishing in September 2022); as well as his new historical fiction novel, *Love in a Time of Hate* (August 2021). Encircle will introduce a new mystery series by Cost in December of 2022 with *Brooklyn Eight Ballo*, featuring private detective Eight Ballo, and set in Brooklyn, New York, in the 1920s.

Cost now lives in Brunswick, Maine, with his wife, Harper. There are four grown children: Brittany, Pearson, Miranda, and Ryan. A chocolate Lab and a basset hound round out the mix. He now spends his days at the computer, writing.

If you enjoyed reading this book,
please consider writing your honest review
and sharing it with other readers.

Many of our Authors are happy to participate in
Book Club and Reader Group discussions.
For more information, contact us at info@encirclepub.com.

Thank you,
Encircle Publications

For news about more exciting new fiction, join us at:

Facebook: www.facebook.com/encirclepub

Twitter: twitter.com/encirclepub

Instagram: www.instagram.com/encirclepublications

Sign up for Encircle Publications newsletter and specials:
eepurl.com/cs8taP